# THE PIMLICO KID

It's 1963. Billy Driscoll and his best mate, Peter 'Rooksy' Rooker, have the run of their street. Whether it's ogling sexy mum, Madge, as she pegs out her washing, or avoiding the local bully, Griggsy, the estates of Pimlico have plenty to fire their fertile imaginations. After years of being the puny one, Billy is finally filling out. He is also taking more than a passing interest in Sarah Richards, his pretty neighbour. But Billy isn't her only admirer – local heartthrob Kenneth 'Kirk' Douglas, likes her too – and something drastic must be done if Billy is to get his girl.

# THE PIMLICO KID

# THE PIMLICO KID

*by*

Barry Walsh

**Magna Large Print Books**
Long Preston, North Yorkshire,
BD23 4ND, England.

British Library Cataloguing in Publication Data.

Walsh, Barry
    The Pimlico kid.

    A catalogue record of this book is
    available from the British Library

    ISBN    978-0-7505-3902-9

First published in Great Britain by Harper
An imprint of HarperCollins*Publishers* 2013

Copyright © Barry Walsh 2013

Extract from 'Burnt Norton' taken from *Four Quartets* © Estate of
T. S. Eliot and reprinted by kind permission of Faber and Faber Ltd.

Cover illustration © Lee Avison by arrangement with
Arcangel Images

Barry Walsh asserts the moral right to be identified as the author of
this work

Published in Large Print 2014 by arrangement with
HarperCollins Publishers

Magna Large Print is an imprint of Library Magna Books Ltd.

Printed and bound in Great Britain by
T.J. (International) Ltd., Cornwall, PL28 8RW

# ACKNOWLEDGEMENTS

When you start writing late, you need all the help you can get. I got a lot. Thanks to: my marvellous agent, Broo Doherty, for keeping faith; Kate Bradley, my kind and tolerant editor at HarperCollins; author, Jacqui Lofthouse; the Richmond Writers' Circle; fellow writers on Word Cloud; The Arvon Foundation; Christine Matthews; David and Lesley Byrne, and Jim Sinkinson. Special thanks to Susan Chadwick for her insight and invaluable support. I owe most to my friends in Quad Writers; without Serena Cook, Martin Cummins, Rob Ganley, Kevin Kelly, Vesna Main, Jarred McGinnis and Bernard Miller, writing would have been much harder – and a lot less fun.

For Bronwen

Also for my father, Thomas Walsh and my brother, Terry Walsh. The best men I've known are the first men I knew.

In memory of Sarah McCormack (1978-2006), a wonderful Pimlico Kid.

*"Footfalls echo in the memory
Down the passage which we did not take"*

From *Burnt Norton*, T.S. Eliot

# PROLOGUE – OCTOBER 1975

Taunton 20 miles. The road sign slips past and another, listing local villages, glides towards me. One name stands out like my own on a guest list. A door into the past swings open and releases a locked-away ache. The car slows, behind me a horn blares. I pull into a lay-by.

Lower Sinton: part of an address written above two kiss crosses on a sheet of lined paper. I have never been here but I know it from what she told me: narrow lanes of pale yellow cottages; black window boxes crammed with flowers; main street pavements that rose three feet above the road. Her grandmother's house stood next to the village post office and in the road outside her father's black Humber gleamed. Beyond the back garden lay the wide meadow and further still there was the river. She spent her holidays here: where the sun always shone. When she returned to London, I marvelled at her golden skin and the extra light that had crept into her hair. It's what happened in Somerset. It should have been Summerset.

I close my eyes. Back they come. First, as always, her face: bright, elfin, thanks to a short hairstyle, known at the time as *Italian Boy*. Beside her, my friend is making a circle with thumb and forefinger to tell me that everything is OK. And the other girl, with shining blue eyes, is hiding a smile behind her hand.

Scar reverts to wound. I tell myself, again, that we were children; that we couldn't have prevented what happened; that when the most we might have been expected to deal with was a first kiss or a dying grandparent, we were undone by love itself, and violence – and that adults betrayed us.

Childhood love can endure but childhood promises are hard to keep.

# LONDON

## August 1963

# FABULOUS FLESH

High summer in Pimlico. After days of fierce sunshine, the meagre lawns of the prefabs in Grims-
dyke Street are bleached and balding. A breeze
churns the baked urban air and releases a faint,
blended odour of street dust and dried dog shit.

In the afternoon heat, even the flying ants are
walking. Rooksy and I have stopped moving
altogether. We're draped over the chest-high wall
of Madge Smith's garden, savouring the smell of
wet soil in her hosed flowerbeds, and admiring
her lush, watered grass.

I rest my head on my arms. It would be easy to
fall asleep on the hard-sponge bricks, except that
Madge is here. We pretend not to look as she
bends to set down the large basket of washing on
her terrace, which is an extension of the concrete
slab on which the prefab stands. Rooksy props
his chin on his hands. Sweat beads down his face
in glistening lines. He sucks in air around his
clenched teeth, and sighs. 'Do you think Madge
would show us her tits if we asked her nicely?'

'Jesus, not so loud!'

Rooksy says thrilling things but he has sod-all
volume control. Madge hasn't heard what he's
said but her frown makes it clear that she
wouldn't have liked it. I ignore his question, but
it's got me wondering, again: what is it about tits?
Hearing the word said aloud excites in a way that

bosoms can't. Mum has bosoms, so does my Aunt Winnie; hers are enormous and stretch her cream blouses and twin sets with more weight than push. Madge has tits.

How, and at what point, they become bosoms is a bit of a mystery. Perhaps they are tits that are no longer exciting? For now, imagining Madge naked from the waist up makes speech difficult and, not for the first time, Rooksy has conjured up images that I'll be thinking about later.

He straightens up. 'You know, I think she might. She must be so proud of them.'

'Don't be stupid, Rooksy.'

Madge will be doing no such thing. She's little Jojo's mum, and she isn't much younger than mine.

He closes his eyes. 'Oh the fabulous flesh.'

'Rooksy, please!'

I turn away but he puts his arm around my shoulders and steers me back to stand alongside him as if we're in a urinal. Madge glides to her back door where she lifts a cloth peg bag from its hook and returns to drop it on top of the washing.

Rooksy starts moving up and down against the wall, forcing me lower as he rises and shoving me up as he drops. I resist but after a few upward scrapes against the warm bricks, I'm moving under my own steam. A 'love it, can't bear it' feeling grows in my groin and Rooksy's tight smile makes him look as if he's trying to whistle through a Polo mint.

Madge looks across at us and our bobbing figures freeze. Rooksy is down low and I'm at the top of my stretch.

'What *are* you two doing?'

'Whoops,' says Rooksy.

'You standing on a biscuit tin Billy? Or are you in a hole Peter Rooker?'

'If only,' he whispers.

'What?' says Madge.

We return to our proper heights and I speak up to stop Rooksy saying any more. 'Nothing, Mrs Smith.'

'You have grown though haven't you Billy, filling out a bit too. What with those blue eyes, you'll soon be...' She winks.

My face burns. Thank you Madge. But soon be what? Please say what *what* is. I've started to grow, at last: a little taller, a bit less skinny. Mum and Aunt Winnie have said as much recently, but to hear this from Madge ... who has tits.

Rooksy nudges me. 'Ooh, I'd watch her.'

'What's that?' says Madge.

'Four nil,' I say.

'What?' says Rooksy.

'Four nil.' I shrug as if it's obvious. Football scores can divert the attention of those who've heard something they shouldn't have. It hasn't worked; Madge is frowning again. Please Madge, don't change your mind about me; you're my only fan with tits. Her eyes narrow but she relents and gives me the smallest of smiles.

She picks up the basket and carries it to the far end of the clothesline, using the top of one thigh to provide extra lift with every other step. At the far end, furthest from prying eyes, she begins pegging out the family's underwear. First, her husband's and Jojo's Y-Fronts, then her whiter, more slender knickers. Knickers: a word as potent as 'tits'. Could those she's hanging out be the kind she's wearing right now? I swallow hard.

Even fully clothed, Madge looks wonderful. A red headscarf squeezes her dark hair into a pony-tail. She's wearing a sleeveless white frock with buttons all down the front. Each time her sun-tanned arms reach up, her breasts stretch the fabric either side of the brown V of her chest. When she bends down to the basket, they settle back and her cleavage narrows and darkens.

'Oh, definitely tits.'

'Without a doubt Billy,' says Rooksy.

Blimey, have I really said that out loud?

Rooksy jogs me with his elbow and starts whispering a commentary like the mad woman on telly who jollies ladies through health and beauty exercises.

'That's it Madge, bend and stretch, bend, sort, pick and stretch.'

One of the pegs fails to close over a shirt and slips down the front of her dress. As she picks it out, Rooksy groans and Madge glares at him.

The clothesline rises as it reaches the pole near us, forcing her to stretch higher. Rooksy can't help himself. 'And stretch up... Oh Billy look at them.'

I'm looking, I'm looking!

'And down...'

Closer now, she stoops to rummage in the remaining washing, allowing us to see further into the 'happy valley' – another Rooksy term.

'And feel...'

Madge's bum pushes out before she straightens up. Oh god. I should leave now but my legs aren't up to it. I cling to the wall.

Rooksy is covering every movement. 'And stretch...'

Now that the basket is lighter, she shoves it along the ground with the outside of her foot. This highlights the curve of her thigh and widens the unbuttoned split of her dress to let us see higher up her suntanned leg. Too much for Rooksy, who puts a forearm over his eyes. 'Oh, fabulous.'

'Rooksy, please.'

He grins. 'What? What have I done?' A bubble appears and collapses on his shining white teeth.

He knows what he's done, and he's doing it from his favourite position: within earshot and out of reach. Rooksy is almost fourteen, only six months older than I am but he knows things that I'm still guessing about.

He's a 'dirty bastard', which is what his cousin called him when she caught him watching her dry herself after a bath. He happily admits that this is exactly what he is.

It's all very well being a dirty bastard in private but Rooksy makes it public and takes things too far. Some of the parents in our street say he's been spoiled because he's an only child. However, if having more money, better clothes and amazing confidence is being spoiled, what's so wrong with it?

'Hello Madge.' His voice is a poor imitation of Humphrey Bogart but his smile is real Errol Flynn – except that saliva has collected at the corners of his mouth and stretches like bubble gum between his lips as he speaks. Above his brown eyes, fair hair sweeps back in glossy waves. Like Kookie in

23

*77 Sunset Strip,* he grooms it constantly with a comb, which he tracks with his other hand to smooth down or push up where necessary. And he stares ahead so intently that you'd think he was looking in a mirror.

'Don't you *Madge* me, you cheeky bugger. Mrs Smith to you.' She puts her hands on her hips. 'Billy Driscoll, what are you doing hanging around with the likes of him?'

'Nothing much, Mrs Smith, is Jojo around?' Like mentioning football scores, asking your own questions can help to change the subject.

'Over East Lane Market with his dad.'

'Can I give you a hand Ma– isis Smith?' says Rooksy.

'Give me a hand, you dirty bleeder? You'll get my hand around your ear if you come it with me. Go on, out of it. Why can't you play football like other kids?'

Football? Rooksy? On the rare occasions he joins in our street matches, his short-lived efforts range between bored wandering about and surprisingly aggressive tackling. We play 'first-to-ten' and when one side reaches five, we change ends. This is when Rooksy sods off.

'Sorry Madge, I mean Mrs...'

Blasted by her fierce look, we turn and squat down behind the wall. Rooksy cowers, ready for her to lean over and aim a clout at him. When she doesn't, he sits back, closes his eyes and starts rubbing his crotch, whispering, 'Oh Madge, fa-abu-lous flesh.'

I want to run away but sit tight rather than let him know I'm a bottler, especially as I'm now looking into the grinning face of the one person who *does* know this. I've forgotten that John is with us. My younger brother is crouched by the kerb and smiling, not so much at Rooksy's antics as at my 'scared face'. His eyes widen as he opens and closes his mouth like a goldfish. He claims this is how I look when I'm frightened. I haven't seen this face myself but I suspect that it's a fair description. John has his faults but he rarely tells lies. I'd like to show him what *his* scared face looks like but he hasn't been frightened often enough to develop one. As far as I know, he has no interest in Madge or the differences between bosoms and tits. This should make me feel more grown up than he is, but it doesn't.

He turns away and, with his fingers, starts killing the winged ants that are filing suicidally in columns along the gutter. We all kill crawlies but John uses bare hands to squash large spiders and beetles that we would only tread on. As he presses down on the ants, his back broadens into a smaller version of our dad's, and the sight of John's flat shoulder blades moving under muscle has me straightening up.

On our sideboard there's a photo of me, taken a couple of years ago by a beach photographer at Brighton. I hate it but Mum keeps it because, she claims, she likes my smile – *not* because it's a big print and the only one that fits her favourite silver frame. I'm standing on Olive Oyl legs and wearing woollen swimming trunks that sag from non-existent hips. My arm is raised in an embarrassed wave that accentuates the white hoops of my ribs.

Skinny arms may have given me a whip-like

25

throw but they're no good for the important skills, like fighting or looking good in short-sleeved shirts. However, things *are* getting better at last and there are clear signs that I am going to have biceps after all. Others have noticed too, not least Aunt Winnie, who has stopped putting her arms around me and John to present us as Charles Atlas *before* and Charles Atlas *after*.

Rooksy, eyes closed, is chanting softly while pretending that he's wanking '...ninety-nine, a hundred, change hands, don't care if I do die.'

I shuffle away from him and settle for just thinking about girls and what nestles under bras and knickers. I often ache, really ache, to see breasts close up on women like Madge – or girls like Christine Cassidy, who sticks hers out in case you don't notice them. Some chance, she's built like a young Aunt Winnie. I'd still love to know what they feel like. I've seen naked women on a pack of Rooksy's playing cards but the pictures were disappointingly indistinct in areas where I'd have welcomed more detail. When you flicked through them, the women cavorted about, arching back or bending over, while always managing to look as if they were about to give you a kiss. Of course, I made the appreciative noises that Rooksy expected but closer examination revealed that there weren't fifty-two different women but a hard-working half-dozen. Viewed one at a time, there was nothing happy or sexy about their smiles and, although I didn't mention it to Rooksy, their flesh was far from fabulous.

The best pictures are in my head. Lying in bed, eyes shut; I can picture girls I actually know,

26

without their clothes. These images are hard to hang on to and my brain could do with a 'vertical hold' button to stop them sliding from view. But no matter how fleetingly they appear before me, at least their flesh *is* fabulous.

'You still here?'

Madge's face looms over us like God's on the church ceiling.

Rooksy rolls to one side, pulling his hand from inside the top of his trousers. Madge notices but she focuses on me. 'Get out of here, Billy Driscoll, now, and don't think that what he's doing is clever, 'cos it's not!'

'No, Mrs Smith.'

Rooksy catches my eye. His smile disappears and I wince at having betrayed the shameful truth that I agree with Madge.

As he scrambles to his feet, he makes the mistake of pushing down on John's shoulders. John spins around, fists clenched. 'Get off me.'

'John!' Madge screams. John freezes. Rooksy's smile returns as he holds up his hands. Madge points a finger at him. 'And you, Peter Rooker, next time you'll be sorry.'

'Sorry... Cheerio then Madge.'

'What?' She scoots after him as far as she can along her side of the wall.

He jogs away laughing.

Before she goes indoors, she flashes me an angry glance. When I look at John, he gives me the gasping-fish face.

# FISH, FAGS AND DEVIL CAT

I'm sitting, feet up, on the bench in the shady corner of our backyard. *Lord of the Flies* is face down on my knees while I picture the dead parachutist swinging in the trees.

I've just come to the uncomfortable conclusion that if I were one of the boys on the island, I'd soon be exposed as less than heroic. For relief I ponder the easier subject of how quickly the dead parachutist's face would rot in heat like this.

'Billy, ducks, run and get us a packet of Weights and a bit of fish for Chris will you?' Ada Holt is leaning out of her kitchen window above me. What could be her last fag is hanging from the corner of her mouth.

'Up in a minute Mrs Holt.'

Ada lives on the ground floor. Getting to her flat involves going up to the street and in through the main front door. It's never locked because no one in the flats upstairs wants to answer knocks that might not be for them. Our street is made up of large terraced houses that were once Victorian family homes but have now been carved into flats and single-room lets. The houses are fronted by iron railings at street level from where stone steps dogleg down to the 'areas' belonging to basement homes like ours. In another era, our front door would have been opened only to tradesmen.

On the wall at the top of our steps, the cheap

cream paint fails to cover the words AIR RAID SHELTER and an arrow pointing down to our two coal cellars. During the War, they were damp, distempered refuges from German bombs. Ada cowered in one of them the night her house next door was firebombed. Today she lives on the same floor in our house with only a party wall between her and the charred shell of her old home. Twenty years on, it remains open to the weather and when it rains, damp seeps down through to our flat and glistens on the passage wall. In winter, John and I can play noughts and crosses in the condensation.

Only one cellar is used for coal. The other is used as a storeroom, where all the things that Mum won't throw away, 'just in case', are packed in. She went on at Dad for ages to seal the manhole cover above it. He finally got around to it, and did a thorough job, the day after a new coalman opened it to pour in five hundredweight of best anthracite – proving Mum right, again, about doing things straightaway. Being right isn't her most endearing trait.

Ada does her crushed-slipper shuffle to the door.

'Hello ducks, come in.' She's wearing her quilted 'all-day' housecoat that, in Ada's case, could be described as 'all week'.

'No thanks, Mrs Holt, think I'll get going straightaway.'

Wafting past her is one reason for staying outside. Our house has its own smell; the main ingredients are cabbage and cigarette smoke. Ada's flat is a prime source. A second reason crouches behind her, glaring at me, tail twitching. Chris is a black-and-white tom that terrorizes other cats,

29

most dogs and me. A real sour puss, his mouth is already open in full feline snarl. Only Ada is allowed to stroke him and even she waits until his mealtimes. Get within range and he slashes like Zorro at exposed skin, and he's undeterred by gloved hands or trousered legs. His lair is by the fire, inside the fender on the scored brown tiles – an ingrate in the grate. Because Chris hasn't been 'seen to', he adds a bitter edge to the distinctive smell of Ada's flat and of Ada herself.

She calls his malevolent behaviour his 'funny little ways' and carries the livid lines of his affection on hands, wrists and legs. She deems most of them 'he's only playing' scratches. But she has deeper wounds from his 'you little bugger' attacks, usually provoked by absent-minded attempts to brush cigarette ash off his back as he snoozes beside her.

Ada squints at me through smoke rising from the fag that clings to her bottom lip. 'Just ten Weights and a tanner's worth of whiting please, ducks.' Her right eyebrow arrows up above her open eye and the left crouches around the one that's closed. It makes her look as if she doubts everything she sees.

She takes a deep drag, which pulls her jaw to one side and gets her goitre on the move. The cigarette rises and falls like a railway signal but fails to dislodge the lengthening ash, which also resists the buffeting of her speech. Only when it's longer than the unsmoked bit does Ada notice. She taps it into a cupped hand and goes inside to cast it vaguely towards the fireplace and provokes an acid spit from Chris. She returns with a string bag and, with a nicotine-stained index finger, stirs the money in her purse to find the right coins. 'Here you are, ducks. Keep the change.'

Ada isn't the nicest of old dears but she's not tight, and errands to get fish for her devil cat always bring a bit of pocket money.

'Oh, just a sec,' she says with an irritated lift of her chin. 'I think her ladyship upstairs wants you to get her something.' She's referring to Miss Rush, who lives on the first floor. Ada doesn't her like because of what she claims are her posh, hoity-toity ways. But she dislikes her most because everyone else *does* like her.

Miss Rush opens the door just enough to frame her tiny body. She tucks a duster into a full-length floral pinny; I've caught her 'mid clean'. She's bright-eyed and her rosy cheeks seem out of place on her bony face, which is haloed by a perm of white hair. Miss Rush neither smokes nor, as far as anyone can tell, does she ever eat cabbage. The smell emerging from behind her is a blend of Mansion floor polish and Sunlight soap. Her passion for cleaning extends to polishing the lino outside on the landing; a practice that Ada thinks is showing off. Miss Rush's home must be spotless but no one knows for sure because, unlike Ada, she never asks anyone in.

She has run out of Bournvita. 'Very kind Billy and that's for you,' she says softly, and hands me a threepenny bit extra. Like Ada, she tips in advance. Mum encourages me to be especially polite to Miss Rush because she's a 'lady'. Whenever neighbours indulge in raucous behaviour or use bad language, Mum says, 'What *will* Miss Rush think?' But Miss Rush doesn't seem to mind and she's the only tenant who manages to stay on good terms with everyone. She isn't all that genteel either because she reads the *Daily Mirror* and calls lunch 'dinner'. She's old, clean and speaks quietly. It doesn't take much to be a lady in our street.

'Won't be long Miss Rush.'

Before closing the door, she nods towards the rope blocking off the stairs to the second floor and the empty top flat. 'Terribly sad.'

Old man Fay died of TB and his flat is waiting to be fumigated before it can be re-let. He was 'a right stinker,' according to Ada, who could have run him a close second. Mr Fay rarely washed and he had a strong smell, even out in the street. He was also deeply religious and did weird things, like laying crosses made of two matchsticks on the pavement and asking people to mind where they walked.

Our landlord, Mr Duffield, found him lying naked in bed, eyes open, staring in terror along an outstretched arm to where his fingers curled around a large wooden crucifix. Scores of empty matchboxes were piled in the corner of his bedroom and matchstick crosses dotted the floor like tiny Christian land mines that had failed to protect him. When they took him away, the sooty outline of his body was stained on the bedclothes. Mr Duffield joked that, unlike the Turin Shroud, Mr Fay's sheet bore only a rear impression.

It's exciting to have known someone who has died and I've been embellishing Mr Fay's death with tales of strange noises coming from his empty flat at night. When John hears these stories, he shakes his head but, like most of our friends he wants to believe that spooky things can happen in our street. For the little kids, Old Man Fay is becoming a bogie man.

Mum and Dad are desperate to move to a flat on the new estate by the Thames. However, they're a long way down the waiting list. The home they want most of all is on the back of Shredded Wheat packets. The Swedish-style 'dream house' stands bathed in sunshine above a sloping lawn. By the garden gate, a man, his wife and a boy are waving while a younger girl crouches to pet a Scottie dog. They're all smiling, even the dog. The house could be ours if we can come up with a winning description for a Nabisco breakfast. Mum has had several attempts, each one sent off with its three packet tops and a catchphrase. She thinks her latest try is a potential winner: 'Shredded Wheat, your morning treat'. We're not holding our breath.

If this one doesn't win, Mum says it will be her last try and she's already eyeing the matching kitchen cabinet, table and chairs that are up for grabs on the back of the Corn Flakes packet.

Dad is an even more committed competitor and he's convinced that sooner or later he'll predict eight draws on the Football Pools. When he does finally line up his 'Os' against the right games in the coupon's little squares, he says we'll all be on the pig's back and able to buy the Swedish house outright – Scottie dog and all. Mum tells him to get away with his nonsense but pays secret attention when he checks the results in the Sunday paper.

Back in the street, I run into John who is bouncing a tennis ball on a cricket bat as he makes his way home. 'Where you going?'

'To get stuff for the old girls.'

'Sharesy.'

'Yeah.'

We share whatever is earned from running errands. It's one of Dad's rules that covers most things we do, even when there's no real money at stake. We've never finished a game of Monopoly because as soon as one of us runs out of money, the other lends him enough to carry on.

## BACK SEAT DREAMS

'Watcha Billy.'

'Watcha Josie.'

Josie Costello is sitting on the 'Big Step', a foot-high terrace of black-and-white tiles that surrounds Plummer's corner shop.

'What are you doing?'

I hold up the string bag.

'Been to get stuff for Ada Holt and Miss Rush.'

Josie sits a lot to ease the strain on her callipered leg – the result of what she calls her 'brush with polio', which she cheerily tells everyone is better than being swept away altogether. Even in summer, she wears a heavy brown shoe to match the clamped boot. When you meet Josie, you have to cope first with her face, and the purple stain that

34

rises on one cheekbone and spreads down to thicken part of her top lip. A smile-wrecker, but it doesn't stop her smiling. When she does, she raises a hand to stop you seeing the birthmark's flat weight tugging at her face. She would look ashamed if her eyes dropped at the same time, but they resist and look straight at you.

'How's your breathing?'

'Pardon?'

She's talking before I'm listening. Her face no longer shocks, but it takes time *not* to notice.

'Your breathing.'

'Oh, fine.'

She's asking about my asthma. At primary school, it had often meant having to stay in the classroom at playtime. Josie would be there too, with her bronchitis. While I wheezed, she coughed, which made her face go red and her birthmark turn dark blue. Those who stayed in, with anything from a sty to a broken arm, had Josie for company. Even when she wasn't ill, she preferred being inside to loneliness in a crowded playground. In class, she sat at the front to one side with her birthmark close to the wall, so that when she turned around the rest of us saw only clear skin. She was always the last to leave the room.

Being asthmatic has set me apart and gets me quite a bit of sympathy. When I get one of my 'attacks', there are small white pills to take and vapour to breathe from an asthma pump. These help my breathing but they've also become props for my role as 'plucky Billy', an image I try to portray with subtle references – at least I think they're subtle – to what I manage to do in spite of being out of breath so often. Truth is that on the days when my breathing is OK, I'm no different to any other kid. Josie doesn't have 'good days'. Aunt Winnie says that, like Josie's disabilities, asthma is my cross. It's also a bit of a crutch.

'What are you doing?' I ask.

'Oh, just waiting. Christine and Shirley are going over the park this afternoon; I might go too.' She pats the tiles next to her. 'Want to sit here for a bit?'

I don't think so. Being seen talking to any girl guarantees piss-taking from mates, even though we talk a lot *about* girls and, especially, tits. Some even claim they've done more than talk about them, but clam up when asked for detail. However, no one talks about Josie, even though she's well endowed in the chest department.

If I don't sit down, I'll hurt her feelings. Most kids find it easy to say no to Josie, or to leave her company when there's something better on offer, but I can't bring myself to do it. I sit down where she beckons me, on her good side.

'Where did you go on holiday? Scotland, wasn't it?'

'No, Carlisle. It's in England.' This has sounded harsh. 'But it is *near* Scotland. What about you?'

'We're going to Ireland again in a couple of weeks. Mum says we might visit some holy place where sick people get cured, and this,' she flicks a hand up to her face, 'might...'

'Oh ... that would be great.'

'Yes, but it only works for a few people. You have to have faith you see, really believe that Jesus will help you.'

'Oh.'

I try to imagine her face without the purple stain, and whether she would be pretty. She does have the shiniest dark hair and Mum says that the skin on the clear side of her face is beautiful. Josie's blue eyes can be fierce while she waits for people to take in her birthmark, but sparkling and kind once they have.

'I hope it works,' I say.

'Thanks. Mum thinks that saying prayers helps, the more the better.'

'I see.' No, I don't.

Her head drops. 'Will you say one for me Billy? For my new face?'

'What, now?'

'Oh no, whenever you…'

She looks at me full-on and I'm reminded of what is at stake. So, yes, I will say a prayer for her new face, as well as for the end of my asthma, for Arsenal to win the League and for a Charles Atlas physique.

'OK Josie.'

'Thanks Billy.'

She leans closer. As I look into her eyes her face blurs and I see no blemish. She sits back, wraps her arms around her knees and stares at the ground.

'Josie Costello and Billy Driscoll, what are you two up to then?'

Sarah Richards has a neat accent that turns most of her 'rs' into 'rrrs'. Rooksy once said that she sounded like the country yokels who sing the TV advert for cider: *Oh Coates comes up from Somerset, where the cider apples grow.*

37

She told him it was better than sounding like a Cockney. Then she sang the real song, as she called it, which ends with, 'because we loves it so'. Fair enough. *Maybe it's because I'm a Londoner* ends with: ''Cos I love London so'.

Sarah's question has pleased Josie and I think that she meant it to.

'We were just chatting,' says Josie. True but not what I'd have said; chatting is what girls do. Sarah sits down and gives Josie's knee a little squeeze. Josie covers Sarah's hand with her own. If she could have a new face, I think she'd choose one like Sarah's.

Sarah Richards came to Pimlico two years ago when her dad, a chauffeur, followed his employers up from Somerset. His large black Humber looked strangely out of place, like it could be visiting Sarah's house for a funeral or something. There were no more than half a dozen cars in her street and even fewer in ours. Mr Richards is forever washing and polishing the car outside his house and looks askance when the elderly cars and vans of his neighbours pass by.

At first, Sarah was the skinny new girl who sat in front of me in my last year at primary school. However, in the final term, things changed. Not that *she* had changed much – she was already pretty – but I was finding her more likeable. I observed her more closely, noticing things, like the way she wore ribbons in her hair when most girls thought them babyish, and how she never waited after school for friends to walk home with, but that others waited for her. Soon I was thinking about her a lot and even guessing, the night before,

38

which of her dresses she'd wear the next day. My favourite had thin blue and white stripes with piping at the neck. I'd stare at her back, at the straight seam between her shoulders, and admire the way she held herself square to line up with it. And whenever she pushed up her hair to reveal the back of her neck, the hairs would stand up on the back of mine.

I even played a game in which seeing her face by getting her to turn around in class was worth twice seeing it elsewhere. One way was to answer the teacher's questions. My hand was usually first up. Christine Cassidy and Shirley da Costa, my rivals for being top of the class, would scowl from their front-row desks. But Sarah would swivel round, head-on-hand, without taking her elbow off the desk and give me a smile that said, *Go on then, clever clogs, tell 'em.* And I did, although seeing her face sometimes made me forget the question and there would be jeering.

When there were no questions to answer, I'd stare at her back, willing her, like Svengali, to turn around. On the only occasion it seemed to work, she grinned as if to say, *OK, just this once.*

Then came the 11-plus exam and the traumatic move to an all-boys grammar school. Sarah surprised Christine Cassidy and Shirley da Costa by passing the exam too and joining them at the local girls' grammar school.

Even in my new uniform, I no longer felt special. At my new school, everyone was clever and almost everyone was bigger than me. In my form room I sat behind a fat kid with body odour. In my darker moments I'd superimpose

39

Sarah's slender blue and white dress on his black blazer, dreaming of her swivel and smile. Thankfully he never turned around when I put my hand up as he was too busy waving his own. He, too, had also been top of his class at primary school.

I saw little of Sarah during my first year and this was just as well. She was maturing fast, while I wasn't. Even worse, she had grown taller than me and, in the company of her school friends in their grey school uniforms, she seemed reluctant to have much to do with me. I felt young, small and left behind. So while I continued to look for her, I avoided any meetings. Even in the holidays I saw little of her as she spent most of the time at her Nan's in Somerset.

However, at the end of this year's Easter holidays, I met her again. She was sitting on the Big Step with Josie. For the first time since primary school she seemed pleased to see me and said how tall I'd got. She asked me all sorts of questions about my school and what I was up to. I forgot to ask her any questions in return, something that often happens when talking with girls. Then, as I was leaving, she said 'see you later then?' At the same time, she turned her head and pushed her hair up. With that glimpse of her neck, everything and more that I had felt for her at primary school came flooding back. I've looked for her most weekends since but with school cricket matches on Saturdays and the agony of quiet family Sundays our meetings have been restricted to brief hellos, often in the company of our respective parents.

In the two years since primary school, her face has grown slender, and her cheekbones seem to have moved closer to the surface. I'm struck more powerfully than ever how pretty she is and dismayed to realise that this is what her woman's face is going to look like. Panic rises in my chest about how much I need to grow up, to catch up, to get better looking. I've been checking my own face daily in the mirror. There has been some improvement, but one or two spots seem to have become as permanent as my nose.

She must have been on holiday in Somerset because she's suntanned and blonde strands streak her light brown hair where it's brushed past her ears. A pale green cotton frock snugs her slender body from her bony square shoulders down to her waist. Each time she smiles, tiny dimples appear either side of her mouth and I have to catch my breath. Even though she's so pretty, the boys say they don't fancy her because she's flat chested. This has become such an important issue that even ugly girls are OK, if they have tits. I wouldn't let on to my mates, but I think that if a girl has a face like Sarah's, breasts are worth waiting for.

'My dad's cleaning his car. Would you both like to come and sit in?'

I'd love to get behind the wheel of a Humber, although it's not one of my favourites. A vertical chrome grille and big headlamps give it a smug, snobby face and it has a fat-arse boot that can swallow not only cases but also the large trunks that wealthy people use. I've only ever ridden in cars like the Morris Minor belonging to my aunt in Cumberland, and I can't wait to get inside a limousine similar to the one used by the Prime Minister, Mr Macmillan.

I'm thinking this as we get up from the Big Step when Josie's bad leg gives way and she tumbles forward on the pavement. Instead of trying to get up, she rolls onto her back clutching the elbow that has taken the brunt of the fall.

'Oh Josie,' says Sarah.

Josie's eyes fill with tears. 'Blinking leg ... goes to sleep on me.'

Sarah looks at me, expecting me to take action. This makes knowing what to do even harder. Josie doesn't look as if she wants to be helped up, and touching a girl isn't so straightforward any more.

Sarah kneels down. 'Come on Josie, let's get up.' She strokes her hair.

Josie doesn't move and covers her face with her hands. Sarah shrugs and looks to me again.

My cowboy hero, Audie Murphy, would simply lift her in his arms. I don't know why I always think of Audie in difficult situations because it only highlights everything that I'm not up to doing: punch the baddie; dive into deep water; lift girls off the floor. Anyway, Josie is probably as heavy as I am. Faced with her tears and Sarah's expectations, I look away to hide my confusion. Then it comes to me: I'll give her my 'Norman Wisdom'. This may not be the place for the elbows-out rolling walk or his famous trip, of which I'm especially proud, but I lie beside Josie and prop my head on one hand – a horizontal version of the way Norman leans on walls and other, less solid, objects. I give her the high-pitched voice. 'Now Mrs, up we get, can't lie here all day, got an appointment in that nice big car over there.' Her fingers part and she peeps through to see Norman's yawning grin and his eyes going up into his head. Her shoulders start shaking.

Sarah frowns before realizing that Josie is chuckling. I roll onto my back, exaggerating Norman's laughter. Sarah joins in and I feel a little guilty at how much more her laughter means to me than Josie's. With Sarah's help, she gets up. From her frock's short sleeve she pulls out a hanky to dab her eyes and wipe away some tear-snot.

Mr Richards calls over to say it's OK to sit in the car but only in the back, and not to make a mess as he's just 'brushed out'. The girls get in and sit back on the deep bench seat. They pat the space between them for me to sit there too. Mr Richards closes the door and soon has the car rocking gently as he polishes the bonnet. In the carpeted hush, we talk in whispers and before long we fall silent, breathing in the heady mix of car wax and Windolene – and when I squeeze the seat's soft leather, it releases a faint smell of cigars. Josie puts one hand through the looped strap and waves with the other like the Queen. Then she touches the gleaming ashtray in the door and snatches back her hand when she sees her fingerprints on the chrome.

'Oops, sorry.'

Sarah smiles and gets up to wipe the ashtray with the hem of her frock.

Mr Richards has moved into the road on Sarah's side. He squats lower to polish the door and we catch him making a cross-eyed face. We smile but he doesn't smile back because he had

43

done it only for Sarah. The vertical wrinkle between his eyebrows deepens and he stands up.

'Blimey, this is smashing,' says Josie. 'Fancy being driven in one of these wherever you want to go. He's got a great job your dad. Will he give us ride?'

Sarah shakes her head. 'I don't think so. He's only taken Mum out a few times, on his way to work.'

Christine and Shirley arrive. Josie's proud tap on the window is too loud and Mr Richard's face goes into full frown. The girls wave but don't stop.

Josie clambers out. 'Thanks Sarah, see ya.' Christine and Shirley carry on, shoving each other playfully, unconcerned whether Josie follows or not. She limps after them but stops briefly to wave at us with little shakes of her upright hand that only we can see. Sarah waves back. Josie resumes her struggle to catch up. Then something about the girls' cruel giggling, their turned backs and their sound legs gets me to my feet. I jump out of the car. 'Wait a minute, can't you!'

They stop, glaring, but they wait with eyebrows raised and cheeks sucked in. When Josie reaches them, they set off, arm-in-arm, and as quickly as they can. Once again, Josie struggles to keep up.

I get back in the car. Sarah reaches across me to pull the door shut and I catch what she feels for Josie in her fading smile. I'd give anything for her to feel like this about me.

'I like Josie,' she says.

'Me too.' This is true, although I wouldn't normally say so.

'It was nice what you did for her.'

44

'Well, they could see she was trying to catch up.'

'Yes, but I meant when you rolled on the ground to make her laugh.'

'Oh.'

'It was kind.' She's talking about me! Silence. My turn to speak, but I can't. 'She's got lovely blue eyes, Josie, hasn't she?'

'Yes,' I say.

'Like yours.'

Bloody hell Billy, say something! There's so much I'd like to tell her but my words stick, like too many people trying to get through a door at once. I eventually mumble something about Josie's trip to the holy place for her face, and how it's important to have faith.

'Really?'

'You know, praying a lot... Josie asked me if I'd say a prayer for her.'

'And will you?'

I hesitate. 'Yes, I will.'

'That's nice of you, Billy.'

I have never felt nicer.

Her father appears again, polishing the door on the nearside. This time his smile is for both of us, but he doesn't mean it.

'I'd love to have a car, to be a chauffeur, like your dad ... to drive all the time.'

'Where would you go?'

'Oh, all over, everywhere.'

She leans closer. 'Would you take me with you?'

A weird fluttering fills my chest. Something has changed, like the moment in cowboy films when the hero and heroine first notice each other. I can see her face so clearly: the little mole beside her

45

nose and the tiny bleached hairs above her lips. I'm not sure what to say but I know what I want to do: for the first time in my life, I want to kiss someone.

'Well?' she says.

'Oh yes, yes, I'd take you.'

'Where?'

'Well, to Cumberland ... maybe. It's a long way. We'd have to take food and things for the journey.'

Her face comes closer. 'What's it like?'

'It's smashing. Near my Aunt's, there's a big river where we fish for trout, but we only ever catch eels. There are caves in the riverbank, where my cousin smokes a tuppenny loose. My aunt has a Morris Minor and drives us to the Lake District where there are huge mountains and er ... lakes. In Carlisle Castle, one dungeon has a licking stone.'

'A what?'

'It's a curvy-shaped bit of wall made smooth by prisoners licking water that seeped through from the moat. And we go to the seaside at Silloth, where there are huge sand dunes to jump from, and the best ice cream: it's Italian. And there's a funfair with flick-ball machines; if you get three balls in the holes, you get one cigarette. And my aunt never stops baking, there are always cakes and different kinds of tart at teatime, and lemon curd, although they call it lemon cheese up there. Her kitchen table is as big as our kitchen.'

I'm out of breath. She's looking at me and I want to tell her more to keep her looking.

'Sounds wonderful.' She puts a hand on mine. 'Shall we go then, one day?'

I have to swallow to start breathing again. 'Yes.'

Then, instead of telling her how I feel, all I manage is, 'It does rain a lot though. And we never get brown like you do in Somerset.'

'Would you take me to Somerset too?'

'Oh I would, yes.'

'Then I could show you our village, Lower Sinton. My Nan runs the post office but it's not like the one here; it sells sweets and food and newspapers. There are haystacks in the fields where hares hide, but I've never seen them. The man next door has ponies and we get free rides. In a cottage on the edge of the village there's an old woman called Miss Walthough. She looks a bit like a witch but she isn't, although she does know about potions for curing sick animals, and she grows the best raspberries for miles around. We've also got a river; it runs across the fields behind Nan's garden. There are all kinds of beautiful stones in it and you can wade across, except in winter when it's too deep.'

Her face is so close. Talking has made her breathless too. Embarrassed, she shifts forward on the seat. I'm afraid that she's getting up to go, but she's pushing down with her feet to sit further back. Now the sunlight can reach her hair through the rear window and her face shines like it's a Technicolor close-up of the heroine in a Western. I move closer. She looks away but slides her hand over mine. To the sound of our breathing, we stare ahead. Through the windscreen, the roads of Cumberland and Somerset stretch before us in a sunny world in which I will drive a sports car with Sarah beside me, and she'll put her head on my shoulder. After several minutes I

47

say, 'I can't wait to be able to drive.'

The door opens with a rich click. Mr Richards ducks his head inside. 'All done, time to lock up.' His eyes narrow and he sniffs. 'What *is* that? It's not fish is it?'

I haven't noticed the smell until now. The whiting has soaked through its paper wrapping and there's a damp patch on the beige carpet. The Bournvita will be OK but I fear for the flavour of Ada's Weights.

I snatch up the string bag and stammer, 'It's for Mrs Holt.'

'Well, whoever it's for you can take it *out* of my car.' He holds the door wide open and for a moment it feels as if he's *my* chauffeur.

I step past him. 'Thank you.' I'm only being polite but Mr Richards doesn't see it that way and he's about to say so, when Sarah stops him. 'Dad, please ... it's all right.'

I walk away.

Sarah calls out, 'Bye.'

I wave and keep going. I turn the street corner and start running as if I could keep it up for ever.

# STRENGTH, THRIFT AND GIGLI

Dad breaks clocks. Every now and again, a snap and a metallic uncoiling signal the end of another innocent Westclox. Death follows a brief whirring of detached innards failing to turn the luminous hands. This is when Mum starts shouting.

This evening she has caught Dad as his hand settles nonchalantly on the mantelpiece. She reaches around him to snatch the clock and hold it safely against her stomach. He throws up his hands and smiles.

'*I'll* wind it,' she says.

He winks at John and me. 'Fair enough, Maureen.'

She lifts the winder's butterfly top and turns it with the tips of her fingers to demonstrate how it should be done: a gentle ratcheting that doesn't go too far. Showing him, for the hundredth time, how every task in hand needs careful attention.

She sets it back on the mantelpiece. 'Now leave it, I'll bring it when I come to bed.' During the day it's a kitchen clock, at night it sits on the table by their bed.

Dad is nothing if not thorough, but he can't resist the final turn that destroys the heads of already embedded screws, or the last twist of the tap that chews up washers. At Christmas, he literally blows up balloons. John and I have hidden the bicycle pump since the time he continued pumping a rock-hard tyre after a squeeze convinced him that it was well short of its right pressure. The bang from the exploding inner tube lifted Chris from his slumbers on Ada's windowsill and dumped him spitting and wailing in our backyard.

Accuracy isn't his strong point either but we love watching him miss at the coconut shy at Battersea Funfair just to see the vertical ripples that roll around the canvas marquee wall after each thump of a wayward wooden ball.

To placate Mum, he picks up the dinner plates

49

from the table and slides them into the sink with enough noise to get her to bar him from clearing the rest. He stands back, eyeing the clock furtively, his big fingers twitching. Mum catches John grinning.

'It's not funny. Your father's lack of self-control wastes our hard-earned money.'

We stay quiet because she's taken the deep breath that means she hasn't finished. Dad, too, is paying close attention; he's heard what she's about to say before but he's going to have to hear it again.

'Nothing is safe when he gets his hands on it.' She catches Dad winking at us. 'What *is* wrong with you? It's not as if you don't know your own strength, you *do...*'

John and I struggle not to laugh. She takes a threatening step towards us but weakens when she realizes that Dad, too, is choking back laughter.

She returns to the sink. 'I give up.'

'That's the way he is,' Aunt Winnie told us when Mum wasn't around. 'Easygoing chap, your Dad, but when something gets in his way, he has to push.' With a phlegmy chuckle, she added, 'Then it's best to back off, ask the Colquhoun brothers.'

The Colquhouns are beefy scaffolders who used to throw their weight around in the Queen Anne until Dad got them to apologize for picking on Michael O'Rourke's father. Aunt Winnie told the story as if Dad were Burt Lancaster seeing off the Clantons in the *Gunfight at the OK Corral*.

When he left the navy, Dad didn't go back to Ireland because he'd met Mum when on shore leave during the war. She had left Cumberland looking for excitement in the capital but found only long days in a munitions factory. When the war ended, they decided to stay in London because even bomb-blasted Pimlico gave them more than they could hope for in Ireland or Cumberland, so they stayed and made it home. As a result, even though John and I are Londoners, we have no relatives living nearby, unlike our Cockney friends, who have loads of cousins and two homes: their own and their Nan's.

Dad wears a cap to work and on Sundays he sports a trilby that he tugs down over his right eye: the *'Connemara side'*. On the days he doesn't go to work, he's bursting with energy. This is often expressed in a shouted 'hup' as, with a flip of his heels behind him, he accelerates to complete short trips, like crossing roads or climbing steps – or, sometimes, to end tricky conversations with Mum.

When we were little, he used to wait till we were walking ahead of him before tearing past us, shouting 'zing' and jogging backwards, challenging us to catch him. Then he'd turn and run in slow motion until we overtook him. 'God, if these boys haven't wings on their feet,' he'd complain, before shaking our hands to congratulate us on another fine victory.

Most evenings, a whistled Joseph Locke song and the slap of the rolled up *Evening Star* announces his arrival. He has a key but he prefers to rap the knocker. When one of us opens the door, he crouches like a boxer and lunges to lift and clinch, and to administer a rub of his day-old

51

beard and fill our nostrils with the smell of sand and cement from his clothes.

He's a ganger for a group of men who lay concrete on building sites: tamping it down with a big beam of wood to even out floors, or pouring it into shuttering for walls and pillars. The more concrete a gang lays, the more it earns. It's heavy work and he often falls asleep in the easy chair after his dinner. This is when Mum looks at him most tenderly and insists that we keep quiet. While he dozes, she picks bits of hardened concrete from his shirt but leaves those that are clinging temptingly to the small hairs of his cheekbones.

Dad gets a bit 'soft' in drink and regularly throws his pennies in the air for the kids to scramble after when he leaves the Queen Anne on Sunday afternoons. This infuriates Mum because she will walk to Victoria rather than take the bus to save fewer coppers than she sees bouncing around on the pavement.

'If we all treated money the way your father does, there'd be little food on the table; what with giving money to tramps and buying drinks when it isn't his turn, anyone would think we were made of money.'

Money isn't something that worries Dad who's convinced that it's only a matter of time before we win the Football Pools. Every week, he slides the coupon into the Littlewoods envelope and insists that we all kiss it for luck: Mum, me, John and then him. Mum does so grudgingly because she believes that you get richer only by working hard and saving. His belief that we'll win the Pools and chucking money to kids provides more fun than going on about how much things cost, but if Mum's right, and she usually is, it's probably a good thing she's different to Dad.

Looking after what money we do have is Mum's preserve. At the back of the kitchen cabinet, she keeps three tea caddies: one for the rent; one holds shillings for the gas meter; and the third is for 'clothes, holidays and Christmas'. This one gets raided most, usually by Dad, who puts back what he owes on payday – Thursday in the building trade. This is when Mum gets her housekeeping and Dad is extra cheerful because he's had a couple of pints on the way home.

In a weekly ritual, they sit at the kitchen table and he hands her the brown envelope. She teases out the white ribbon and pulls it through her fingers to examine the pay details. He gives her a nod – 'job done' for another week – and she puts most of the money into the tins. Then she hands him a pound and some change and drops the rest in her purse.

'Thrift' is Mum's favourite word. We rarely have the pleasure of using a new bar of Pears soap because, rather than waste the old sliver, we have to press it into the depression on the new one.

Our clothes are bought to 'grow into'. I once had to wear pyjamas with eight-inch turn-ups. 'Bound to shrink,' she said when I protested. This was embarrassing enough at home, but humiliating during a stay in hospital, when the turn-ups rolled down during the night and, on pulling back the sheets in the morning, the nurses joked about their little 'double amputee'.

Mum makes us all feel lazy because she's forever

'doing'. Even when listening to the wireless or watching telly, she sews, knits or does other thrifty things, like cutting old washing-up gloves into rubber bands. This requires the big light to be on in the front room and stops us watching telly in the dark to make it feel more like the pictures.

When we were small, Dad's stories made us the envy of our friends. And we'd get him to tell, again and again, while Mum closed her eyes, how he killed a shark with a knife when swimming close to his ship in South Africa. And, for years, we thought he knew Italian because while shaving on Sundays he renders in beautiful gibberish the arias sung by his favourite opera singer, Gigli. Dad's a fine light tenor, like John McCormack. In the Queen Anne, they're always asking him to sing his Irish songs and on the rare occasions that Mum drinks too, he makes her cry by singing, 'I'll take you home again ... Maureen'.

Mum says that exaggerating and inventing are the same as fibbing, even if it does make people laugh. He defends himself with, 'A bit of colour, Maureen. Where's the harm? Just a little salt and pepper on the meal?'

Aunt Winnie once stopped coming to see us after Mum told her that her breath smelled of cigarettes. Mum eventually apologized for upsetting her, but not for *what* she had said. 'There you are Maureen,' said Dad, with a wink at us, 'the truth is not something to be trotted out on just any old occasion.'

Although Mum isn't quite as shapely as Madge Smith, she's prettier, and her eyes are as blue as Josie's. She has a mole on her cheek that she darkens with a brown pencil. I tell her it makes her look like Elizabeth Taylor. It doesn't really, but I do think that to be beautiful, women have to look something like Mum.

Before she goes out, or when someone knocks at the door, she smoothes invisible creases at the sides of her skirt and flicks real or imagined strands of hair from her forehead with her little finger. When she gets wolf whistled outside building sites, she pretends to disapprove, but she's betrayed by her freshly flattered look, and can't resist pushing up the back of her hair with the palm of her hand.

Mum and Dad don't *act* as if they're in love, not like Rooksy's parents, who hold hands in the street. However, they seem happy enough and never have screaming fights like some of our friends' parents.

Their rows usually involve the subject of John and me having been christened Catholics, something that Mum, a relaxed Methodist, says she'll always regret. Life isn't made easier by the nuns of St Vincent de Paul who haven't given up trying to get us to go back to Westminster Cathedral, even though we've only ever been to a Church of England school. Their disapproval of 'mixed marriages' infuriates Mum. 'Anyone would think that your father had married a black woman.'

Sister Phillipa, a tall nun made taller by her sailing-ship wimple, once said to me, 'Your father knows best which church you should go to.' After I told Mum, she tore into Dad as if Sister Phillipa were *his* sister. When Sister Phillipa made the mistake of calling in to see Dad on the following

55

Saturday, Mum answered the door, potato peeler in hand. After apologizing that her husband (she didn't like Sister Phillipa referring to Dad by his name, Dan) wasn't in, she laid into her about trying to influence her sons with Roman Catholic mumbo jumbo. The affronted nun left muttering about returning when Dad was home, when she might be received with better manners. That's when Mum followed her up the stairs shouting 'and another thing'.

She came back in, teeth gritted, and we waited for another stern warning about talking to nuns. Instead her face crumpled into smiles. 'She ran ... when I went up the stairs after her, she speeded up! By the time she reached the top of the stairs, she was running and I could see her little white socks!' She bent double laughing and lifted her pinny to dab her eyes.

Dad was angry and embarrassed about the incident but he said nothing because this was the one subject about which he knew he'd always get a fight. In any case, he's far more tolerant than either Mum or Sister Phillipa, and doesn't mind which church we go to, as long as we go. He's also pretty good about going himself, even after a late night at the Queen Anne.

On Sundays, if there is a working alarm clock in the house, it doesn't go off until 9.30am. This gives him time for a lie-in and a cooked breakfast before he goes to eleven o'clock mass, when I suspect he asks forgiveness for his volatile wife.

# COMANCHE SPITE

John and I are playing *knockout*. The game involves kicking the plastic football at a goal on the primary school wall and, with one touch, returning it on target, a sort of football squash. The rules are enforced as much by what we hear as what we see. The goal is an oblong of cement render surrounded by glazed bricks. Hitting its crumbling surface makes the flat sound of *goal*; striking both render and brick is *post* and the ping of ball on brick, means a miss. Neither of us is trying to win but simply to keep the game going in satisfying thuds that eventually bring Mrs Johnson to the front door of her prefab.

'Boys, I hope this wretched game will be over soon, the Archers is starting shortly.'

Plump Mrs Johnson is Akela for the local cub pack. Her loud voice is ideal for conducting games for excited small boys in the church hall but she has trouble speaking quietly, even when she's standing close. At Sunday Service, hymns don't really get going until she joins in.

'OK, Mrs Johnson.'

'Thank you, Billy.' She gives me smile and goes back indoors.

John kicks the ball extra hard against the wall. 'OK Mithith Johnthon.' He points to the sign on the nearby lamppost. 'This is a bloody Play Street!'

In Play Streets, kids have priority and passing cars have to slow to walking pace. No one knows this better than John. When motorists toot him to get out of the way, he goes into slow motion, or kneels down in the road to do up a shoelace. If they toot again, he puts his hands on his hips and tells them that kids have rights here.

He's a natural resister, who meets requests or orders with silence or slow, sullen acceptance. His standard answer to challenges from other kids, no matter how big they are, is 'gonna make me?' He prefers to leave me to do the talking when adults ask questions but he's quick to attack goody-goodness. Grown-ups like me. Kids prefer John.

Michael O'Rourke is perched on the end of Mrs Johnson's garden wall. Behind him, smoke rises from a concealed cigarette. Between hunched, furtive drags, he looks up and down the street like a spy in a doorway. He blows the smoke down between his legs and his fat cheeks flap out to 'thtup' real and imagined bits of tobacco from the tip of his tongue, followed by a squirt of saliva through the gap in his top front teeth. Michael admits to being a 'heavy ould lad' and his bulk makes describing sport easier than taking part. He's reporting our game as if it's the Cup Final.

'A great attempt by Billy Driscoll, roising star of English football ... and what a clearance from his kid brother, surely de foinest young fullback in de country.'

Today he's broadcasting from his commentary box but he often strolls around in the middle of our football or cricket matches, speaking into an imaginary microphone. It's like having Kenneth

Wolstenholme or John Arlott down on the pitch. However, Michael's knowledge of cricketing terms remains extremely Irish. 'Driscoll is after firin' de ball past de bowler's kisser.'

Michael loves all things American, especially Westerns and gangster films. So do we, but he wants to *be* an American. In the weeks after he arrived from Ireland, we knew him as 'Gene', after the cowboy, Gene Autry, until we heard his mother call him Michael. When explaining, he said, 'Tell me now, what kinda cowboy, goody or baddy, was ever called Michael?' He had a point.

I was delighted when he christened me 'the Kid' to go with my name and, with most of the street cowboys, I was won over by his colourful language in our Wild West games. Outdrawing the fastest gunslingers and saving settlers from marauding Indians had never been more fun. And he'd never say, 'stick 'em up' when he had enemies cornered; instead he'd slowly waggle his revolver under their noses and say, 'Now I'd be obloiged if ye'd be after hand'n me your weapons, and den reachin' for de skoy.' Sometimes, in the heat of battle, he'd confuse cowboys and gangsters, 'vamanos muchachos, dey're packin' heat' or 'dirty hoodlums are speaking wid forked tongues'.

We no longer play cowboys but Michael continues to 'mosey on home', eat 'chow' and greet you with 'howdy'.

Further along, Madge Smith's son, little Jojo, is astride the same wall, spurring it to a gallop while swivelling left and right to fire his cap guns at chasing Indians. He's wearing a fawn Roy Rogers hat that was once John's pride and joy. He gave it grudgingly – to Jojo last year when I told him he was too old to be playing cowboys. John wanted so badly to be a real cowboy. Even now, it irks him that the Wild West is no longer a place he can go to fight outlaws and Indians.

Cowboys are the kind of men we all want to be. Other TV heroes like Robin Hood, William Tell or Ivanhoe can't hold a candle to Flint McCulloch in *Wagon Train, Bronco Layne* or scary Richard Boone in *Have Gun Will Travel* – it's something to do with guns or 'equaloizers', as Michael calls them. In the cinema, our favourite is Audie Murphy whose films we sit through at least twice when they're showing at the Biograph.

Jojo is blasting away when, worse than Indians, he sees David Griggs loping up behind him. 'Griggsy' is the son of 'Scrapman' Griggs, who rides around calling out for 'old iron' or 'any lumber' from a cart pulled by a muscular skewbald pony who is as gentle as a lamb, until he gets near enough to bite.

Like his dad, Griggsy is a street scavenger, only he takes stuff from other kids: sometimes sweets, sometimes money and – always – any fun they might be having.

He's a year older than I am but we were in the same class for the last year of primary school as he was too thick to go on to secondary school. He hates anyone cleverer than him, which is most people – especially me, ever since an encounter at the bus stop on Vauxhall Bridge Road. As a bus approached, he jabbed me in the back because I hadn't put my hand out to hail it.

'You want this bus?'

60

I couldn't help myself. 'Why, are you selling it?'

He jumped ahead of me on to the rear platform and as he grabbed the white pole, swung a fist into the side of my head. 'That's all I'm selling today, shitbag, very cheap.'

Pretty good for a moron.

Today he's wearing a baggy plaid shirt with the sleeves rolled up his beefy arms and, even in high summer, he's in heavy brown corduroy trousers held up with braces. He bounces towards us on spring heels that launch him on to the balls of his feet the moment they touch the ground. He comes to a halt in front of us, rising and falling on the spot like a nasty copper.

Jojo sits petrified on his brick horse as if the whole Sioux nation has appeared on the skyline. Michael stares at the ground and I smile an appeasing welcome. John, who smiles only when he finds something funny, waits.

'Gis a kick then, brains.'

This is no friendly request to join in. I pass him the ball. He steadies it and thumps it against the wall. The kick is hard and uncontrolled, like Griggsy himself. The loud thud on the bricks is intimidating and he knows it, but he's missed the goal. This angers him and he smashes the returning ball back at the wall; another miss! He makes a mess of retrieving the rebound and lurches after the ball. Once he has it under control, he folds his arms and scans us for any sign of piss-take for his complete absence of skill.

Why doesn't Mrs Johnson or, better still, her big milkman husband come out to complain about the thumping noise now? Why do bullies always have so much time?

He beckons me forward by flicking up the fingers on his upturned palms. 'Come on then Brains, try and geddit.'

The thing to do is fail but make the effort look genuine. Even so, I risk a clump once I'm in range. My attempted tackle is to one side, making it obvious, even to Griggsy, that he should go the other way. He does but the ball bounces off my shin, and he has to chase it again. He gets one foot on the ball and calls to John. 'Now you, come on then.'

John refuses. With widened eyes, I silently urge him to do what Griggsy wants. He shakes his head. I'm about to shout at him, when Griggsy relents and dribbles towards him.

The one person John takes notice of is Dad, whose advice on tackling is 'follow through and you won't get hurt'. But it *can* hurt, especially against someone bigger, and if the follow-through contains too much flinch, as it usually does in my case. John shrugs and leans in hard to block the ball. The tackle takes Griggsy's leg away and sends him sprawling. Silence. Griggsy springs to his feet in a ludicrous attempt to make it look like he's gone down deliberately. Jojo starts laughing. Griggsy, checks for a smile on my face – not a chance – before dashing over to cuff Jojo across the mouth. Jojo burst into tears.

'Ah now, Griggsy, de little fellah meant no harm...' says Michael.

'You what, fatso?'

Michael has many one-liners for facing down Comanches and other baddies. But this isn't Jesse James, it's mental Griggsy. Instead of replying, he holds his chin in the air like Randolph Scott in *Colt .45*.

Griggsy paces up and down, nodding his head, working out his next move. As he passes Jojo, he yanks the cowboy hat from his head, but the chinstrap holds and pulls him off the wall. He hits the ground hard and stays silent until he realizes he's not badly hurt and starts screaming.

'Shuddup you little bastard. Cowboy eh? Well, cop this, Roy Rogers.'

He snatches up the hat in both hands. The tendons in his neck stand out as he snorts up phlegm with such force you'd think he had a muscle inside his forehead. He spits into the hat, throws it on the ground and stamps on it. Forgetting he's no longer the owner, John dives to rescue it. Griggsy grabs him around the neck.

'And you ... fink you're an 'ard tackler do ya? Well, this is 'ard.'

He runs John at the wall. I close my eyes until I hear the thud-scrape of his head on the bricks. Griggsy lets go and John wheels round, ready to fight. This startles Griggsy but he recovers and grabs John's shirt collar, twists it around his fist and shoves it up under his chin.

'You little shitbag.'

'Leave him alone, you fucking bully.' I can't believe I've said this and after one step towards Griggsy, I regret it. He hurls John to the ground and turns to face me. I lose momentum and freeze in the no-man's land between spontaneous bravery and rising fear.

'Oh yeah? What's big brother gonna do then?'

What's he going to do? Nothing. Anger and

courage drain from me as if plugs have been pulled in my ankles. John gets up and shakes his head to tell me to 'leave it'. This is exactly what I'm going to do. I lift my hands like a cowboy starting to surrender.

Griggsy moves forward. I wait for the first punch, praying that my legs won't give way *before* he hits me. The punch doesn't come. Instead, he drops his fists and takes a penknife from his pocket. He opens it and circles the blade inches from my face. John barges between us, fists clenched. On top of his head, blood is gumming up his blond hair.

Griggsy lowers the knife and steps back sneering, not at John but at me for standing behind my younger brother. Being stabbed couldn't hurt as much. He makes the quivering arsehole sign by curling and uncurling his fingers. 'Chicken windy fucker, got your number.'

He has, and I'm close to tears. He swaggers over to pick up our ball and stabs it. The air hisses out and John rushes forward. I grab him and hold tight while we watch a grinning Griggsy plunge the knife in again and again. Then he goes over to Jojo, who is crouching on the kerb.

''Ere's a cowboy 'at for ya.'

He moulds the ruined ball into a bowl and jams it on Jojo's head. Jojo curls up, humiliated but not daring to take it off.

Mrs Johnson appears at her window. Griggsy puts the knife away and says to me as if everything is back to normal. 'Got any money to borrow me?'

'No.'

For once, he believes me and I'm not forced to

empty my pockets. Instead, he gives me a contemptuous pat on the cheek and bounces off down the street. 'See ya, windy.' Before he turns the corner, he snorts again and spits in our direction.

Jojo hurls the squashed ball to the ground, pulls out his guns and fires wildly after Griggsy. And I want to be Audie Murphy, to gallop after him and drag him through the dust at the end of a lasso, before running him out of town.

'A Comanche if ever I saw one,' says Michael. He knows no greater insult. Comanches are the lowest of the low; treacherous bastards even attack wagon trains at night.

John gives the remains of our ball a last violent kick down the road and Jojo picks up his soiled cowboy hat.

Michael eases off the wall. 'Jojo, y'ill need dat disinfectin'. Sure, ye might catch TB, or even vinurial disease.' Jojo looks at him, then at me, mystified.

Michael strokes the few dark hairs above his lip that he hopes make him look a bit like Richard Boone. 'Dat bastard deserves a bit of his own Comanche treatment: staked out in de sun, bollick-naked, near an anthill dat I'd be after givin' a good kickin'.'

I join in. 'Yeah, balls smeared with honey to get the ants in the mood for something sweet.'

Jojo giggles and our humiliation fades as we imagine ever more painful retribution.

John doesn't laugh, even when we're removing Griggsy's dick with a tomahawk. His revenge isn't going to be in the Black Hills of Dakota.

65

# SIZE MATTERS

'Go on then,' says Rooksy, 'show us.'

Raymond Dunn's dick was big even when he was a toddler. His nickname is 'Swole'. It comes from the time he was having a bath with his little cousin who, noticing the difference in sizes, pointed between Raymond's legs, and said to Mrs Dunn, 'Look Auntie, it's all swolled up.'

This remained a private family joke until the day Rooksy saw it during a piss-up-the-wall contest. He claimed it gave Raymond an unfair advantage that should be taken into account when measuring the height of the wet stains. Caught between pride and embarrassment, a flustered Raymond mentioned the story of his cousin in the bath. Rooksy's growing smile told him that this had been a terrible mistake. Soon, everyone knew about 'Swole's snake', and no one called him Raymond again.

Rooksy, John and I are sitting on Swole's bed. He's the only kid we know who has a 'double'. Swole's home is an 'apartment' rather than a flat. Flats are what we and Peabody tenants live in, although 'Peabodies' are posher because they have bathrooms. Our bath is in the kitchen beneath a lift-up board. It doubles as a high table top that we sit around on stools. Inside, the bath is chair-shaped; so there's no lying back under bubbles as women do in the Camay soap adverts. This is one of three things that would mean luxury to John and me, along with a fridge, so we can drink cold Gold Top milk all year round, and a telephone. We'd like a car most but Dad doesn't drive.

Swole's bedroom is above the entrance to the large wood yard that stretches up Morton Hill. We rarely have to call for him by ringing the bell because he sees us first from his window, where he spends a lot of time propped on his elbows and spitting on the timber lorries as they pass through the gates below.

Swole's bedroom is also his playground. He's rarely allowed out. His dad doesn't like him mixing with us because he thinks we're common. Swole doesn't have any uncommon friends and he lives in fear of being sent to a boarding school, where he'll sleep in a dormitory with posh boys and probably have to become a queer.

On the rare occasions his dad isn't around, Swole invites us in and his mum gives us cold lemonade: the kind you make by adding water to yellow powder.

The shelves beside his bed are stacked high with books and board games but Swole doesn't read much and he has no brothers or sisters to play games with. His pride and joy is the huge wooden battlefield, painted green and brown, on which battalions of British and German soldiers line up against one another. There are hundreds: running or marching across the uneven terrain, lying down or kneeling to fire from black trenches, or from behind balsa-wood rocks and bushes. Some are frozen in action, arms flung back in the moment of being shot, while others are charging enemy lines with fixed bayonets, led by officers armed only with pistols. Each model is immaculately painted: the British in khaki and the Germans in grey with contoured helmets that are so much smarter than the British pudding bowls. 'Dad made everything, apart from the soldiers,' says Swole. He tells us this with pride but little affection.

He was proud enough recently to take me into the separate area of the wood yard adjacent to their home where his dad makes his own stuff. When working here, Swole says that he always wears a full-length white apron instead of his overalls.

'Take a look at this,' he said, carefully lifting the sheet from a large cabinet whose delicately shaped doors lay unattached beside it. 'It's for keeping trophies in. Look at those joints, they're called dovetails.'

I ran my finger across the interlocking wooden teeth at the corners and could feel only smooth wood.

'I said, "look" not "touch"!' He leaned close to check for incriminating fingerprints before he put the cover back, and tugged it left and right to make it look undisturbed.

'Let's go.'

'Jesus, Swole, what's the matter?'

'My dad, he'd kill me if he knew I'd let you in here.' The look on his face made me as keen to get out of there as he was.

John and I used to play with toy soldiers but Swole deploys armies. Today, John is eyeing them longingly. If he were on his own, he'd happily lead them into battle. Swole regularly rearranges the formations and we would much sooner help him to do this than look at his dick, again. Rooksy, however, is persisting.

'Come on then Swole, let's see if it's got any bigger.'

I hate these moments because they can lead to Rooksy suggesting cock comparisons, which only involve establishing whose is next biggest after Swole's. I always refuse. Although things are starting to happen for me down there, progress is depressingly slow. Rooksy and Swole have pubic hair. So do I, but unlike them, I know exactly how many I've got. We've seen Swole's dick before because he likes showing it. He spends a lot of time in his bedroom, making do with his solitary games of soldiers, reading American comics, playing chess against himself and, we suspect, playing *with* himself. Rooksy says that it couldn't have got that big without hours of attention, something that could work for us if we do the same. We're obviously not devoting enough time to it.

Swole looks like Alfred E. Neuman, the kid on the cover of *Mad Magazine*; his ears don't just stick out but are cupped towards you by invisible hands. He's aware of his less-than-film-star looks but his dick is a consolation and, although his ears turn deep red when others refer to it in front of girls, he's secretly pleased and fondles it gratefully in most idle moments.

Rooksy gives him a shove. 'Give it some air Swole or it might stop growing.'

Swole grins. 'OK, shut the door Billy.' He unbuttons his trousers. And there it is on his open palm,

69

like Mr Bevan our butcher showing a lamb chop to a customer. Only the greaseproof paper is missing.

'You lucky bastard,' says Rooksy, poking at it with a German lieutenant. 'Can you make it bigger?'

Swole is ahead of him and everything is swelling nicely until we hear his mother coming along the hall. He grabs a comic from the shelf and throws himself face-down on the bed. Rooksy stands bolt upright. John and I whip round to study the soldiers but crash into the battlefield. The resulting earthquake sends the British and German armies bouncing into one another. Mrs Dunn flings open the door to the silence of illicit activity rapidly abandoned.

'Four nil!'

Mrs Dunn raises an eyebrow. 'What's that, Billy? I hope it's not four nil to the Germans.'

She's a sharp one is Mrs Dunn, a skinny woman with short, violently permed hair. She purses her lips while her darting, nervous eyes probe the room.

'Now what are you up to, Raymond?' she asks, in the way mums do when they really mean everyone present.

'Nothing, just playing.' The choked squeak betrays his excitement.

'Why don't you go out now and get some fresh air.'

'OK Mum.' His voice is closer to normal.

'Well, up you get then.'

'In a minute, Mum, I want to finish something off.'

Rooksy snorts. Mrs Dunn's eyes flash but she says nothing.

'Quick about it then, Dad's home you know ... and that comic is upside down.'

Very sharp, Mrs Dunn.

Swole won't be finishing off anything. Mention of his dad has drained the colour from his face. After his mum closes the door, he rolls on to his back, frantically doing up his fly buttons. John starts setting the soldiers in khaki back on their feet to show a British victory. Rooksy looks disappointed enough to ask for his money back.

'Let's go,' says Swole.

In our house, 'Dad's home' means noise and what Mum calls 'foolery'; at Swole's, it brings a scary hush. Even when out with us, Swole behaves as if his dad were standing behind him, and whatever he's about to do, he takes a look around first.

Mr Dunn is a cabinetmaker. He hates running the yard and the business of buying, cutting and selling wood when all he wants to do is work with it. According to Swole, he's happy only when he's making his own furniture. But most of the time, he seems to be waiting to get angry and the red marks that we often see on Swole's face show that he doesn't wait for long. Sometimes it's worse: a black eye that Swole swears comes from being bashed up by kids from the other side of Vauxhall Bridge Road. Even if this were true, they'd never hit Mrs Dunn. So where does she get *her* bruises?

It's not as if other parents don't hit their kids; some fathers even use their belts. John and I have been spared this. While Mum used to slap out spontaneously at whatever part of us was closest,

Dad has never hit us, or threatened to. His own father beat him and Mum says we're lucky that he's decided to be different. Not that he doesn't make his disapproval clear: he can freeze you with a look. But it lasts only long enough to make a point before a tilt of his head and, sometimes, a smile tells us it's over.

At the foot of the stairs, Swole's wide-eyed warning brings us to a halt by the open door to the wood yard. On the workbench, Mr Dunn, in his white apron, has the carcass of the trophy cabinet on its back and he's rubbing it with sandpaper wrapped around a small wooden block. His work-thickened shoulders and Popeye forearms couldn't be moving more gently. After each pass, he runs his fingers over the smoothed surface and holds them close to his face to examine the white dust as if he's about to taste it. He wipes it on his apron and rubs again.

He hasn't looked at us but he knows we're here. He stops working. We've interrupted him and he isn't going to start again until he's told us so. He closes his eyes, tilts his head forward and stretches his neck by easing it from side to side. We wait. Swole is shaking. His dad opens his small, dark eyes and his instantly accurate gaze makes me want to run away.

'Where do you think you're going?' His soft, menacing voice makes me forget he's only our mate's dad.

'Just going out for a bit,' says Swole.

'No you're not, upstairs.'

'But Mum said I...'

'Now!' His whisper is more frightening than a

shout. Swole's head dips to his chest and he climbs the stairs to his room.

Rooksy, John and I stand there, waiting to be dismissed.

'Well?' he says and shows us the way out with an angry flick of his eyes.

'Miserable bastard,' says Rooksy, once we're in the street. 'Do you think Swole's mum told him what was going on?'

I shake my head. 'No, she's scared of him too. He blames her for anything Swole does.'

Rooksy shrugs. 'Jealous then, Swole's got a bigger dick.'

# JUBBLIES, PIGEONS AND LIES

Wooden crates of R Whites and Corona empties are stacked four high on the Big Step outside Plummer's corner shop. The sun has turned the black-and-white tiles into a chequered hotplate. I'm sitting on its edge holding a Jubbly that was frozen ten minutes ago but is already turning to orange juice in its collapsing tetrahedron carton.

'Hello Billy.'

Sarah's slender silhouette stands before me. A fizzing in my chest has me rising to my feet. But a bigger outline moves alongside her and I sit down again. It's Kenneth 'Kirk' Douglas. He's blond, very blond. Girls like him, giggle when they see him, send him anonymous notes, and the younger ones use his name in their skipping games.

*On a mountain stands a lady*
*Who she is I do not know*
*All she wants is gold and silver*
*All she wants is a nice young man*

The rope turns faster.

*All right Susan, I'll tell your mother*
*Kissing Kirk Douglas around the corner*
*Is it true?*

Faster still, to catch the girl's legs.

*Yes, no, yes, no, yes, no, yes, no, yes...*

The rope invariably traps their legs on yes.

I listen out for my name but never hear it. When I was little, the girls never caught me in kiss-chase because I didn't want them to. Even if I'd made myself catchable, they would have rushed past me in pursuit of Kirk, who was a good runner but enjoyed being caught. At the time, it made him a sissy. Not now, it doesn't.

I didn't care much about girls at the time but it bothered me that they liked Kirk so much. They still do, especially his 'lovely long eyelashes' and his blond hair. What makes him bearable is knowing that he's not too bright. Not backward or anything, only a little slow on the uptake.

'Hello Sarah, watcha Kirk.'

His push on my shoulder is heavier than play-ful. 'Watcha Billy, hot eh?'

He has this likeable, irritating way of talking

without thinking, while I waste time searching for clever things to say that, once said, are rarely worth the effort. Inside Kirk's head, there's no space between thinking and speaking and although what he says isn't funny or that interesting, it's OK. I can't stand him.

'We're going to have Jubblies too,' he says.

'We're'? Because they're both going to buy one? Or because they're boyfriend and girlfriend, and he's buying? An ache spreads in my stomach as I hold up my Jubbly.

'Just the job in this heat, it's ... melty hot.'

Melty hot? Melty bloody hot? Thankfully, they don't seem to be listening. Kirk goes into the shop but Sarah waits outside. He is buying hers and she's avoiding looking at me.

Kirk emerges with a Jubbly in each hand, tearing along the top strip of one with his teeth to reveal the orange ice. He holds out the other one. 'Here you are Sarah.'

'Thanks Kirk.'

It hurts to hear them say each other's names. And is Kirk standing between us to make it clear she's *his* girlfriend?

Sarah squeezes the orange ice out through the edge that Mr Plummer has cut with scissors; girls ask for it to be cut, boys tear it. Kirk sits down, and jostles me to move over, pretending to be friendly but determined to make room between us for Sarah to sit next to him. I'm about to leave when I catch her glance at the space Kirk has made for her and pretend she hasn't seen it! She walks in front of us to sit down beside me. One in the eye for Kirk, long lashes and all.

She is wonderfully close and her bare arm is touching mine. She stretches out her brown legs on the pavement and, with her free hand, pushes her frock down to her knees. I clutch my Jubbly too hard and orange juice squirts on to the pavement.

'Ha,' says Kirk, 'what a waste.' He leans over, knocking me against Sarah. His bulk doesn't threaten in the same way that Griggsy's does but with Sarah next to me, I hate him for being bigger than I am.

'Kirk, do you mind?' she says.

'Looks like he's peed on the pavement.'

It does.

'No, it doesn't,' she says.

He smirks. I swig long and slow at my Jubbly, trying to think of a clever response. Nothing comes to me and we sit in awkward silence until relief arrives in the shape of Michael, who is toiling towards us, arms straight down like he's carrying an invisible rucksack. One hand is cupped backwards as if ready to draw a gun; it's hiding a cigarette.

He flicks the brim of an invisible cowboy hat. 'Howdy M'am, Kork, and if it isn't Billy de Kid. Buenos dias, how are ye?'

'Hello Michael, what're you up to?' says Sarah.

'Not much señorita but I'm just after hearin' on de wireless that de bandits who robbed that train vamoosed with more than two million pounds. Jesse James would have been proud of 'em.'

'Oh yeah?' says Kirk, dropping his jaw to mock him.

Michael spits a shred of tobacco from the tip of

76

his tongue. 'I'm too late for de Jubbly swallying contest den?'

'Contest? It's not a contest,' says Kirk.

Michael winks at me. 'Just as well, doesn't Billy have yiz both well beat?'

Sarah laughs.

Kirk takes the bait. 'Anyway, he started before us.'

'Dat's de way to win muchachos, dat's de way.'

'If we'd started at the same time...'

'Ah Kork, if de moon were made of cheese...'

'What?'

'Oh nottn', just a bit of poetry.'

I suppress a laugh. Michael looks away, eyes narrowed against the sun and prairie dust, like Randolph Scott. He drops what's left of his cigarette and shreds it with the sole of his shoe. 'Will yiz be at the hoedown on Sunday?' He's referring to our street party that has been held ever since the Coronation, except that it now takes place in the school holidays. We nod. 'Me ould fellah's doin' de announcements. Isn't he after gettin' ahold of won of dem loudhailer yokes to help with de organizin'?'

Other Irishmen have difficulty understanding Michael's dad's accent and our Cockney neighbours will be taking the mickey as usual. Kirk shakes his head and smirks at me. I refuse to smile. Dad sticks up for Mr O'Rourke because he says it's better to be a doer than someone who watches doers.

Behind Michael, some pigeons scatter as a Morris Minor burbles by. It's white, like my aunt's. I'm about to mention this when Sarah cries out and puts her hands over her eyes.

Michael gasps. 'Jesus, Mary and Joseph.'

In the road, a pigeon is flapping, straining to pull itself off the tarmac. Several times the squashed body peels up but can't break free of its own goo. Small, surprisingly white feathers swirl like snowflakes around the grey body and some settle on the dark red intestines that have wormed out on to the road.

'Yeuch,' says Kirk, dropping his head between his knees.

Sarah clutches her hair and turns put her face against my chest. 'The poor thing, the poor thing...'

The pigeon rests, then tries again. It must be in agony but its face just looks puzzled. If only it would stop flapping. Its neck writhes up between wings that are scraping the ground like a weird dustpan and brush. Please stop flapping! I ease Sarah away from me and she looks at me like she did when Josie fell over, expecting me to make things OK. My head swirls with pride – and the need to be sick. I stand up and grab a bottle from a crate.

When I reach the pigeon it stops moving. Relieved, I spin round to announce its death when the bloody bird flutters back to life. I raise the bottle to strike, but the bird is still again, watching me with its orange-bead eye.

'Do it Billy, de poor yoke's buzzard meat.'

I bring the bottle down but miss the head and make a greater mess of its body.

Sarah screams, 'No, stop!'

The neck lifts. This time the eye is closed. With

the next blow, I crush its head. Jubbly-flavoured vomit rises in my throat.

I wobble back to the Big Step. Michael takes the bottle from me and puts a hand on my shoulder to reassure me as if I'm Roy Rogers and I've had to put Trigger out of his misery.

'How could you? The poor thing,' says Sarah.

'T'was for de best Sarah. Sure wasn't de bird dyin' in agony?'

I want to say something too, but my head is too full of what I've just seen, and done. I sit beside Sarah, breathing hard to stop myself being sick. Until now, I've killed only insects and worms, which can't look you in the face as you're doing it. I put my hands over my eyes and can still see the pigeon's writhing neck, and its accusing orange eye. Even when I was bringing down the bottle on its head, I could think only that here was a living creature that would soon not be alive anymore, because I was killing it. I tuck my shaking hands into my armpits, unsure whether I'm proud or disgusted by what I've done.

The Corona lorry pulls up at the kerb to screen the corpse from view. Michael holds out a hand to me. 'Well done compadré, it had to be done.'

We move to sit on the other side of the shop to let the deliverymen load the crates. No one speaks until Michael gets up and squints into the distance, as if checking whether Sioux or Comanches are waiting up ahead for the wagon train. 'Hasta la vista, muchachos. I have to be gettin' back to de ould hacienda ... chow time.'

Squashed pigeon or not, a meal is not something to be missed.

Kirk looks at Sarah and winks at me. 'Hasn't that put you off eating Michael?'

'Not at all Kork. But aren't ye looking terrible pale in de face. Was it all a bit much for ye?'

'What are you talking about? I could have done it if Billy hadn't.'

'Not easy when ye are sat der wid your head in your hands. Sure wouldn't de bird be dead of ould age before he got a belt from ye.' He grins at me. 'See ya around Kid.'

He lumbers off at a pace that will get him home before hunger sets in. For me, meals are interruptions to whatever I'm doing; for Michael, they're vital staging posts in a day that consists of eating, short periods of satisfaction and longer, more difficult, times spent looking forward to eating.

'What's Fatty O'Rourke on about?' says Kirk, who should keep quiet, as it's the best thing to do when you've had the piss taken out of you.

Sarah and I don't answer.

After a while, she says, 'Well Billy, what about the round-the-block race on Sunday? Are you running?'

'I am,' says Kirk, with a forward one-two shrug of his shoulders.

Well, Kirk, aren't you the bloody marvel.

The 'round-the-block' race is four times round an oblong circuit that takes in our street and the next one. Last year Kirk won it. This year, I think I've a chance of winning if I can stay free of asthma. Sarah hasn't answered him. She's waiting for my answer!

'Maybe.'

Maybe? Of course I'm running in the race but I

80

don't want Kirk to think that it matters that much.

'Well, may the best man win,' she says.

'Yeah,' says Kirk, 'hope it's me ... again. Last year, I won two big bottles of Cream Soda.'

That's where he gets it wrong: boasting is worse than being thick. Sarah misses my modest smile, which is a pity, because it's like Audie Murphy's before he beats up bigmouth baddies.

I change the subject. 'How was your holiday in Somerset?'

'Oh, marvellous ... didn't want to come home.'

'At your Nan's?'

'Yeah.'

She can see I'm trying to exclude Kirk and decides to be fair, 'What about you, Kirk? Going hop picking again?'

'S'pose so.'

I envy Kirk his late summers in the hop fields, when his whole family goes down to Kent to live in wooden dormitories with other Cockney families. They have a great time and, according to Aunt Winnie, it isn't only the kids who get up to all kinds of mischief. And everyone comes home brown as berries.

We don't get much sunshine in Cumberland. When John and I returned from holiday last week, Kirk greeted us with a rare joke, 'Nice tan, Driscoll brothers, been moonbathing?' Of course, he's at his best in the summer, when his hair goes 'straw blond'. Bastard.

Everyone looks better with a suntan. It makes Rooksy's dad look like a film star. My dad goes dark brown in summer when working on the building site but because he keeps his vest on, he

81

looks like he's wearing one even when he isn't. I've been sitting in the sun myself at every opportunity because it's supposed to shrink spots – and Mum says a tan makes my eyes look bluer.

I pick up my empty Jubbly carton. Punching down over the hole at the corner can get it to burst with a satisfying bang. I place it nonchalantly on the step and bring the side of my fist down hard. It's my day for missing targets. The blow fails to cover the hole and instead of a small explosion, there's an embarrassing 'phut' as the carton collapses.

'Ha, he's farted,' says Kirk.

My face burns.

'Billy Driscoll's farted.' He's rolling backwards on the step, forcing himself to laugh.

Sarah smiles. Does she think I have?

'Don't be stupid, it was the Jubbly packet,' I say.

'Wasn't. You farted, we'll get the smell in a sec.'

My voice goes sissy-thin. 'I have not farted.'

'Pooh, the whiff,' says Kirk, like some five-year-old.

'It was the Jubbly packet,' I say.

'It was a faaaarrrt.'

'It wasn't a fart. I don't fart.'

'Yes you do.'

Then I say it. 'No I don't, I've never farted.'

Kirk throws his arms in the air. Sarah's eyebrows rise. I stand up, desperate to get away.

'Never farted? Ha! Everyone farts,' says Kirk.

Embarrassment boils through me but now I can't help myself. 'I haven't.'

'You're not only a farter, Billy Driscoll, you're a liar too.'

It's true. I'm unravelling in front of them.

'It was the Jubbly packet,' says Sarah.

Kirk stops smiling, 'But he said he's *never* farted ... liar.'

'Have you ever heard him?'

Unlike me, Kirk doesn't lie. 'Fart? Well, no. But...'

'How do you know he has then?'

His mouth opens and he looks around for an audience to share his disbelief. 'But everyone...'

'You don't know, Kirk, do you? So stop it.'

Her words cut through the shame roaring in my ears.

'But...' He flashes her a furious look and thrusts his face into mine. 'You bloody liar.' He storms off.

Although Kirk can be dim, he's made me look dimmer. I hate him. But not as much as I hate myself for being a lying idiot in front of Sarah.

She gets to her feet. 'I have to go now ... see you at the street party?'

I can't look at her. 'Yeah, see you.'

'The pigeon ... it was brave.'

I tingle at hearing 'brave'. Now I can look at her while her 'brave' competes with the other voice in my head screaming 'liar'.

'Thanks. Look, sometimes I say ... *want* to say things that don't come out like they should...' She stops me with a shake of her head.

'I hope you win the race.' She touches my arm with Jubbly-cold fingers. Guinevere is tying her favour to my lance before I go jousting with Sir Bad Knight.

'Thanks Sarah, yes, see you there.'

She walks away, pushing a hand through her hair and revealing the back of her neck. I wonder, again, if it's normal to find this so exciting. I watch her until she reaches her doorstep half way down the street. She turns and gives me a wave, and goes indoors before she can see mine.

## BEACH MAGIC AND SUNRAY STORIES

I sit down again on the Big Step and squeeze my palms into my eyes. Why not be like Kirk and simply say what comes into my bloody head? Being dull has to be better than being a liar.

I don't often get caught out lying because I rarely tell complete lies. At a hint of doubt in someone's face, I can adjust smoothly back towards the truth. I fib because in that second before speaking, there's enough time to make things funnier, smarter – and I can't resist. However, my 'improved' versions are often pathetic. Melty hot?

It's when I'm scared or ashamed that I lose control. 'Never farted'? For God's sake! While I can laugh when others talk of bodily functions, I can't bear it if it has anything to do with me. This goes back to when I was four years old. I was at sanatorium on the Kent coast: a 'fresh-air haven' for the chesty kids of smoggy London.

My stay began badly. On the first morning, the nurse stood me on the bed to pee into the wide-necked bottle. When she thought I'd finished, she took the bottle away. But there was more and my arc of pee splashed on to the floor. 'Billy!' she screamed and lunged forward to field the waning stream. Startled, I swung round, spattering her white apron and dribbling over the blankets. She stretched again to get the bottle between my legs but slipped to her knees on the wet floor. The bottle flew from her hand and spun along the ward, sprinkling left and right. The other kids scrambled to the ends of their beds to cheer its progress.

I was frozen with shame until I had to jump, two-footed like Spartacus in the gladiator school, above the nurse's slap at my legs. Before she could aim a second swipe, sister arrived, scrubbed arms on hips.

'What in the name of sweet Jesus is going on? Nurse, will you please clean up this urine immediately.'

Then the sister took my hand and led me, without my pyjama bottoms, past jeering inmates to the bathroom where she washed down my legs with a flannel. The next night I 'urined' in the dozy warmth of my bed. On subsequent nights before 'lights out' I was taken to the lav and had to stand there with the door open until I convinced the nurse that I didn't need to go.

A week later, I caught whooping cough, which extended a fortnight's convalescence to two months and, for a while, confined me to my own room. On sunny days, my bed was wheeled out on to the veranda from where I watched enviously as other children played games on the vast lawns. Apart from eating before meals, taking medicine and going to the toilet, there was little to do except fill in pictures in books. The coughing made this difficult and jogged my crayon over the lines. As soon as I knew a picture couldn't be perfectly coloured, I'd abandon it and begin the next one. The more I messed up, the angrier I got, until I couldn't even stand having the spoiled pages in the book. After I tore them out, the nurses took away the crayons and colouring books.

They replaced them with old illustrated story-books that had words in a box at the bottom of each page. I couldn't read but the pictures fascinated me and I made up my own stories to match them. Once I was back on the main ward, I needed only these books. When the nurses encouraged me to play with the others, I feigned asthma in order to be left alone with my pictures and stories.

Part of my treatment involved ultra-violet light sessions in the Sunray Room in the company of boys and girls who, with their hunched shoulders and narrow white chests, looked like my relatives. Wearing only baggy navy shorts and stinking rubber goggles, we squatted on low benches around the lamp as if it were a campfire. Through green lenses, I watched skinny, glowing bodies shifting impatiently on the benches while the lamp flickered and fizzed. None of us spoke until one day I asked if they'd like to hear one of my stories. Some of them nodded. I was only half way through the tale of a racing caterpillar, when the lamp was switched off and we had to go back to the wards.

That evening, after 'lights out', the boy recovering from TB in the next bed asked me to finish the story I had started in the Sunray Room. I was less sure of myself in the hushed ward but, under cover of darkness, I began. On following nights, I whispered stories into the dark until everyone had fallen asleep. When I ran out of the tales from my picture books, I made up my own. Soon I was telling stories in daytime too. I must have overdone it because the nurses, who had encouraged me to talk to the other children, now called me 'chatterbilly'. This felt like being told off. However, it was after we were taken to Broadstairs Beach that I got into my storytelling stride.

I was one of five boys kneeling, almost head to head, around a deep hole in the sand. The sun was extra hot on our backs as we had been told to keep our shirts on. Beneath us, our shadows merged and parted as if trying to keep out the sunlight that was flashing past us in bright slashes and crescents to bounce off the pool of seawater at the bottom of the hole.

A toy galleon bobbed on the water and the bigger boys were taking turns to describe the adventures of the pirates on board. I knew exactly what the pirates should do next but each time I tried to take up the story, I was told to shut up. I listened while the tales unfolded in whispers and the air seemed to thicken with our breath. The noises from the beach became remote and the hole felt as secret as a cave. As I grew drowsy, a godlike hand reached down to agitate the water and send the ship lurching violently. 'It's going to sink,' I shouted. It didn't sink but keeled over on the sloping side of the hole. Another hand scooped up the ship and set it back in the middle of the pool, where it rocked gently. Then it disappeared.

I reached down, scrabbling around in the pool to locate the wreck but this caused me to slip down the hole's collapsing side. Warm seawater, smelling vaguely of piss rose above my elbows.

'Help!' One of the boys dragged me out by the legs. 'The ship, the ship has gone...'

He wasn't bothered. 'Has it?'

Another boy offered an explanation: 'Magic.'

'Yeah, made invisible by magic,' said my rescuer. He was smiling.

'Magic?' I asked.

'Can't be explained.'

'Invisible?'

'Means it's there but you can't see it. It's vanished.'

'Oh.' And then, 'Vanished?'

'Gone, disappeared.'

The boys exchanged smirks. One of them had nabbed the ship while I'd been distracted. He brought a hand from behind his back.

'No!' I spun round to avoid seeing. I would believe only the magic version.

I tore across the beach, hands clamped over my ears. The ward nurse got up from the picnic blanket when she saw me holding my head. 'What's the matter?'

'The ship, it got invisible.'

'Did it?'

'Yes, and it vanished.'

'Just look at your shirt, it's soaked.' She pulled it over my head and rubbed my arms and chest with a towel.

'It was magic!' I'd used my three new words.

'Stand still.'

'But it was magic.'

'Of course it was Billy, if you say so.'

I thought she meant this, and that people would believe what I told them. I began to tell ever more fantastic tales that usually involved me and magic. Soon none of the nurses was saying, 'if you say so, Billy'; now it was, 'I don't think so, Billy'. When other children started calling me a liar, I stopped my stories altogether. I had abandoned colouring-book pictures once I'd drawn over the lines and I gave up telling my stories unless they could be told exactly as I imagined them.

Only at home with John did I risk giving full rein to my stories, told before he went to sleep. At first, he didn't even understand them but he grew to like them and they became part of a nightly ritual. Eventually, the stories turned into plays in which, under my direction, we acted out a variety of heroic roles.

Since my time at Broadstairs, being myself – like Kirk manages to be himself – never feels good enough because I can always imagine a better version of who I am. Like it says on the signs outside building sites, I'm *under construction.*

## BIKINI CLOSE-UP

The suffocating afternoon heat has driven Rooksy and me deep into the shade of the church porch. Looking back from the dark end, the wrought iron gates at the entrance shimmer as if they're being

X-rayed by the sun. We could be sheltering from a light storm. We lie on our backs on the black and ochre tiles. From under the heavy church doors behind us, a draught smelling of stone and furniture polish streams across the floor to cool our necks and outstretched arms.

Rooksy begins rubbing his crotch.

'Not here Rooksy. I mean, we're almost in church.'

'What?' He props himself on an elbow. 'Just thinking of Madge, fancy coming to see her? In her bikini?'

'Where?'

He sits up. 'At her house, where do you think?'

'How do you know?'

'Jojo told me. She sunbathes out the back on a long deckchair thingy.'

'But we'd have to go into her garden.'

'Just for a peek.'

'But what if?'

'She won't.'

'No, I mean Siddy, what if he...?'

'He's out.'

Madge's husband may be out but he doesn't go to work like most dads. He could come home at any time. We don't know what he does exactly but we have an idea from the company he keeps: big, scary blokes in Ford Zodiacs and, sometimes, Jaguars. Anyone who sees him unloading cardboard boxes from his little van gets a 'whatchoo lookin' at?' sneer. Jojo claims that the boxes contain towels and tablecloths for sale at East Lane market. No one believes him.

'I don't think so, Rooksy.'

'Don't think so? Don't think you want to have a look at Madge in her bikini? In knickers and bra?'

'Knickers and bra?'

'Good as.'

Is it though? This is another puzzle. A bikini provides no more cover than undies, except that when women wear bikinis they're usually on view, at the beach or a swimming pool. This is OK. Underwear, on the other hand, does a similar covering job yet it mustn't be seen and has to be kept *under* clothes.

Mum's *Ambrose Wilson Catalogue* shows women posing in corsets, knickers and suspender belts. And we can see ladies' underwear, close-up, on half-bodied models in the Army and Navy Stores, where Mum tells John and me to scarper while she looks around. So, in a bikini, women are dressed; in only their underwear, even if it covers more, they're not.

Rooksy says that if it's their bodies you want to see, there's no difference. Maybe, but why is it so much more exciting to catch sight of a girl's knickers than to see her in a swimming costume?

'Come on, think of it Billy, Madge, in a bikini, a couple of minutes away. Those tits...'

The magic word.

'And you don't want to go?'

No, I don't. I half-close my eyes, pretending to look excited while trying to think of a way out: a sudden asthma attack or, more truthfully, an overwhelming need for the toilet. Rooksy stares at me, mouthing 'Maaadge' and cupping an imaginary breast on his chest.

'Madge, Billy, in only her knickers and a bra.'

I'm beginning to hold on to this image.

'Come on. Just a quick decko. Something to remember, to keep in your wank bank.' He gets up and thrusts out his hand and I let him pull me to my feet.

Outside the Smiths' prefab, Rooksy says, 'I'll go first.'

He rolls over the wall and creeps along the side of the house. On reaching the corner, he stops and sits back on his haunches, expecting me to be right behind him. I haven't moved. His eyes flick to the corner of the prefab and he holds a finger to his lips, like Audie Murphy outside the baddies' hideout. Then he makes a circle of his thumb and forefinger to tell me it's OK.

I clamber over the wall and scoot up to him on legs as limp as string. From around the back of the house, the Searchers are singing *Sweets For My Sweet*.

'Right, here goes.' He moves on to hands and knees and stretches his neck like a tortoise to look around the corner. He jerks his head back. I get up to run but he grabs my shirt and grins. 'She's there. She's there … yellow bikini.'

I hope that that's it but he takes another, bolder look and waves me alongside to see for myself. On all fours, I peek past him. Madge is lying on a canvas lounger, eyes closed and lips pursed, while she concentrates on her tan. White-framed sunglasses are pushed back into her dark hair. Her bikini is covered with thin wavy frills, like the one Jayne Mansfield wears. The yellow is luminous against her brown skin and the oil on her

pared with the rest of her body? Like turkey, you know … the white bits are best.' He doesn't think this is funny, so I get more explicit. 'I'd love to feel under her bikini and…'

And what? I'm running out of steam. Rooksy stands back and his smile fades. Truth is, I don't know what I'd do after the 'feel' bit. I know what I could do, but I can't see myself doing it, not with Madge.

'And I'd…'

'Well?' says Rooksy.

'Dunno … not much, I suppose.'

'Oh?'

'Well … she's a woman.'

His eyes widen. 'Er, yes Billy. Don't you like women then?'

'Yes, no, I mean, it's just that she's grown up and … well, big.'

He nods and looks away. Does he think I'm queer?

'Rooksy? She's Jojo's mum. I mean if it was someone else like…'

'Like who Billy?'

Why is he standing so close?

'Oh, I don't know … if she was a girl, you know.'

Rooksy takes a deep breath and closes his eyes.

'Look Rooksy, it's not that, you know, I didn't like it. I mean, I'm not a bummer or anything.' I accompany this with a forced laugh that makes my claim sound false.

'No, sure.'

'I'm not.'

'Course not.' He shoves his hands in his pockets. 'See you later then?'

'Yeah, OK ... but what do you think Madge will do? I mean, Siddy...'

'Don't worry about it, Billy. What harm did we do? She might even have liked it, you know, been a bit flattered.'

'But do you think she'll tell him?'

'Don't know ... don't care.'

I care, and fear has lodged a lump in my stomach that will be there for days.

'Don't worry. She won't blame you. Anyway, I've got to go.'

After he leaves, I sit on an old car tyre, praying that Madge really did see only one 'filthy bleeder'. And despite what Rooksy said, the fury in her voice has convinced me that the last thing on earth she wants is to be lusted after by her son's mates.


## BOOKS, EMPIRES AND DICKENS

Miss Birkett unlocks the library door.

'Are you my only customer then, Billy? Breathing not so good?'

'Not so good, Miss Birkett.'

I'm a bit shaky and in need of a sit-down. Asthma and ephedrine tablets have kept me awake through the night with the same stubborn thoughts looping around in my head like a stuck record. Not for the first time, I got angry at how my brittle gasps for air contrasted with John's deep breaths, and the unconscious ease with which he took them. He can't conceive of how difficult

96

breathing can be – except, maybe, when watching me. Does Josie feel like this when watching others walking normally? You don't think about the things that you can do without thinking. Breathing or being brave never cross John's mind but I think of them all the time.

It's a library day. No point going with John to meet the others. Asthma can get me sympathy from adults but if I'm not up to playing cricket or football, it only confirms me as a pune. On days like this, I either play or I'm not there – an absent sportsman, not one who is incapable of sport. So, today it has to be reading, which can be as effective as pills for calming my breathing.

The Children's Library occupies the basement of a large Victorian house. In between rows of high wooden bookshelves, heavy toast-rack radiators are ranged against the pale green walls. Freestanding lines of shelves divide the infants' corner from the main section, where four tables form a reading square in front of Miss Birkett's desk. Few kids read, or even pretend to read, under her gaze. But it's my favourite spot. While she's on guard, I can relax and read for hours.

It's going to be hot again. Miss Birkett has steeled herself to open the large, high windows but she's already having second thoughts now that cool morning air is inflating the long net curtains. In summer, the library feels less library-like: too light, too airy, too noisy, not least from kids who enjoy shouting down from the pavement outside to break Miss Birkett's rule of silence from a safe distance.

Winter is best: windows closed and centrally

heated air, thick with the smell of floor polish, cough sweets and the warm tang of the books' cellophane covers. Close to Miss Birkett's desk, the air is sweetened by her eau de Cologne, which she keeps in a large blue bottle in her right-hand drawer.

All year round, I love the smell of the books, even the old ones, with their palmed and fingered pages that can be made whiter by rubbing. And most of all, the brand new books with their unblemished white pages crying out to be read and their fresh, pear-drop smell that is never as intoxicating on a second opening, even if it's only moments later.

Slender, strange Miss Birkett is a restless lady who seems unsuited for the calm that she imposes on her library. She has a chilly manner, and she feels the cold. Her cardigans are generally buttoned up, her skirts reach her ankles and her shoes are slim versions of those that men wear. In winter, when the radiators keep the temperature in the 70s, her coat stays draped over her shoulders.

It's a bit of a puzzle why she works in a children's library because she scares children. Her witch-of-the-west eyebrows squeeze up to points while she checks the condition of returned books. As you wait before her desk, her eyes flick up from your books to regard you over her half-lens spectacles – as if it's her job to check you too. When she leans down to place the books on her 'RETURNS' trolley, her glasses slip forward to reveal small livid loaves of red skin either side of her nose, where her near-white face powder has worn away.

'Do you eat while reading?' she once asked me, while shaking breadcrumbs out of my returned

*Sherlock Holmes*.

I was about to say 'no' but her face said 'just you dare'.

'Er, yes ... sometimes.'

I often read during meals, except when it's Sunday dinner.

'Books and food do not go together. I don't see why other borrowers should be presented with scraps of your meals. Do you?'

'No.'

'Well then, read or eat. Not both at the same time.'

'OK.'

'OK?'

'Er, yes, I will, I mean I won't.'

I wanted to tell her that when it comes to reading or eating, she should do more of the latter.

I was eight years old when my class was taken to Miss Birkett's library to be shown how it worked. She stood in front of a big sign saying SILENCE and frightened everyone with her loud voice. She didn't say much about books but took time over explaining how to borrow them: 'a special privilege' and 'woe betide those who fail to return them in pristine condition.' Few kids went back to face the responsibility of membership. I did. Not that she didn't scare me too, but on days when asthma prevented me playing out it was much better to be at the library than sitting alone at home.

At first, I went less for the reading than the pleasure of being there, especially the borrowing: handing over the blue lending cards; watching Miss Birkett tuck them into the cardboard pouch with my name on it in her beautiful italic writing;

and, best of all, the plunging date stamp.

Our bookshelves at home were filled with Mum's ornaments. In our 'library' the only story book was *The Mill on the Floss*, which contained no pictures among its hundreds of pages of forbidding, tiny print. There was also *Enquire Within Upon Everything* – everything except First Division football – and a black, floppy bible which couldn't stand up like a proper book.

I went to the library most days after school to read more of the fairy stories I had heard during class 'story time'. I moved on to darker tales set in forests and castles, which Miss Birkett told me came from Russia and Germany. Next came Greek and Roman Myths, and children's histories of the great empires, Assyrian, Egyptian, Persian, Greek and, best of all, the Roman.

I picked up speed with Enid Blyton and raced on to adventures like *Coral Island*, *Ivanhoe* and the Alan Quatermain stories, which I re-enacted in games with John. Once Mum switched off the bedroom light, he would plead, 'Please Billy, let's have an adventure.' Yes, we could, as long as I was the hero. Each night, I'd lead him into jungles, across stormy seas, through space to hostile planets to fight and conquer our enemies. Facing down Indians or Martians was easier than real-life challenges, like standing up to Griggsy.

Only Miss Birkett knew how many books I was getting through. One day, as I finished *Treasure Island*, she plonked *The Strange Case of Dr Jekyll and Mr Hyde* on the table.

'This might be of interest, given what you're reading at present.'

I was flattered that she might think me clever, which, apart from Mum and Dad, everyone else seemed to think was no big deal. I hadn't liked Miss Birkett much before but she was growing on me. I've never disliked anyone who likes me.

Later on, when I handed back the *Three Musketeers*, she said, 'Now, what about Charles Dickens?' I'd seen the film *Great Expectations* on the telly. 'Ever read any of his books?'

Not fair, I thought. I was only eleven years old.

'No. Not yet.' I said, making it sound like 'but of course I will soon'.

'Well, I think it's time you met Mr Dickens.'

She put a copy of *A Christmas Carol* down in front of me and pressed it open at the first chapter. The print was tiny but there weren't as many pages as I'd expected.

'Well, go on then, make a start. There's an hour till closing time.'

*Marley was dead.*

'Time to go home, young man.' Miss Birkett was closing up as the ghost of 'Christmas yet to come' was showing Scrooge what life was like in the Cratchit home. She saw that I didn't want to stop reading and a rare smile lit up her face. 'Take it home with you.'

Dickens and small print came to mean even better stories, which made me laugh out loud – and cry – more often than I did at the pictures.

'You shouldn't read those Dickens books if this is what they do to you,' said Mum, when she found me in tears at the death of Betty Higden.

Until then, I had believed that heroes had to be handsome, brave and strong, like Jack in *Coral*

*Island* or Leo Vincey in *She*. In Dickens' stories, being good and kind was enough, and smaller characters, such as Smike and Joe Gargery, were as memorable as Nicholas Nickleby or Pip. I wouldn't have wanted to be like Betsy Trotwood or Wilkins Micawber, but I liked them more than David Copperfield. The people you most want to be like aren't always those you like the most. If Dickens were to write about the people in my street, I think Josie and Michael would be my favourites.

Now I read not only when I'm wheezing, but whenever I can: walking in the street; at bus stops; in the lav; and, despite what Miss Birkett might think, during meals. I've also become a bit vain about it. When I finish a book at home, I close it with a big-headed flourish – yet another book devoured by this clever young man – to get Mum saying, 'Surely you haven't finished it already?'

'Come in then. You look tired,' says Miss Birkett. She waves a finger towards my face. 'And you've those lavender smudges under your eyes. I'm making tea, would you like a cup?'

'Thank you.' I'm not bothered about tea but I know she wants to make me some. She goes into her little back room, which is more like a big cupboard. It contains a deep square sink and a greasy wooden draining board on which sits an electric kettle. In the corner, a damp mop stands permanently in a metal bucket. Behind another door, there's a toilet, which I'm allowed to use when no one else is in the library. I may be Miss Birkett's favourite but she won't let on in public.

While she's out, I have another look at the fading, slightly tatty display that she put up in May for Commonwealth Day, which Miss Birkett insists on calling Empire Day. It was Queen Victoria's birthday – 'The Queen Empress, you know.'

She comes up behind me, hands me my tea in an Ovaltine mug. 'I really must change all this.' I remain standing in front of the display to drink my tea as she wouldn't countenance it being taken to the table.

Miss Birkett gets out her little Union Jacks at every opportunity. One side of the patriotic display is a map of the world. The other half plots, in different colours, the extent of ancient empires around the Mediterranean. When I first saw it, I was pleased to find that my favourites, the Romans, had the most territory. It was like seeing Arsenal top of the league.

'Do you know which has been the world's biggest?'

'The Roman Empire,' I say. I've done empires.

'Look again.'

I do but she directs me to the world map next to it. '*Our* empire. On which the sun never sets, and big enough to contain those old empires many times over. Look at all that pink! Australia alone is bigger than Europe, then there is Canada, much of Africa and hundreds of islands – our navy had only to land on them, you know, to claim them for the Queen.'

She flicks a finger at India, which is still pink. 'Such a shame that that Mr Gandhi, a troublemaker if ever there was one, should have got us to give up India.' She sighs and her eyes glisten.

She takes my empty mug.

'Do you know what kind of asthma you have?' she asks out of the blue.

'I didn't know there was more than one kind.'

'There's something about it in here.' She goes to her desk reaches below it and comes back to put *Common Ailments* on 'my' table 'Apparently you can grow out of childhood asthma.'

This is rubbish. Mum used to believe that our bodies change every seven years but a week after my seventh birthday my worst ever asthma attack put me in hospital.

'There's also nervous, and bronchial, asthma.'

This makes more sense. I usually wheeze on the first day of holidays and during exams, and in winter I get bouts of bronchitis, which is like asthma, only with a bad cough.

'See what you think,' she says and goes back to her desk. I sit down at the table and after reading about asthma, I flick through, stopping at illustrations of bunions, carbuncles and a split-open head that shows how ears, nose and throat are connected. Under 'Fits' a man lies on the floor with his eyes closed and foam around his lips like a dog with rabies. Another man is putting something between his teeth to stop him biting his tongue.

Venereal Disease, or knob-rot as Rooksy calls it, is caused by sexual contact but there is nothing about catching it off toilet seats or wanking or, as Michael fears, from 'anny ould gerum dat might sneak under your foreskin.'

Miss Birkett clears her throat behind me and I whip the pages over to Warts.

'I think you're probably ready for this. I've just

got it in from the main library.' She hands me *My Son, My Son* by Howard Spring.

Now that I'm thirteen, I should be going to the main library but Miss Birkett gets books sent over to her, to save me a long walk to the other side of Westminster. I think she doesn't want to lose me.

'Thank you. What's it about?'

'Two friends, two close but very different friends. Do you have a best friend?'

'Yes.' And, you could say that we, too, are very different.

I settle down to read. Other kids arrive to return books and wander around looking for new ones. None of them stays to read at the tables until Christine Cassidy sits down opposite me and shuffles her folded arms under her tits.

'I've just seen Sarah,' she whispers.

'Oh yeah?'

She lifts her breasts higher and smiles. 'Can't see what a nice-looking boy like you sees in a skinny ooh arr girl like her.'

A compliment from Christine Cassidy? But she's also having a go at Sarah, so I ask her, 'What's so good about London girls?'

The smile turns to a scowl. 'She was with Kirk.'

'So?'

'Just thought you'd like to know.' She smirks and closes her eyes against my hatred.

Her smug pursed lips invite a slap. 'Sod off, who cares anyway!'

She's shocked that I've said this so loudly with Miss Birkett close by. So am I.

She leans forward. 'See, you *do* care, don't you, lover boy.'

'Sshh.' This is no discreet request for quiet, more a small locomotive letting off steam. Christine's smile vanishes. Miss Birkett stands over her. 'You're in a library, young lady ... shouldn't you be reading?'

Christine blushes and gives me a 'sod you' look: nose wrinkled and tongue pushing out the flesh below her bottom lip. 'He was talking too.'

Miss Birkett is in no mood for being fair. 'He,' she pauses, 'has a book.' She says this like you'd say, 'checkmate'. Close to tears, Christine scrapes back her chair and rushes out. Miss Birkett's lips get even thinner and her nostrils flare. Her sharp nod is like a tick for her own right answer.

She returns to her desk. I read and reread the first pages of *My Son, My Son* but nothing sticks. I look up to see Miss Birkett looking at me. There's no smile but her eyes sparkle kindly out of her narrow face. She reminds me of someone. When she pushes her glasses back up her nose, it comes to me. She's my Betsy Trotwood.

## FEMALE COMPANY

'Do you know what he said to me, the little bugger?' says Aunt Winnie. Mum and I shake our heads. 'Go on, guess.' There's no point, she's going to tell us anyway, for the hundredth time. It happened in the Biograph cinema.

'"Have you got a light?" he said, bold as brass.' She looks at us, her mouth open in full horror at such cheek from a kid who only wanted a light, not her purse or anything. Her big face comes nearer. She could be Tommy Cooper's sister.

She puts a hand on Mum's arm. 'I ask you, Maureen, "Have you got a light? A light?" I said, "how dare you ask a lady for a light, at your age, you cheeky bugger." Do you know how old he was?'

Oh yes. Along with her other favourite story about cruel nuns at her convent school, we know every detail. Mum sits back on her chair to listen and I hunch over my book. Aunt Winnie isn't my real aunt. However, even though she's much older than Mum she's her best friend and the nearest thing we have to a relative in London. Dad thinks she's nuts – nice, but nuts. He once said something about her turning into a Protestant spinster, but he never repeated it after getting one of Mum's old-fashioned looks. Winnie's a demanding friend but she makes Mum laugh a lot.

Aunt Winnie's arrival at our house brings the risk of the slobbery kiss, the nicotine breath and a close-up of the brown stains emerging from her nostrils. If I manage to avoid this, she usually gets me later with a sneaky 'come here my darling' lunge, and a hug that buries my face in her huge, soft bosom and the lavender-ashtray smell of her blouse. My compensation is usually a shilling. She holds the back of my hand to press the coin into my palm and curls my fingers over it. Mum says old people do this because their money has been hard come-by and that it's their way of saying 'keep it safe'. So I flourish my closed fist and say, 'Thanks Aunt Winnie,' with enough enthusiasm to make her believe that I think it's half-a-crown.

'He couldn't have been more than your Billy's age.' She thrusts out her chin, giving Mum time to put on her 'well I never' look. 'I mean to say, in the foyer of the Biograph, can you believe it?'

I'm not sure I do believe it. And foyer? At the Biograph? The Empire, Leicester Square – where Dad took John and me to see *Ben Hur* – has a foyer, and a marble floor. In front of the Biograph's ticket booth there's a narrow stretch of once-red carpet covered in shiny black patches of squashed chewing gum.

Aunt Winnie holds one hand at arms length to examine her nails and with the other hand taps ash into our only ashtray – a red bowl circled by a silver vapour trail forming the words *Trans World Airlines*. Four small troughs sit in the rim for resting cigarettes but Aunt Winnie never puts hers down. Dad says we'll fly with TWA when we go to see his brother in America. John and I would prefer to go on the *Queen Elizabeth* because Rooksy's dad, who works for Cunard, reckons there's nothing like life on a liner.

Aunt Winnie settles back on her chair with her legs a bit too far apart. With a groan, she rubs her arthritis down her thighs, while keeping her cigarette cocked high between two yellowed fingers. Her linen summer coat hangs over the back of her chair but she hasn't removed her paisley silk scarf. It lies in a V-shape down her back and is pinned to the front of her cream blouse by a cameo brooch, from which the two ends drape over the balcony of her bosom. She's kept her hat on too, a maroon beret that covers most of her bobbed hair, except

108

for wayward grey tufts that stick out over her ears. The beret is secured by a long hatpin with a large pearl head, which she whips out with an 'en garde' flourish whenever she wants to demonstrate that she's well armed against 'wandering hands' in the cinema, or those who try to get 'too familiar' with a lady. This always gets Mum laughing, which Aunt Winnie takes for doubt.

'I do, I do, I let them have it, Maureen. They never try it on twice.'

She takes a deep drag of her cigarette and the insides of her cheeks make a fleshy click. She's a jaunty smoker. While Ada Holt feeds a cigarette greedily into her mouth, Aunt Winnie flourishes it through a couple of beckoning circles before her big lips reach gratefully forward to receive it. After inhaling deeply, smoke streams from her nostrils or escapes untidily from her mouth as she speaks.

She closes her eyes: her signal that she's about to say something important. Mum winks at me and we wait. This time I'm the subject.

'He's suffering again then, Maureen ... with his breathing, poor chap.'

I'm in the same room but she talks as though she's come from visiting me in hospital.

'Yes, it's a rotten thing,' says Mum.

I'm sitting on the other side of the kitchen table propped on my elbows, wheezing and reading. They go together: the mouth-organ whines in my ears as my eyes take in the words on the page. Reading is about all I'm up to after a bout of asthma. I'm also feeling light-headed, thanks to the ephedrine that eases my breathing but sends my pulse racing. If I put my hands over my ears, the sound of my heart thumping into my palms, can almost block out Aunt Winnie's voice. Almost.

'And he's quite a reader isn't he,' she says, as if this is another illness.

'Oh yes,' says Mum proudly.

'He should get out more though, don't you think?' She doesn't wait for an answer. 'South Africa's where you want to send that boy. The Transvaal ... clean air, better for him there than here.' The cheeks collapse, the lips kiss out, the cigarette flares and shortens by half an inch. 'I mean, with all the smoke and smog in London.' A lady-like belch puffs a small cloud in my direction and she rattles on about me as if I'm some delicate plant that needs re-potting in foreign soil to grow properly.

'Or we could send him to Switzerland,' says Mum.

What? So Mum has had a similar idea, only the soil would be different.

'Switzerland?' says Aunt Winnie with exaggerated astonishment.

'I've read about special clinics in the mountains. It wouldn't be so far; it was hard enough getting to see him when he was at that sanatorium in Kent. South Africa's such a long way...' Mum pauses. Aunt Winnie's head has been shaking since she heard mention of Switzerland.

'But it wouldn't be warm, would it Maureen?' she says triumphantly. Smoke eddies around her mouth. 'In South Africa, it's an outdoor life, a manly life. It's all very well being clever and that, but he could do with building up, and a bit of colour in his face.'

The 'outdoor' and 'manly' bits hurt, given that I'm indoors and in the company of two women. And why is any mention of my supposed cleverness always followed with a 'but'?

'And think of all that sunshine, I mean, look how strong and healthy it makes those darkies. Oh yes, the Transvaal, where it's high, hot and dry, that's your answer. Nowhere quite like the Transvaal.' She could be a travel agent.

Aunt Winnie gets her 'gen' from the *Reader's Digest*. There's little point in us reading the *Dije*, as she calls it, because she recounts nearly everything that's in it – although her versions restore much of the stories' original length.

I get to read the *Dije* in the doctor's waiting room and I drop words from *It Pays to Increase Your Word Power* into conversations to impress adults. However, I've stopped doing this with my mates, who called me a big-headed git when I used 'impenetrable' to describe Arsenal's defence. They prefer *Tit-Bits*: a misleading title because, although it has lots of pictures of women in swimsuits, the tits and bits are always well covered.

Aunt Winnie wants to join the Salvation Army and would love, above all, to have the uniform. Whenever the 'Sally Ann' band and choir play in the market, she stands in what she calls her civvies behind her uniformed colleagues and sings her heart out, while curling a hand under her coat cuff to allow smoke from her cigarette to go up her sleeve.

She abandoned the Catholic Church of her childhood a long time ago and now considers the 'Army' to be the saviour of all right-thinking souls from the evils of Rome, and its cruel nuns. However, Mum says she'll never get into uniform because joining the Salvation Army properly means having to give up smoking.

Conversations with Aunt Winnie involve mainly listening. And she's a watchful talker, who asks questions at intervals to make sure you're paying attention, or to dramatize what she's about to reveal. I simply nod and Mum, who is already bored, kindly keeps her going with comments like, 'get away,' 'you don't say' and 'she didn't'.

While they're talking normally, I forget they're here, except when they lower their voices about the 'goings on' of the neighbours: 'how she had the nerve to show her face'; 'if he knew how long she was spending in his shop'; 'her youngest looks nothing like him'. I filter out the rest, including frequent references to Mr Macmillan, the cost of living, Jim Reeves and *Emergency Ward 10*.

'I think he knocks her about,' says Mum quietly.

'Does he?'

'I saw the bruise on her face in Bevan's.'

'The wicked...' Aunt Winnie remembers I'm in the room, '... so-and-so. There's something about him, nasty staring eyes, the sort you'd have to watch out for in the dark at the Biograph.'

Mum makes a face to suggest they change the subject while I'm here.

Aunt Winnie gives me her big grin. 'You're not interested in what we're talking about are you, Billy? Not listening with those big blue eyes of yours?'

I take my hands from my ears. 'Pardon?'

She gives me a knowing wink. I put my hands

back over my ears and return to my book.

Mum carries on, whispering, 'Suffers with his nerves, apparently ... and he's got a temper. The boys say his Raymond is terrified of him and that he often has marks on his face and legs.'

Aunt Winnie leans forward, pushing her knees even wider apart. 'Nerves? That's no bloody excuse. I suffer with my nerves, but do I hit anyone? Eh? Eh?' She fingers her hatpin. 'Anyway, what sort of man hits women?'

Quite a few, as far as I can make out. Swole's dad has a scary reputation and no one wants to tangle with him. He's a grown-up Griggsy and it must be just as hard for adults who would like to face up to a bully but aren't brave enough to do it.

Aunt Winnie lights another du Maurier with the chrome lighter, which goes with the posh red and silver packet that opens like a proper cigarette case – unlike the narrow fold-in flap you get with a pack of Weights. Mum believes that you should spend as much as you can on the things you use most, like beds and shoes. For Aunt Winnie, it's cigarettes and something to light them with. She makes our house smell like the Biograph. I don't mind this but the kitchen is now hazy with smoke and I start coughing. I get up to go into the backyard.

'That's it love,' says Mum, 'get yourself some fresh air.'

'Fresh air!' Aunt Winnie splutters and phlegm catches in her throat. 'Here? In London? Air here's no good for that lad. Transvaal is where he needs to go – high, hot and dry. That's the ticket. You should have a word with the doctor.'

# A MAN'S LIFE

I sit on the bench in the backyard until the coughing stops. Behind the kitchen window, Aunt Winnie is waving at me, fag-in-hand. Mum is beside her and a worried smile is asking if I'm going to be OK. They could be standing on the dockside as my ship leaves for South Africa.

I wave back then cross to the shed and climb on to its roof, which slopes from Ada Holt's kitchen windowsill down to our back wall. It's a good place to read in warm weather and feels private, even though it's visible from the backs of the houses opposite – so not quite pick-your-nose private. As soon as I sit down, Chris lands cat-lightly nearby and pads up and down, mewling aggressively to move me from his snoozing spot on the warm asphalt. I keep my head in the book. He stops a yard away, forces his whine up an octave and studies an upturned paw for the sharpness of his claws. Then, as if I were a sparrow, he crouches and wiggles his arse. The attack could come at any time. I don't move and stare at the pages without reading them. Having got me to a state of maximum alert, Chris stretches out to lay siege with his whiskered snout in the sun.

My book is *Love on the Dole*, in which the back-to-back houses seem to be smaller versions of ours, except that their backyards don't meet but have an alley between them. The biggest difference is that their outdoor toilets don't flush and have to be emptied into carts that come along the alley. At one time, our lav was outside, where the shed stands today. Now it's inside, squeezed under the stairs that go up to Ada's floor.

A window flies up in the sooty wall of the house opposite. Mr Cleeve leans out with a carving knife in his hand.

'Hello Billy, reading again?' He shakes his head in disapproval, as if reading is like wanking, that if you've to do it, you shouldn't be *seen* doing it, and certainly not often enough for old bastards like him to be able to add 'again' to their questions.

'No, I'm staring at the pages to make them burst into flames.'

'What's that?'

'Reading, Mr Cleeve.' I hold up the book. Go on, tell me, what else I could be doing with it?

'So I scc. So I see. A young man can have too much of books you know Billy. Action lad, at your age, action is the thing.' Mr Cleeve was a sergeant major during the War. I know this because he tells me every time we meet.

'When I was a sergeant major in the War, I wouldn't let my lads waste their time reading. Too much to do. Young men need to be kept on the move.'

I give him my 'guess you've got me again, Mr Cleeve' grin.

Once, when I met him on my way into the library, he put a hand on my shoulder and, squeezing in each word, said, 'Reading books wouldn't have won us the War lad, it was action, action. Do you understand, Billy? Without action a young

115

man can get up to all sorts of undesirable things.'

In a library?

Mr Cleeve begins scraping the knife back and forth across his window ledge like a conductor who's just keeping the orchestra going. Years of weekly sharpening have sculpted the sandstone sill into the shape of a pouty bottom lip. It's his Saturday ritual; 'action' prior to the challenge of carving the Sunday roast.

'A man's job in the home, Billy.'

Not in my home it isn't. It's Mum who does the carving and everything else to get dinner ready. She keeps our sharp knife sharp not on a windowsill but on the kitchen step. And what is all this 'man's job' rubbish which, with Aunt Winnie's 'man's life in the Transvaal', makes me wonder if they're trying to tell me something?

Mr Cleeve holds the knife up to, as if, from twenty feet away, I can appreciate how well it has been honed. He licks his thumb, lays it lightly on the blade and gives a little flinch. 'Perfect ... could cut through a silk hanky as it falls to the floor.' I doubt this but the roast lamb won't have a chance.

Mr Cleeve ducks back inside. He's another adult who isn't really interested in kids, or what they have to say. He's worked out what kind I am, and what to say when he sees me. If I were to join the Scouts and give up reading, I think he'd be miffed at having to alter his ready-made 'Billy' comments.

Most adults say the same things every time, 'you're the one with the asthma, aren't you?' Or to John, 'you don't say much, do you?' Or to Rooksy, 'is your mum managing all right, with your dad away again?' Conversations start and end with what they think they know about you. I try to keep them short, mainly by nodding, so they don't have to think of anything new to say. Only Dad and Miss Birkett at the library regularly say, 'what's new?' or ask me what I think of something.

Kids aren't much different. Once you're deemed 'crater face', 'four eyes' or 'silver sleeve', it sticks. Harsh nicknames are a way of keeping everyone in their place, no matter how sporty, good looking or clever. And the names rarely change, unless something even more embarrassing becomes known: Swole was 'earoles' until everyone found out about the size of his dick.

Sarah's house is five doors along from Mr Cleeve's, next door to where our friend Derek McCloud lives. I can reach it by walking along the back wall, something John and I used to do all the time until neighbours complained. Even wondering if Sarah will be in gets me to my feet and set to go. I bang the book closed and Chris rears up like a furry-faced cobra. He slashes at my leg. I panic and kick out. One of his claws catches in my jeans and he's swung squealing through the air. He bounces off the back wall and is on his feet in a flash, embarrassed, mouth closed, muffling a rising wail in his throat. I leap over him on to the wall and struggle to get my balance.

'Attaboy, Billy.' Mr Cleeve is back at his window. 'Bloody cat shits on my flowers and onions.'

'Cats, eh, Mr Cleeve.'

'Do you know, he not only shits on them, he scrapes soil over to cover it up?'

Everyone knows this but I don't want to sound too clever. 'Don't most cats do that, Mr Cleeve?'

117

'Not with a bloody shovel they don't.' He roars with laughter. I'm the latest victim of a favourite joke. Aren't you a one, Mr Cleeve. I smile and set off along the wall.

'Not with a bloody shovel,' he shouts at my back, repeating the punch line like lots of older people do. If you're not laughing, they assume you haven't got it – not that it was a poxy joke.

I arrive above Sarah's empty backyard and crouch to look into her kitchen. She's standing with her back to me at the table, holding up a bowl to let her mother wipe the American cloth beneath it. I will her to turn around but it's Mrs Richards who notices me first. She touches Sarah's shoulder and goes into the living room. Sarah comes to the back door. I straighten up in a poor attempt to make out I'm walking past.

'What are you doing?'

'Oh just ... just going to see Derek.'

'Doesn't he work at the garage with his dad during the holidays?'

Of course he does. Shit. 'Oh, yeah.' Exposed and ridiculous eight feet up in the air, I turn to go back as Mr Richards comes out.

'Billy, isn't it? The fish boy?'

Another one that's got me categorized. Now I'm the 'fish boy', and he'll be in no hurry to think anything else of me.

'Yes, Mr Richards.'

He's wearing his grey chauffeur's suit, black tie and impossibly white collar, one of those stiff 'detachables' that allows you to change your shirt every day and not the collar – or the other way round. However, they can't be undone easily when it's hot because the collar pings out both sides from the rear stud. Take the collar off altogether and you look like a miner or someone who works on a farm.

He taps his chauffeur's cap on his palm. 'Make a habit of walking along people's walls?' His smile indicates that he doesn't mind.

'Er, yes.' He stops smiling. He does mind. 'No, not really, I... Mrs Holt couldn't find Chris ... thought he might have come along here.'

He doesn't believe me. 'We've seen no one, have we Sarah?'

'Dad, Chris is a cat.'

She gives me an embarrassed shrug and I fight back a smile.

'He's black and white and he wanders off a lot and we ... Mrs Holt and I, get concerned about him.' The only concern I have about Chris is that he might live to old age.

'Oh *concerned* are you?' says Mr Richards. He thinks the word is too grown-up for me; that I'm showing off. 'No cat been past here.' His *here* sounds like *eeeurr*. Most of the time, he doesn't have a West Country accent like Sarah or her mum because he tries to sound like the people he works for. Rooksy's dad's Cockney accent has largely disappeared too because he spends so much time with wealthy passengers on his ship.

'Oh, right then.'

He turns his back on me, assuming I'll now leave, doing to me what the people he drives for probably do to him. In Pimlico, people can be rude, really rude, but not like this. It's something he's learned from his employers: that you can dismiss people by turning away. It makes me determined to stay.

Mr Richards strokes Sarah's hair. 'Bye my lovely.' He runs his hand down her arm to her fingers, which he squeezes and pulls in farewell. I would love to do that.

'Bye dad.' There's affection in her voice. She loves him, horrible as he is.

Instead of going in, she comes over and looks up. 'So, what *are* you doing?'

'Nothing, I got fed up reading and decided to walk along to see...'

'Boys who aren't at home? That's what you do is it? When you get fed up?' She has me on the run.

'No, not usually, the neighbours don't like it.'

'My dad, for one.' No, he wouldn't.

'I know. Anyway, I'm going back now.'

'Oh.'

'See you.'

She smiles. 'He's not here now though, is he? Just a sec.'

She drags over a small stepladder, climbs to the top step and rests her arms on the wall. It's my turn to say something but nothing can get past the catch in my throat. I sit down on the wall beside her.

'Not going to see your mates today?'

'Oh, no, it's ... well my breathing's been a bit...'

'You smell of cigarettes. Smoking's not good for your chest.'

'I never smoke.'

'Never?' Oh god, is she referring to my earlier 'never'?

'No, I can't, not with my asthma. My Aunt

Winnie's at our place and she smokes a lot. It's why I came out.'

'Isn't she the mad lady who sings with the Salvation Army in the market?'

Despite what Dad once said, I've never thought of Aunt Winnie as mad but of course she is. From now on she'll be 'mad' Aunt Winnie. John will love it.

'That's her. She's not really an aunt, just a friend of my mum's.'

Sarah puts her chin on her arms. I want to stroke her hair like her dad did, and to lift it to see her neck. 'So, what are you reading?'

I've forgotten about the book. Reading indoors is OK, outdoors is definitely swotty.

'It's about poor people who live in Manchester.'

'Oh.'

I push on, 'My mum loved the film, so I thought I'd read the book. It's about two young people who ... who fall in love but can't afford to ... anyway, they go on a trip together, to the seaside.'

'Oh. Where was that place by the seaside you told me about ... in Cumberland, where they sold the nice ice cream?'

'It was Silloth. I said I'd take you, one day.'

'Yes, you did.' She lifts her face to me. 'How old were they, the young couple?'

'Oh, older than us.'

'I see.' Her head drops. I've embarrassed her by referring to *us*, as if we were like them. I think we are. She looks away. 'And do they get married?'

'Don't know, I haven't finished it yet.'

'Will you let me know?'

Oh yes. She changes the subject. 'Will you be

up to running in the "round-the-block", I mean, with your chest?'

'Yes, I think I'll be OK.' It's what Audie Murphy would say: that he's going to be fine and that despite being wounded, he'll be riding out to face the Indians. I straighten my shoulders and sit up, tall in the saddle.

'Good ... do you think you can beat Kirk?'

'I don't know.' I barely manage to say this because mention of Kirk revives the humiliation of the denied fart. I rock forward, unable to look at her. She says nothing and the silence drives me to explain.

'Look, about what I said to Kirk...'

'What?' How could she *not* remember? But she does, 'Oh, that...'

'Sarah.' Her mother is in the kitchen doorway. 'Coming to the shops?' She goes back before Sarah can answer because it wasn't really a question. Mum does this too: Billy, are you going to fetch in some coal?

Sarah shrugs. I touch her shoulder to say good-bye. She starts climbing down, leaving her hands on the top rung. My fingers trail along her arm as she goes lower until, when she lets go, I hook the tips of my fingers under hers in a goodbye tug. She looks up. This is the moment when Audie would lean down from his horse and kiss her. I hesitate and then it's too late. Back on the ground, she looks up at me like women do in westerns as they scrunch up their pinnies to watch the cowboy they love ride off. She drags the stepladder back across the yard and gives me a quick wave before going inside.

'Bye, Billy.' How good it is to hear her say my name. She goes inside and closes the door.

Bye, Sarah.

I start back along the wall, happy until I remember the 'fart' lie and how it's going to disable me every time I see her. I want to tell her that I lost control because Kirk made me angry by saying something stupid and embarrassing and that my response was stupid too, and even more embarrassing. But how? When? She doesn't seem to think it's important anyway. But I do because I'm the boy who claimed he'd never farted. Although I'm on the wall, I break into a trot.

When I get to my house, Mr Cleeve is down in his backyard. Against one wall, he has two coffin-shaped window boxes. One is packed with black and yellow marigolds, the other contains shallots at different stages of growth. A thunderstorm during the night has encouraged slugs and snails to try their luck in his 'garden'. He's captured about a dozen and detained them in a flowerpot.

He holds up the pot for me to inspect. 'What with these buggers, weeds and cat shit, it's a wonder a man can grow anything.' Now that he has an audience, he decides to impose the public death penalty. He tips them on the ground and proceeds to smash and grind them with a trowel, before taking up his watering can to swill the gritty sludge down the drain.

'That'll teach them eh, Mr Cleeve.'

He beams. 'That's right Billy lad, always take the fight to the enemy.'

On the shed roof, Chris is curled up in the sun under Ada's window. He opens one eye and gives

123

me a warning whine. I climb down into our yard and as soon as I'm out of range, shout 'boo!' to get him on his toes.

In the kitchen, Aunt Winnie is on her feet with her back to me. Her knees are going up and down as her arms alternately cross her chest like she's flinging the ends of a scarf around her neck. Mum is doubled over, laughing, begging her to stop. Aunt Winnie sits down at the table, lights a cigarette and says, 'I'm serious Maureen, marching with the Sally Army won't be a problem for me.'

## INDIAN CAMP RAID

I urge the horse forward one-handed, flailing the reins left and right on his shiny black flanks. The wind batters my face and ripples my horse's mane as his head plunges and rises above the blur of galloping legs.

With my Colt .45, I'm shooting Comanches as they emerge from their tepees. Ahead of me stands Griggsy, in full headdress and war paint. He has Jojo's cowboy hat skewered on the end of a lance. With his other hand, he yanks a rope that binds Sarah's hands together. Next to him, in long golden plaits, a bare-chested Kirk raises his bow and takes aim. The arrow whistles past my ear. I shoot. Kirk spins and falls. Griggsy runs off, dragging Sarah after him. She is calling out to me over her shoulder. I gallop alongside them and swing out a leg that sends Griggsy tumbling in the dirt.

He rolls over and springs up brandishing a Bowie knife. I jump from the horse, dodge his first lunge and knock him cold with a single punch. I pick up his knife and cut the rope around Sarah's wrists.

Other Indians are whooping towards us on their ponies. I remount and hoist Sarah up behind me. We gallop away but barring the road ahead is a flat-topped wagon. Siddy, dressed in buckskins, kneels on top of boxes of Winchester rifles that he's been selling to the Indians. He's firing at us, snapping the rifle's trigger guard down and up after each shot. We speed towards him as bullets zip around us. When we leap the wagon, the horse's hooves send Siddy flying.

Sarah clasps me around the waist as we splash across a shallow river and I urge the horse up the steep far bank. We reach the cavalry fort as the sun is setting. On top of the sunlit wooden walls, John, Michael, Rooksy and Josie are waving and cheering.

'The End' rises on the screen behind us.

The screen goes black. I struggle to hang on to this final scene, but it's hopeless. I'm finding it hard to breathe.

'Time to get up!' John lifts the pillow off my face.

I can't for the life of me understand how he was one of the goodies in my dream.

# FRONT ROW TOUCH-UP

John and I are in the queue at the Biograph when we spot Rooksy talking to a young man in a suit on the far side of the ticket booth.

'Watcha, Rooksy.'

His surprise turns to a smile. The young man leans closer and says something into his ear. Rooksy shrugs and the young man leaves. Rooksy comes over.

'Coming to see it?' I ask.

'It's another bloody "cowboy",' he says, as if I'd invited him to watch *Noddy and Big Ears*.

But this is an Audie Murphy film and John is having none of it. 'Suit yourself Rooksy, we're going in.'

'All right then.' Rooksy pushes into the queue beside us.

I love going to the pictures. The magic starts at the ticket booth, where coloured tickets chug out of slits in the brass counter top and I slide my hand through the space under the window to draw them back like dealt cards. Next, it's the heavy door with the little round window, and the brush trim around its edges that 'pfaffs' open to let us into the smoky dark, where the booming sound is always a surprise. From one of two tiny windows the shining cone spreads over the audience and, although it's circular and passes through rising smoke, the picture on the screen is oblong, clear and full of vivid colours and the giant faces of the actors in close-up. In these early moments, I expect every film to be wonderful.

Inside, an usherette with long blonde hair shines a light on our tickets and leads us down the sloping aisle in her high heels, holding the torch against her bum to cast a bobbing bright disc on the floor.

The first four rows of seats are cheap wooden tip-ups that can be arse-achingly hard during a bad film. We sit right at the front in the middle, our favourite position since the days of Saturday morning kids' matinees. From here, we had most room to throw stuff when the serial's hero arrived to save the day and the screen would dimple with flak from saved bits of lolly, ice cream tubs or Kia-Ora orange juice cartons.

Ten minutes into the film, Audie Murphy, knotted neckerchief to one side, is climbing a large rock in the *day-for-night* blue light. We know it's not really dark, but we don't care. He's circling 'round back' of the outlaws' shack while his sidekick fires from the front to 'keep 'em busy'.

I feel a light touch on my thigh. At first I think it's John but when I look down the hand belongs to someone sitting behind me. Between the thumb and index finger a sixpenny bit is glinting in the light from the screen. The hand stops moving and lifts to offer up the corn like bait. I shuffle to the other side of my seat, too scared to turn around to see who's holding it. Another tap on my thigh. I look down again and the fingers snap the sixpence down beside me on my seat. The hand gives a brief thumbs-up sign before turning into a fist.

I catch my breath and try to focus on the screen. The baddies have spotted Audie and a loud gunfight breaks out. This time the hand prods me, like someone saying, 'Oy'. The fist is swinging from left to right, fingers-side up, banging against my leg, covering and uncovering the shining sixpence. My brain races but my body can barely move. I nudge John, who is irritated at first but smiles when he sees my scared face. I point at the hand cavorting between us and he stops smiling. He jogs Rooksy and sits back while Rooksy leans across him to have a closer look. Rooksy slides out of his seat and keeps low as he moves past John and around in front of me. He puts a hand on my knee to steady himself and taps the swinging fist, which relaxes and opens, as if ready to shake hands. I clutch the front edge of my seat and watch aghast as Rooksy tickles the palm. The hand tries to close around Rooksy's finger but he pulls it away. The man grabs my leg instead and in a whoosh of bad breath and *Old Spice*, his bald head comes alongside mine. I leap to my feet. Rooksy grabs his hand and yanks it through the back of my seat. The man grunts and hisses, 'Let go you little sod.'

Rooksy holds fast and jams his foot against the seat-back for leverage. Shouts of 'sit down' and 'get out of it' are coming from the audience. Rooksy is undeterred but he's losing his grip on the man's sleeve.

'Grab his arm Billy, dirty bastard.'

I can't do it. I should be angry but I'm more embarrassed, and barely strong enough to stand up. The complaints from everyone sitting behind us get louder. I plead with Rooksy to let go but he hangs on. John shoves me aside and steps back to kick at the man's other hand with which he's bracing himself on the seat-back. There's general uproar and no one can be watching the film. Rooksy is unstoppable. 'Bummer ... bummer here.' He won't let go and raises one arm above his head like a rodeo rider, yelling 'Lights, lights please.'

The man breaks free and scrambles past legs and shoving arms towards the aisle.

'Lights, bummer on the run!'

Amid general booing and whistling, the film stops, the scalloped red curtain drops and bleaching light floods the cinema. John and Rooksy are laughing. I've done nothing wrong but I want to run away as if I have.

Rooksy gives me his OK sign.

The usherette harries the culprit up the aisle, shouting at him to keep his filthy habits out of her cinema. John and I are about to leave too but Rooksy sits down and invites us to do the same. We slide low in our seats, praying for it to go dark again. The usherette returns. In the unforgiving light, she isn't blonde, or young. Her long hair is grey, and thick beige make-up has stained the white collar of her uniform. She asks if we're OK. We nod.

'Fine thanks,' says Rooksy.

She looks at him askance. 'Well, you're not short of confidence, are you young man?'

Rooksy shrugs and gives her the Errol Flynn grin. It feels like an age before the lights dim and the film restarts.

More outlaws arrive to surround Audie and we settle down to enjoy the next gunfight. But Audie's blazing guns can't get what has happened out of my head. So, the bald bloke was one of them – and that's the sort of thing they do. Wandering hands don't only bother ladies like Aunt Winnie. I guess I've been what she calls 'interfered with.'

'He was a bummer then,' says John, on our way home.

'Yeah but he didn't touch my arse, only my leg.' I want to make this clear.

But John is quite clear. 'Yeah, but he wasn't a "legger" was he? He was a bummer.'

Rooksy hands me a sixpence. 'This is yours.'

'Mine?'

'You were the one he gave it to. He fancied a bit, to feel your dick, or for you to feel his. Blokes like him try it on all the time. Think they can touch you up for a tanner.'

John laughs.

Rooksy laughs too. 'It's nowhere near enough.'

He sees the look that flashes between John and me and laughs extra loud. 'I mean, pity it wasn't a ten-bob note or a quid.'

'Yeah,' I say, forcing a smile about something I haven't found at all funny.

We fall silent.

'Best stick to kids' matinees if you want to avoid that stuff,' says Rooksy.

# DIFFERENT DADS

John, Michael and I are beneath Swole's bedroom window. There's no sign of him so we step inside the wood yard gates. The screaming circular saw warns us that, even though it's Saturday afternoon and the other men have gone home, Swole's dad is working. Through the sawdust mist swirling under the shaky fluorescent light, we can make him out in his navy blue overalls, bending to lift several six-foot lengths of four-by-two timber and shove them together into the saw's whirring bite. Once they've been halved, he pulls them back and lines them up for another pass. He clamps the quartered lengths between his big hands to lift and stack them against the wall. He kicks into place any that stick out.

Swole says his dad is quite deaf, yet even in the din of the saw, a half turn of his shoulders tells us that he knows we're here. There's little chance of Swole coming out now, so we back towards the gates, hoping Mr Dunn won't turn around.

I once suggested to Rooksy that it was working in this terrible noise that made Mr Dunn such a miserable, scary, deaf bastard. 'Nah,' he said, 'only the deaf bit.'

As we reach the gates, Dunn slowly cocks his head, from one side to the other. He looks at us and an exasperated closing of his eyes makes it clear that we've interrupted important work. We know he likes disappointing people and we wait to hear him say, 'He won't be coming out.'

Swole has never heard his dad say, 'Raymond, your friends are here.' Or, 'go on in boys, he's up in his room.' Mr Dunn's dark eyes glare at us from his dusty face. He strides over to the big red and green buttons on the wall and thumps the red one. The saw whines to a halt and in the quiet that follows he becomes more menacing. We hurry through the gates into the street. He follows us. We wait to hear what he's going to say. He takes a tobacco tin from the pocket on the front of his overalls, pulls off the lid and starts to roll a cigarette.

I glance up. Swole is standing at his bedroom window shaking his head, signalling to us to go. Poor Swole, even when he's allowed out, it's only after he's been put through the 'have you dones?' list: washing up, tidying room, errands for your mother, blah, blah. Even if Swole has done them all, his release is conditional: 'If I hear that you've been up to anything...' or 'don't you dare be late back'.

Mr Dunn puts his tin away. 'What do you want?'

Michael, who is sucking on a gobstopper, says, 'Oh we were after wonderin' if our compadré, Swo... Raymond was in.'

'What?'

Michael speaks louder. 'Er, Raymond. Is he in at all?'

'Yes, and "in" is where he's staying. He has jobs to do. Unlike you lot.'

With a bulge in one cheek, Michael says, 'Ah well, Mr Donn, I wonder, would he be after comin' out when he has dem finished?'

'What?'

'If he moight be headin' out when he has de chores done?' says Michael, loudly enough for the hard-of-hearing.

Dunn frowns and shakes his head.

Michael persists as if Dunn is completely deaf. 'Maybe tomorrow den? We moight meet up for a spell?'

Dunn comes closer. 'Don't you get cocky with me, you fat little Irish git.'

Michael steps back and flicks his imaginary cowboy hat in farewell. 'Adios, den Mr Donn.'

Dunn isn't sure whether he's taking the piss, neither am I.

'I've told you once, now go on, clear off!' He waves his arm in a 'sod-off' fling that sends his newly rolled cigarette spinning to the ground. Michael can't suppress a laugh. Dunn steps forward and cracks him across the mouth with the back of his hand. The gobstopper squirts out. John, an instinctive slip fielder, fails to catch it before it hits the ground and smashes into multi-coloured shards. Michael tries not to cry. Dunn stoops to pick up the cigarette. Swole's Mum scurries out with her hands clamped to her face.

'Oh Arthur, what have you done? Michael, come here love.'

Dunn grabs her arm and swings her around, 'And you can shut up too, get inside.'

She turns back to us, shaking her head in silent apology.

We pull Michael away. 'I'm goin' to get my old fellah on you,' he screams.

'Get who you bloody like. Now go on, out of it, all of you.'

Dunn steers his wife back into the wood yard and closes the big gates behind him. Up at his window Swole has an arm raised in a fixed, sad wave.

We make our way home and as soon as John thinks Michael is up to answering, he asks, 'Are you really going to tell your dad?'

Michael wipes away the tears. He's rethinking things. Everyone knows what Dunn is like. If Michael doesn't tell, he'll save his dad from having to make a hard decision.

'Feckin' Comanche. Yeah, I tink so.'

John doesn't think so. 'Oh yeah?'

'Probably,' says Michael. His shoulders sag. 'But he *is* a big bastard, like feckin' Cheyenne Bodie.'

We nod. No one is as big as Cheyenne but Dunn is the biggest of the dads. If only there was someone to stick up for Mr O'Rourke like Alan Ladd did for Van Heflin in *Shane*.

John looks at me. What would we do in Michael's place? A fight involving your own father, especially one that he might lose, is a frightening prospect. We've seen fights outside the Queen Anne. They tend to be sprawling, swinging affairs with most punches missing – none of the satisfying thuds you hear in cowboy fights – and too much grabbing, slipping and swearing. When it's clear that no one is going to win, other men usually intervene to stop it.

Michael won't tell his dad. Mr O'Rourke is a mild man, good at making kids laugh, and getting

134

drunk on Saturday nights. The most aggressive he's ever been, according to Dad, is to shed a few angry tears when 'roaring for his mother's people' after he has had a drink. Dunn is rarely seen in the pub but Swole says he drinks whisky at home and that that's when he gets really scary.

When I tell Mum what happened, John opens wide to signal 'big mouth'. He has a point but I find it hard to resist passing on news. Later, when Dad asks us about it, John says nothing but I tell the story, and chip in about how Dunn often beats Swole. John is wide-eyed with disapproval. Our parents exchange glances and Dad says, 'Mr Dunn has never touched you boys, has he?'

'No,' we say together.

'I want you to keep well away from him. And I hope, also, that you've not been giving him any cheek.'

'No Dad,' I say. 'Michael wasn't being cheeky, it's just that Swole's ... Raymond's dad gets so angry, so quickly.'

'Some people are treated best by keeping away. Are you with me boys?'

We nod.

'Getting involved with them can be...' he swivels his open hand like he's turning a large doorknob '...tricky.'

'Yes Dad.'

'Good. And...' He hesitates. 'I want you to be sure to let me know if Mr Dunn ever does anything like this again.'

'Yes Dad.'

After he leaves the room, John breaks out in a grin.

'What?' I whisper.
'If Dunn hit me, I'd tell Dad all right.'
'Me too.'

# KISSING KHRUSHCHEV

Rooksy and I are half sitting on the children's roundabout, swivelling it left and right with our feet. The Peabody Estate's sooty balconies rise around us on three sides. Rooksy offers me his frozen Jubbly, squeezing it up through the slit cut along the top. The ice looks like old snow as most of the orange has been sucked out. I bite a lump off the corner that still has some colour. Rooksy does the same and we lie back, moving the ice around in our mouths like a sweet.

'I want a word with you.'

We sit up. Siddy Smith is standing in front of us, arms held wide to block any escape. On his shirt, sweat stains are spreading out from his armpits. His face looks like it's coming to the boil. He grabs Rooksy by the throat. 'If I find you've been anywhere near my house again, anywhere near my Madge, I'm gonna cut your dirty little dick off.'

His lips draw back over clenched teeth and he squeezes hard enough to make Rooksy gag.

'Please Mr Smith, don't.' My voice is little more than a squeak.

He gives me fierce look. However, it's one of irritation, not one that says, 'and you're next'.

He lets go of Rooksy and gives him a couple of

136

finger-knuckle cracks to the side of the head that knock him back on the roundabout.

Rooksy springs up screaming. 'Get away from me, you bastard.'

Siddy leans in to him again. 'Want some more do you?'

'Just fucking leave me alone.'

Siddy cuffs him again; Rooksy curls up and goes quiet. Siddy stands over him and waits. Rooksy doesn't move. Siddy gives a gangster's shake of his shoulders and walks away.

I grab Rooksy's shoulder, 'Are you OK?'

He rubs his head but instead of answering, shouts, 'Bastard, bastard!'

Siddy stops and looks back. Rooksy leaps from the roundabout and runs for the nearest staircase, where he turns to face Siddy and to my horror starts running his tongue around his lips.

'I saw it, I saw plenty. Her fabulous flesh. It was loverlee...'

Siddy rushes at him but Rooksy is away, pausing long enough to hurl his Jubbly into Siddy's chest before legging it up the stairs. Siddy follows him into the stairwell but he'll never catch him. We've played run-outs in these buildings for years. Once you've made it on to the stairs, it isn't hard to evade chasers because they have to pause on each floor to check whether you've run either way along the balcony. Six floors and four staircases offer scores of options.

Siddy appears on the second floor, looking around and down. On the balcony above, Rooksy is grinning at me, pointing down at Siddy and making the wanker sign. Siddy catches me smiling.

'Think it's funny do you?'

I shake my head. Rooksy tears along the balcony to the next staircase and emerges on the first floor to wave at me. Siddy comes out on the fifth floor and leans over the balcony wall, gasping for breath. Rooksy ducks back and begins 'stair calling'. Crouching by the stairs, he calls out in loud, ghostly tones – first along the balcony, then up and down the stairwell.

'Oh Madge, ooooh, ooooh. I've seen it, her fabulous flesh. Ooooh. Seen it, seeeeen it.'

The point of stair calls is that you can't tell where they're coming from. Siddy sprints along the balcony and down to where he thinks Rooksy is hiding only to hear a taunt from two floors up. 'Ooh, Madge!'

A crowd of small kids has gathered to watch the chase and Derek McCloud's mum comes by on her way to the baths with a pushchair loaded with washing. Mrs M is a big woman who shouldn't wear slacks because, according to Mum, 'she has a behind on her like a Suffolk Punch'. A headscarf, tied in a large knot at the front, almost has her frizzy hair under control. She cares little about her appearance and devotes most of her attention to her six kids, or to those she looks after for other people. Today, she's flanked by two of Derek's little sisters, and her youngest toddler grins from his perch on top of two full washing bags. You never see Mrs M without seeing children too.

With Rooksy's jeering echoing around us, Siddy returns, defeated, to the courtyard. He stands

138

close to me, hands on hips, scrutinizing the balconies. I admire Rooksy but his daring appals me. He's incapable of thinking about what might happen next, while I think of little else. Siddy may not catch him today, but Rooksy won't be able to avoid him for long.

Siddy drops his arms to his sides, fists clenched. The sweat patch now covers most of his shirt. Out of sight, Rooksy keeps up the abuse in a drawn out Cockney crescendo, 'Fabulous flay–yesh.'

Mrs M finds this amusing.

Siddy rounds on her. 'What you looking at then? Eh? Think it's funny do you?'

She turns away in a huff. General sniggering breaks out among the children. Red-faced, Siddy roars up at the empty balconies, 'I've got time, you little bastard. I can wait. You and me have a fucking appointment, and we're gonna keep it.'

'Language, really, in front of children,' says Mrs M.

The invisible Rooksy remains defiant. 'The flesh, the flesh!'

Siddy surveys the growing audience for his humiliation and picks me out. He comes over and pokes me in the chest.

'Leave that boy alone, you great bully.' Mrs M lets go of her pushchair and marches towards us.

He ignores her and shouts into my face loud enough for Rooksy to hear, 'It won't be long. I'll see him soon. Thinks he's got away, does he? We'll see.'

He scowls up at the now silent balconies and storms off, taking care to go around the immovable Mrs M.

On the top floor balcony, Rooksy pops up to make vigorous V-signs at Siddy's back. A few minutes later, he ventures down. Mrs M takes him by the arm. 'Now what have you done to get him so mad?'

Rooksy is eyeing the entrance to the yard. 'Oh nothing, Mrs M.'

'Well, if that was for nothing, you'd better watch out when you *have* done something. It's all right, he's gone, for now. He's a nasty bugger to get the wrong side of. Is your dad home at the moment?'

'No, still away.'

'Well, I hope he gets back soon. In the meantime, you'd better make yourself scarce.' She sets off with her pushchair and its escort of kids.

Rooksy's dad is in the merchant navy. He's at home only a few times a year, when Rooksy shows us the exotic things he brings back, like a fossil of a fish that's two million years old, or a mini totem pole carved by savages. His dad is always suntanned and wears starched, white short-sleeved shirts in summer. The only time we see much of Rooksy's mum is when his dad is home. When they're out together, they look like a pair of film stars.

Many women like Rooksy's dad.

In Plummer's, I once heard Welsh Beryl Street say to Madge, 'Who wouldn't find him attractive? I mean he's hardly ever here. Wouldn't you be happy with a husband who's at home only a few weeks a year, with money in his pocket? Eh? And then buggers off when you're starting to get on each other's nerves? Easy then, like being on

140

bloody holiday, really.' She cackled, 'Handsome bugger though, wouldn't mind his boots under my bed, now and then like.'

Mr Plummer was mortified. 'Now really, is there any need for that?'

'Need? *Need*, lovely boy? Oh yes, I'm afraid there is; if there wasn't any need, what woman would put up with any man's bloody nonsense. Packet of Tide and ten Senior Service please.' She winked at Madge and burst into lewd laughter.

Without Beryl there'd be a lot less to talk about in our street. She's from Cardiff and has what Dad calls a fiery Celtic nature. Mum says this is no excuse whatsoever for her filthy tongue. She's the only woman we hear swearing like a man. If we need a bit of excitement, we have only to play knockout against her back wall. Within seconds, the bedroom window is thrown up and she dinks her head out to invite us to 'fuck off and take your fucking ball with you'. We roar with laughter and before long Beryl is laughing too. She can go from snarling to smiling and back again in seconds.

Rooksy and I wander around cautiously until we reach the deep bombdie, where eight houses were blitzed in the War. The cellars under the pavement have survived but the open space is covered in rubble, rubbish and weeds. We climb down and sit on an overturned couch. Rooksy touches his face, testing for the coming bruise.

'Jesus Rooksy, that was scary.'

'Bastard.'

'Are you all right?'

'Yeah.'

'I thought he was going to kill you.'

I reflect on the painful fact that I'd just sat there, saying sissy stuff like, please don't Mr Smith.

'I'm sorry, I didn't ... you know, help much.'

'What could you do? Anyway, it might have been worse if you hadn't been there.'

This is what I want to hear. 'What are you going to do? Will you say anything? Tell anyone?'

'What for? My old man won't be home for ages, and what can mum do? She'll only want to know what I've done to make Siddy so angry.'

'But why do you *do* that? Why can't you just leave it?'

'Don't know. Can't help it. I saw his nasty red face and I couldn't stop.'

Fancy not being able to resist saying what you really want to say; it's something I do all the time.

He smiles. 'Anyway, he said I had a dirty little dick, and it's not, little that is. And I knew he wouldn't catch me in the flats.'

'But we live here Rooksy, you can't avoid him.'

'Yeah, tricky. But I don't think he's the kind of bloke who'd come around your house ... not after a kid, do you?'

'I hope not.'

'Don't worry about me.'

I'm not worrying about him, I'm worried about me and about seeing Siddy's angry puce face at my front door.

'Anyway wasn't it worth it to see Madge in her bikini that time ... and those tits? You liked that didn't you. Wouldn't you have liked to give them just a little squeeze?'

'Oh, yes.' I'm lying. I haven't thought much about seeing Madge in her bikini but I've thought a lot about what might happen to us because we did.

'So you weren't impressed?'

'Oh no, I mean, yes, I was, but...'

'Well?'

Silence. For once, I manage to say what I'm thinking. 'Her face could be prettier.'

'Her face? Her bloody face?'

'Well, yes. I mean, you kiss, too, when you feel tits ... don't you?'

'Not necessarily.'

'And if her face isn't...'

'Isn't what?'

'I don't know... I mean, I wouldn't want to kiss Madge.'

'That's not the point.'

'No?'

'No. You don't have to look at the mantelpiece when you're stoking the fire, you know.'

This takes me time to work out. When I do, I think it's funny but not true.

I force a laugh. 'Oh yeah.'

'Well, who would *you* like to kiss then?'

'No one really.'

'Really? There must be someone you fancy.'

'Fancy? Me? No.'

His face comes closer. 'Oh yeah?'

'Sarah Richards is quite pretty.'

'Sarah?' He steps back.

'She is, quite, pretty.'

'No tits though.'

'So what?'

'So, *no* tits!'

Instead of Marge's tits, I'm holding on to an

image of Sarah's face, but it's alternating weirdly with the mantelpiece in our front room.

'No, but she will ... probably, one day.'

'One day?'

'Have them.' I realise that I don't want to use the word 'tits' when talking about Sarah. 'And girls like Christine Cassidy and Shirley...'

'Fine tits, Christine's.'

'Yes, but they won't get any prettier.'

'Her tits?'

'No, Christine and Shirley.'

He gives me his Errol Flynn smile. 'So tits aren't top of your hit parade then?'

'Well yes, but...'

I'm not going to say so but the more I think of it, the more I know I'd rather kiss Sarah than feel anyone's tits, especially Madge's. Rooksy goes quiet. I search for something to say. He stares at me, cocks his head and takes a deep breath. I'm expecting him to say something about Sarah. Instead, he sighs and shakes his head. 'Fair enough. See what you mean ... I think.'

'And, well, look how old Madge is.'

He thinks for a moment and grins. His face comes closer. Saliva has gathered at the corners of his mouth. He sees that I've noticed this and clears it away with his little finger. 'Yeah, you're right. Think I'd sooner kiss you than Madge.'

I laugh, 'Yuck.'

He laughs too, after a pause.

'Yeah, right,' I say. But Rooksy waits, as if he hasn't heard me. 'I said, "yeah, right"!'

Should I be saying, 'piss off Rooksy, you bummer'? I would if Michael and John were here but they're not and now it's tricky to say anything. And if Rooksy is trying to be funny, why isn't he laughing? I know that men kiss men in Russia, I've seen Mr Khrushchev do it on the telly. But isn't that only when meeting people? Mr Khrushchev doesn't look like a bummer. Neither does Rooksy.

He mock punches me on the arm, 'Der, joke Billy, it's a joke.'

I laugh, relieved, and give him a shove in return. But for a few seconds too many, it hasn't felt like a joke. 'Don't worry, I won't ... unless you want me to.'

I force another laugh. 'No thanks. I'd sooner kiss Mr Khrushchev.'

Rooksy thinks about this and laughs. 'Oh thank you very much.' He puts a hand on my knee and pushes himself to his feet. 'Sarah Richards, eh?'

'Well ... you know.'

'Yeah, I know. See you later.'

'Yeah, see you later.'

Rooksy climbs back up to the street and lifts a hand to acknowledge John who has swung one leg over the bombdie's brick wall.

'What's up with you then?' says John. I must be looking scared.

'Nothing.'

'Who clumped Rooksy?'

'Dunno.'

'Big red lump on his face.'

'It was Siddy Smith.'

'Knew it wasn't you.'

'Yeah.'

Of course he knows, but why say it? Everyone is saying too much today.

# FISH PASTE AND FLAMING TURDS

It's the day of the street party and the 'round-the-block' race will be starting in a couple of hours. I've already run the race during the night, and lost. In my dream it was so hot that the melting tarmac sucked at my shoes while Kirk sprinted to the finishing line.

From the top of our basement steps, John and I are watching the party preparations. Strings of faded colour triangles, curling like old sandwiches, criss-cross the street between lamp-posts and weave untidily along the railings. Six doors along, Mrs McCloud's house is the centre of operations. From their mooring on the front door knocker, two-dozen balloons float under her first-floor window. They will be handed out after the party but are already losing height and, even in the shade, their stretched shiny skins are turning matt.

Several trestle tables are set end-to-end in the road, close to the pavement. The tablecloth is the reverse side of long rolls of wallpaper that have been Sellotaped together. Because there aren't enough benches, an assortment of kitchen chairs provides extra seating. Most are wooden and worn, but some are metal-framed with padded plastic seats and backs that are part of the cabinet-and-table sets that Mum would like for our kitchen. Piles of newspapers are on hand to boost small children to table height.

146

Excited toddlers whose mothers are helping to set up, skip about and chatter at a well-behaved distance. Further back, other kids have gathered, trying not to look interested but watching for the signal to come forward.

'Another jug for the end table, please Maureen,' says Mrs McCloud to Mum, with her fat-finger wag. Mum dutifully carries out her order and gives me a tolerant smile.

Mrs M lifts and drops one of her dinner-lady arms as she counts the paper plates and plastic spoons, and matches them with the number of seats, 'eleven, twelve, thirteen'... She carries on as she breathes in, 'ffourteen, ffifteen, chthicteen, chtheventeen...' Other mothers, in sleeveless frocks and clean aprons, lay out large oval plates, piled high with jam or fish-paste sandwiches, Lyons cupcakes – everyone's favourite – and sponge cakes, topped with powdered icing sugar and cut into wedges. Several Pyrex bowls contain custard creams and Bourbon biscuits. Large jugs of orange squash and bottles of lemonade have been allocated to each table. The ice cream and jelly will be served later. In the meantime it's safely stored in Madge Smith's huge fridge.

The women stand back, arranging themselves behind the seats. The little children press closer against the soft cordon of mothers, reaching for their hands. Behind them, the bigger kids jostle for position in the happy panic of ensuring that they sit next to friends.

'Just a tick girls.' Mrs M frowns. She's looking at what appear to be too many children for the number of places at the table she has just checked.

The kids eye her warily, as they will do throughout the party. She's an accurate slapper of hands of those who want to start with cakes, or to grab for more before finishing what they've already taken.

From her doorstep, Ada Holt calls out, 'Be a love Billy and fetch my kitchen chair out.' I hesitate and she laughs. 'It's all right, I've fed Chris.' As if this is in any way reassuring.

'Don't worry about that Billy, she can come and sit on my lap.' It's Kirk's granddad shouting from across the street. He's wearing no shoes or socks and his trousers are rolled up to the knees because he's been cooling his feet in the enamel basin that stands beside his chair. Even in the heat, he wears an old suit waistcoat and shirt over an off-white vest.

He holds his arms wide. 'Very fetching Ada.'

Still in her hairnet, Ada is wearing her short housecoat that doesn't cover much of her white, vein-splattered legs. 'Get out of it, you cheeky old bugger. Even if I was Diana Dors, you'd need Robin starch in your underpants.'

'Ada, please, the children,' says Mrs M.

'Sorry, love.' Ada chuckles and shuffles across the street in her slippers. On reaching the other side, she calls out, 'Don't worry about the chair Billy ducks, I've got a date.'

Granddad Douglas gets up and feigns running away to the jeers of the other old men who are on their doorsteps to watch the party. They're as excited as the kids, cheeking the women and laughing at their own comments. Some have already been given sandwiches, which they're washing down with bottles of light ale.

Mrs M stands back from the table, 'Are we ready then, girls?'

She looks meaningfully across at Michael O'Rourke's dad, Brian. Mr O'Rourke is the only man present who's doing something *for* the party. In the heat, his florid complexion looks like permanent sunburn. A bit of an 'ould redskin', according to Michael. This is as far as you can take the comparison. Mr O'Rourke is short with a pronounced potbelly over which braces hoist his trousers to within inches of his armpits. He's an object of ridicule for many, as is 'bossy' Mrs M, but without these two there'd be no party.

Mr O'Rourke is testing his loudhailer by whispering into it. The sound quality and his accent aren't making for clarity, 'Testin', ssccchhh, awon, atwo, atree, afour ssccchh.'

Good enough for Mrs M. 'That'll do Brian, let's get going, shall we?'

'Right ye are, Alice.' He smiles, crouches and lurches towards the end of the table, holding the loud hailer to his mouth like Groucho Marx's cigar. The adults laugh and the kids cheer. He can't resist one more try. 'Ahem, yiz are all welcome to our annual street party. And tanks must go to de ladies for all der work and for settin' out such a foin spread.' The shriek from the loudhailer could be a complaint about his accent. 'Will de little ones please come forward forst...' Another piercing whistle. He gives up and peers inside the loudhailer to locate the bird that's making the strange noises.

The children cover their ears and move as one to the table. 'Now, don't rush!' They clamber on to the seats, squealing and calling to friends, while the women shout at them, with little conviction, to calm down and sit still. As the party gets under way, the struts of one table give way and a jug of orange squash tips into the laps of two small girls. Their screaming has their mothers rushing to comfort them. Mrs M stands back with her hands on her hips, beaming.

John and I make for the table that's set aside for older kids who won't be sitting down. We're rationed to a couple of fish paste sandwiches, a cupcake and a beaker of Tizer.

'Soppy' Albert Woods and his younger brother Georgie are at the front of an informal queue. Most of us want only the Tizer and a cupcake, but the Woods brothers will actually eat the fish paste sandwiches. Soppy has a huge appetite and will devour anything, and always asks if he can have my core when I'm eating an apple.

Soppy is fifteen and enormous, although he has a small brain. For weeks he's been on about the street party and asking me to remind him in detail about all the nice things that will happen – in particular, the sandwiches and cakes that we'll be eating.

I take my allocation of sandwiches and slip them to him. He puts a huge hand on my shoulder. 'Thanks, Billy.'

I've been his 'best friend' ever since I gave him my old Viewfinder and several picture discs. For days, he walked around the street clicking away to look at the images he loved best – photos of exotic fish – until it broke in his big fingers. He sat in tears on the Big Step until John ran home and returned to swap him his working Viewfinder for the broken one. It, too, was broken in a couple of days.

Soppy has always been a willing listener to my stories but, like a small child, he has his favourite: my version of Disney's *Old Yeller*, in which the dog *doesn't* die. When Soppy saw the film he cried his eyes out but I've convinced him that my story, with the happy ending, is the true version.

Georgie Woods is my age. There's nothing wrong with *his* brain. He's also a good runner and a champion fag-card player, even though he's boss-eyed. To us he's 'Little' Woods, because of his football-pools eyes: one at home, one away.

Soppy and Little's mum is 'Dopey' Eadie. Her husband disappeared years ago. Beryl Street says that he and Eadie had only one brain that they passed back and forth between them in a hanky. She also says that women like Eadie shouldn't have been allowed to have kids. But we're glad she was because we like Soppy and Little, even if Soppy smells. He's dirty too. Griggsy often has dark smears above his collar, but the 'tidemarks' on Soppy's neck come up to his ears. And the nit nurse with her tiny tooth-comb calls at the Woods' house as often as the rent man.

Eadie is the poorest woman in the street but she's always cheerful, although her smile reveals too much of her gums. However, her infectious giggle is funnier than the laughing sailor's at the funfair.

We play a game called, 'Ello Eadie'. It involves walking up to her in single file, shaking her hand and saying, 'hello'. This gets her giggling and it doubles us up too before we hand over to the next in line. It sounds mean but everyone, including Eadie, enjoys it, and we never play it when Little is around.

She earns a bit of money from sweeping up for the barrow boys in the market. I once heard Aunt Winnie whisper to Mum that they 'take advantage' of her and that Little is the spit of the bloke who runs the fish stall. Eadie's painfully thin and always looks tired. Rooksy reckons she's worn out from doing knee-tremblers for a Mackeson behind the Queen Anne.

Soppy and Little spend most of their time with their Nan, who's far from dopey but a bit of a scruff. Her house is crammed with collected newspapers that she bundles with string and takes in an old pram to sell to the rag-and-bone man.

Even though they get loads of free orange juice and malt from the clinic, Soppy and Little suffer from boils. On Soppy's neck they stand out like small volcanoes. We never see Little's boils because he gets them on his arse. Some people in our street think that the Woods brothers are poorly nourished and should be taken into a home. But Soppy is massive; how big would he be if he were better fed?

After we've had our Tizer and cake, John, Michael, Little and I move to the quiet end of the street. Soppy follows at a distance, devouring left-over sandwiches and enjoying a series of baritone burps. Suitably fortified, he crosses the road to perform his favourite trick. He shins up a lamp-post and grabs the iron cross-member that sticks out on both sides under the lamp. To chants of 'heave' from the rest of us, he bends it down until everyone cheers the inverted V.

'Stupid thick bastard.'

Griggsy is behind us, moving up and down on the balls of his feet.

Soppy grins down at him; Griggsy scowls. Because Soppy is 'backward', kids take the piss a lot, but it doesn't bother him. Like his mum, as long as other people are laughing, he laughs too. However, unlike other kids who get bullied, he's far too big to bash up. This infuriates Griggsy, for whom 'bashing up' is the best bit. So he usually picks on Little, to whom he says the same thing every time, 'I'm gonna make you cry, boss-eyes, and watch the tears run down your back.'

Today he starts with Soppy. 'What you laughing at, you spastic?'

Soppy's grin fades, but not enough for Griggsy.

'What's funny?' He tries to give Soppy a 'dead leg' by punching his thigh.

Soppy drops down rubbing the spot with one hand and takes hold of Griggsy's arm with the other. 'What you do that for?'

'Because you're stupid.'

'Oh.'

Griggsy aims a slap at his face but Soppy turns away and the blow clips the boil on his neck. He roars with pain and spins round, dragging Griggsy with him. Behind Griggsy's back, Little starts throwing shadow-boxing punches at his head, urging Soppy to retaliate. When he sees Little's antics, Soppy's grimace turns to a smile but he doesn't understand what he wants him to do. Griggsy catches Little delivering a mock uppercut.

'And you, "boss-eyes", I'm going to make you

cry and watch the tears run...'

Griggsy's mouth clamps shut as he swings round to face Soppy. With an exaggerated shrug, he tries to move away but gets jerked back like he's on a lead. Soppy hasn't let go of his arm and although he's smiling, he's also squeezing! Griggsy is a big, hard bastard but as Soppy draws him closer, he looks wonderfully small.

Little starts dancing around them. 'You're gonna do what Griggsy? Eh?'

Griggsy's face goes deep red as he strains to get clear. When Soppy grabs his other arm, Griggsy curls a hand to dig his nails into Soppy's wrist – to no avail. Soppy's grin broadens as the rest of us repeatedly jut our heads forward, urging him to beat the shit out of Griggsy.

Soon Griggsy abandons any pretence that this isn't hurting and starts kicking out. Soppy holds him at arm's length until Griggsy gives up struggling.

'Don't stop Sopp,' says John. I cringe. Urging him on behind Griggsy's back is one thing, saying it out loud is suicidal. Griggsy flashes us a look of promised vengeance. Soppy lets go with one hand and raises it in a huge fist. Griggsy pulls away as far as he can and holds his free arm in front of his face.

'Bash him, Albert,' shouts Little.

'Yeah, do it,' says John.

Soppy is enjoying the attention but he's confused about what to do next. What's more, he's looking at me with his gentle, puzzled face, waiting for me to tell him. What I want him to do is smash Griggsy. I need only to raise my fist or nod, and

154

that will be that. The others wait like a Coliseum crowd for the emperor's thumb. But I'm held up by Soppy's simple, bewildered smile. For all his size, he has never hurt anyone and it seems wrong for him to start now, even with a bastard like Griggsy. I look around at the expectant, vengeful faces and wonder if not wanting to hurt someone is as feeble as not wanting to be hurt.

I shake my head. Soppy loosens his grip. He's smiling and I think he's relieved.

Griggsy yanks his arm clear and rubs it. 'Stupid fucking spaz.'

Much as he's disappointed, Little knows better than I do that Soppy isn't a hitter and takes his big brother by the hand. John comes up to me. I avoid his eyes. He gives me a light shoulder barge and surprises me by saying, 'Fair enough.' He's a hard one to work out.

'Oy, what do you think you're doing, David Griggs. Leave Albert alone you bloody great bully.' It's Beryl Street, arms folded and hair scraped into a bun behind her bullet head. Griggsy scowls at her but doesn't answer back.

'Well?' She comes forward and we know that unless Griggsy leaves she'll keep coming. He spits on the ground in front of us and takes off, shaking his sore arm but trying to make it part of his swagger.

'Lovely boy, I'm sure,' she shouts at Griggsy's back. He flicks up a V-sign without turning round.

She eyes the lamp-post's new shape. 'Did you do that Albert?'

He takes the credit, grinning and nodding.

'Well, you get right up there and bend those bars back.'

He looks at her bemused.

'Go on, now.'

Little pushes him towards the lamp-post. He climbs obediently and sets about the harder task of pushing the bars back up into place. They move but it's a struggle. Beryl turns on the rest of us.

'You should know better, you lot, fine friends you are, leading him on, letting him do things like that. And you, Billy Driscoll, you specially. What's the point of being a grammar-school boy then, if you're not bright enough to look out for the likes of poor Albert?'

No one can stop Soppy testing his strength. He does it all the time. I've seen him pull the front bumper off a Ford Anglia. The others, including John, are sniggering. I hate this. Except for Mum and Dad, the only time anyone mentions my so-called cleverness is to prove that it's obviously not true, or that I'm letting myself down or, while I might be clever at schoolwork, I have no common sense.

Beryl's attack on me isn't really about what's happened to Soppy, it's about her son Ivor and the chance, which she takes at every opportunity, to have a dig at the only boy in the street who passed the 11-plus when her lovely Ivor failed it.

Soppy drops down from the lamp-post, having bent the bars back almost to horizontal.

'Now, go on, clear off, all of you.' Beryl goes in and slams the front door.

Michael ambles alongside. 'A raw deal der compadré, raw.'

He raises an eyebrow and leans over sideways from the waist, like a cowboy from the saddle. He offers me a Spangle from a stub of four after graciously taking for himself the top one with pocket fluff attached.

'Have yiz ever heard of de flamin' turd?'

'No.'

'De lads in Ireland do it to der enemies.'

'Do what?'

'Just be after holdin' your horses a spell.'

He crosses over to his house and returns with two inches of methylated spirit in a milk bottle, and some sheets from the *Topper*.

'What we need now, Kid, is won of Nelson's specials, de softer de better.'

Nelson is old Beattie Hartop's Alsatian. Some people call them German Shepherds but Nelson's the kind of dog that'd eat sheep, rather than round them up. He's 'top dog' locally and trots everywhere with his tail in the air above a pink pencil sharpener that could put a point on an altar candle.

He shits all over our street, which causes Beattie countless rows with neighbours. She sees off most complaints with the same shrieked response, 'Dog's got to shit hasn't he? Where do you want him to do it? In the bleedin' house?' It's rude, but kind of reasonable.

Michael doesn't have to go far to find his key ingredient. He scoops it up with a piece of cardboard, tips it on to Beryl's doorstep and covers it with crumpled sheets of comic. He douses it with methylated spirit, scrapes a Swan Vesta on the step and lights the paper. He waits for the fire to take hold before rapping on the door and sauntering back to our side of the street.

Beryl emerges. 'Christ.' She steps forward to stamp out the flames.

As blackened bits of burnt paper float up around her, Beryl realizes what lies beneath the flames. Little gives a cheer.

'What the ... ach a vee, you dirty little bastards!' She drags her open-toed shoe backwards, leaving a brown smear across the doorstep. She takes off the shoe, hooks a finger under its slingback and hobbles towards us, screaming. 'Who did this then, eh? Come on, who fucking did it?' Soppy is grinning and holding his nose. 'Was it you, Albert?' He keeps grinning. She grabs his hair, pulls his head down to her level and screams into his face. 'Well it's not fucking funny, see.'

She lets go. Soppy straightens up and bursts into tears. He towers over her while his great frame shakes with sobs. Little hugs him and I go over to take his hand. Beryl's face crumples. She drops the shoe, takes a handkerchief from a pocket in her skirt and starts dabbing Soppy's face.

'All right now, duw duw, Albert, it's all right. Don't cry cariad.'

He stops crying. She sees the black smears on her hanky and her eyes go up into her head. The smell of Nelson's shit on her shoe gets stronger. She turns on the rest of us. 'You filthy little bastards. Get out of here. Go on, take him home, look you – and tell his mam to wash his fucking neck, right? And her own while she's at it. As for you...'

She's ashamed about picking on Soppy, so she targets me again, 'I'm going to give your mam a piece of my mind.' She will too. Her mind must be some size, as she's been giving people pieces of it for years. Like most of my best thoughts, this doesn't get said. She gives Soppy a gentle push towards us, 'Go on my poor boy ... doolally tap and no one looking out for you, is it?' She carefully picks up her shoe and, holding it at arm's length, she limps indoors. Everyone, except Soppy and me, is laughing.

Michael ambles up. 'Mission accomplished, would you say Kid?'

'Oh yeah, now Beryl's my biggest fan.'

Michael shrugs, 'Ah well der ye are, ye can't have everytin' compadré.'

We all move off and drift round the corner. In the next street, we catch Griggsy grunting as he strains to pull down the cross member of another lamp-post. It hasn't moved an inch. Little and John jeer him. Griggsy drops down and marches up to us. Little moves behind his big brother and, except for John, we all move a little closer to Soppy. Griggsy stops just beyond reach, bursting with anger and embarrassment. He stands for a few seconds, rising and falling, unable to think of something to say. So, he does what he does best and spits in Soppy's smiling face before loping off.

## RACE LESSONS

John and I are sitting on the Big Step waiting for the start of the round-the-block race. I'm nervous enough as it is but John is making things worse.

'So what are we going to do about Griggsy?'

159

'Why should we be doing anything?'

'To pay him back, someone should.'

'I don't know, Griggsy's kind of...'

'Frightening?'

'Well...'

John gets to the point. 'He frightens you doesn't he?'

Yes. 'No. Look, he *is* a bit...'

'Scary? Maybe he is, but someone should pay him back.'

He's serious and, not for the first time, it occurs to me that John's the one who's scary. 'Anyway, there's no need to make a big thing out of it...'

'I think it's a big thing. I think he should pay.'

'A big thing? He didn't hurt Soppy, if anything, Soppy hurt him.'

'I'm not talking about Soppy; I'm talking about what he did to Jojo and me ... and the hat.' He shrugs and delivers a blow below the belt. 'Dad would do something.'

I know what Dad would do. I also know he wouldn't want me to get hurt. Truth is, I lack bottle. So what? So everything. It matters more than being strong or good at sport, and it's miles more important than being clever. Hiding a lack of bottle is difficult. I usually manage to leave scary situations early enough for it not to look like I'm running away. But not when John is there. Either he can't see when a fight is likely, or he can but doesn't care. I rarely get him to come away when trouble is brewing but on most occasions the fight never starts or, if it does, John scraps away until his opponent has had enough. Either way, I'm always shit-scared.

'Dad doesn't have asthma.' John shakes his head. The asthma excuse has never worked with him. I press on. 'And Griggsy's not only bigger than me, he's nuts.'

'I know you can't fight him but you can't bottle it.'

Oh yes I can.

'I'm not going to bottle it.'

He holds up a fist. 'If you don't do something, *I'm* going to.'

'You're too small.'

'I'm as big as you.'

'Yeah, too small.'

'He gobbed in my cowboy hat.'

He had his head smashed against a wall but he's more upset by what happened to the hat.

'But it wasn't even your cowboy hat...'

'I'm still gonna do him.'

'No, *I'll* do it.'

'Will you? When?'

'When I'm fucking ready!' He's got me angry enough to believe that I *can* do something about Griggsy. It won't last.

'Not very nice language Billy.' Mrs Dunn is standing behind us with Swole.

Isn't it bloody marvellous? I rarely swear but now Mrs Dunn will assume that I do all the time.

John and I stand up. 'Oh sorry, Mrs Dunn, I...'

She doesn't answer and her smile is surprising. 'Now John, what have you been saying to upset your brother so?' He shrugs.

'Younger brothers, eh Billy? Aren't you glad you don't have a younger brother, Raymond?' says Mrs Dunn. She pats my cheek and walks away. She's never cheerful like this indoors.

Swole stays behind. 'Watcha Driscolls.' His resigned tone tells us not to bother asking if he's staying for the race. Dunn has probably insisted that he and his mum go somewhere less common.

'Where you going, Swole?' says John.

'War museum.'

'How long were you standing there?' I ask.

'Oh, not long.'

'Your mum doesn't miss much, does she?'

He grins. 'Not a bloody thing.'

'Will you tell her I don't normally swear?'

'Yeah, will do. By the way, good luck in the race. I'd have liked to run myself but I wouldn't have had much of a chance.'

'None whatsoever,' says John.

Harsh but true. I can't remember when I last saw Swole run, let alone race. His head dips.

'Come along, Raymond.' His mum is waiting at the corner.

'Never mind Swole, pity they're not holding the kind of competition we all know you'd win.'

John laughs. Swole grins. 'See you later Driscolls.'

Sarah and Josie arrive arm-in-arm.

John turns his back to them and faces me. They stop behind him.

'I'm off. See you later, lover boy.' He says this loud enough for the girls to hear. He gives me a soft punch in the chest, 'Good luck in the race.'

Josie leans against Sarah to ease the weight on her leg. 'Watcha Billy, I don't think your brother likes girls does he?'

'Sometimes I think he doesn't like anyone.'

162

'Josie won the two-ball contest,' says Sarah.

It's one of the few games for which you don't need two good legs. It involves keeping two balls bouncing continuously off a wall and doing tricks, like clapping hands, in between.

I congratulate Josie. The hand she raises to cover her smile is holding a gold medal.

'I came nowhere in the skipping,' says Sarah.

'Oh, bad luck.'

'I'm used to Josie roping; two of the mothers did it today.'

Josie never skips but all the girls like her to rope for them, by herself, with the other end tied to the top of a railing.

'Hope you win the round-the-block,' says Josie. I shrug as if I can't be bothered but I've already been home to the toilet twice.

'Is your chest all right, Billy?' says Sarah.

It's absolutely fine, but now that she's asked, 'Oh it's not too bad, thanks.'

'Hope you'll be OK. Good luck.'

'Thanks. I'm gonna need it.' Cowboys say this before heading out to face hostile Indians.

She smiles and gives my hand a quick squeeze. Now I could face Crazy Horse himself.

The race starts half way down our street, outside the Queen Anne. A crowd has gathered to watch.

Mr O'Rourke is back on his loudhailer. 'De traditional round de block race for bize onder fourteen, step up now bize.'

Everyone knows what he's announcing but they haven't a clue what he's said. He puts down the loudhailer and bends over to waddle backwards,

163

drawing a wavy chalk line across the road.

Mum and Dad are standing on the far kerb behind John. Mum waves and I get a small nod from Dad. John shakes a fist. I take deep breaths to get my nerves under control, followed by a very public puff of my asthma inhaler.

Eight of us line up. Kirk is jogging on the spot as if he's Herb Elliot. Bastard even looks a bit like him in his proper runner's vest. Vests look fine on Dad and John but on me, there's too much 'flop about' under the arms. I've settled for the better covering provided by my aertex Sloppy Jo.

'Watcha Drisks.' Little grabs me good-naturedly around the neck. His fish-paste breath brings me close to retching; and there's no time for a last trip to the toilet.

Mr O'Rourke holds up his hanky, 'On your marks.' Kirk gets down on his hands and one knee, and carefully places his fingers behind the line.

'Hah,' says Little, 'where do you think you are, White City?'

'What would you know?' says Kirk.

'Not much,' says Little, 'only that you look like a dick.'

Everyone laughs but those of us who were going to get on our marks like Kirk won't be doing it now.

'Get set... Go! Away wid yiz!'

In the rush to the end of our street, Little and Kirk are soon out in front. By the time I get to the corner, they've nearly reached the next turn down the long stretch of the street parallel to ours. I want to get after them but running too quickly too soon always brings on asthma. I have to go steady.

At the end of the first lap, more customers from the Queen Anne have spilled on to the pavement to cheer us on. Loudest is Kirk's mum, who's leaning forward, thumping her fat thighs and screaming, 'Go on Kenneth, go on, my darling!'

No one calls out my name and I catch sight only of Mum and Dad, who are concerned that I'm so far behind.

On lap two, Kirk and Little are about thirty yards ahead. Next comes Derek McCloud, who's a fast runner but he's heavy like his mum and won't be able to keep up the pace. The others are beginning to struggle. By the beginning of lap three, the crowd has spread to line both sides of the road but there's no sign of Sarah and Josie. But I do hear 'Come on Billy, get a move on.' At least John is in the crowd somewhere.

By the time I turn out of our street, my breathing has become deeper and easier. I pass a couple of stragglers and I'm gaining on the leaders. When I reach Derek, he clutches his side and gasps, 'Stitch.'

If you say so, Derek.

As we start the last lap, Little is dropping behind Kirk and I'm gaining on both of them. I still can't find Sarah and Josie in the crowd.

Then Josie shrieks, 'Go on, Billy.' She's standing next to Sarah, whose hand is knuckling over her mouth. When I catch her eye, she smiles and gives me a wave. It feels like my private Wembley roar.

I overtake Little as we reach the end of our street.

'Bugger,' he gasps, grinning.

Ahead, Kirk is all 'look at me with my elbows in

and my arms pumping'. Very good, but I'm catching you, you flash bastard! Half way along the final long stretch, he's there for the taking. He hears me closing in and his fancy running style goes ragged. He scowls back at me from a frothy mouth and pumps his arms harder. The gap between us stretches again but he soon weakens. I've got him! By the time we reach the Big Step corner I'm alongside. His face contorts and each exhaled breath is a defeated grunt. Then he does what Herb Elliot would never do: he bursts into tears. I scream 'zing!' in his ear and pull ahead. The final corner is coming up. I'm ready for the cheering crowd, the run to the line – and Sarah seeing me win.

Suddenly, I'm staggering. Kirk has grabbed my shirt and is reaching for me with his other hand. Strangled squeals burst through his clenched teeth. I scream into his flushed face. 'Get off me you cheating bastard!'

Then he gets both arms around my waist, stumbles and drags me to the ground. I kick out and punch but he doesn't fight back; he hangs on until I catch him full on the nose. He rolls away, clutching his face. I get to my feet but my legs have turned to jelly and I struggle to stay upright. When I finally get running again, it feels like slow motion.

A roar goes up as I come around the final corner. This is when Audie would take off his hat to acknowledge the cheers. I tingle with pride and pick up speed. The faces in the crowd grow clearer and as my victor's smile broadens, I find Sarah. But she isn't smiling. She's caught sight of

Little, who is scooting past me and going flat out for the line. I summon up what remains of my energy and tear after him.

Ahead, Kirk's mum is in the middle of the road, hand to her brow, squinting and wondering why her cheating bastard of a son isn't in the lead. Next to her, Eadie and Soppy are holding hands, jumping up and down like Masai warriors to cheer Little. Sarah and Josie have their hands in the praying position in front of their mouths.

I'm catching Little with every step, and I'd pass him if the finish was at the far end of our street, but it isn't. He crosses the line a couple of yards ahead of me.

Everyone is clapping and it doesn't feel like losing until Little comes over to shake hands with the boy who came second.

Kirk limps in, dabbing his nose and pretending to wipe sweat from his face to cover his tears. His mum rushes to comfort him.

He points at me. 'I tripped. He got in my way and tripped me. *I'd* have won otherwise, not him.'

'Billy didn't win love, Georgie won.' This seems to console him a bit and his mum gets him to stand sullenly in line behind me and Soppy, who has put Little on his shoulders. Mrs McCloud is waiting with the prizes.

Although no one is more than ten feet away, Mr O'Rourke insists on announcing the winners through his loudhailer.

'And de winner is... Georgie Woods.' Eadie shrieks with joy and Soppy bounces Little up and down in triumph.

Mrs M reaches up to hang the gold winner's

medal around Little's neck and, one at a time, hands him two big bottles of R Whites lemonade. Georgie passes them down to Soppy, who takes them by the neck in one hand as if they're baby bottles of Britvic.

'Second, and a silver medal, Billy Driscoll.' Above the applause, I hear John shout, 'well done Billy'. The medal is lighter than I expect because it's made of grey plastic.

'Bad luck, Billy,' says Mrs M. I think about telling her just how bad but Mr O'Rourke carries on.

'Turd' – a new and better nickname for him – 'Kenneth Douglas.' Kirk steps forward to receive his medal, which is the colour of a penny. He takes it without saying thank you, gives it to his mum and walks away.

Mrs M is not pleased. 'Well!'

His mum scurries after him, 'Oh Kenneth, don't be upset, love.' After a few yards, she stops, embarrassed, and calls out to Mrs M, 'Sorry about this, Alice.'

Mum and Dad come over with John.

'Bad luck Billy, you did really well,' says Mum.

Dad puts an arm round my shoulders, 'Once down is no battle son.' I'm suddenly on the verge of tears. They notice this and tell me they've got to go.

'Thought you could beat Little,' says John.

'I would have, if Kirk hadn't pulled me over.'

'Did he?'

'Yeah, ask Little.'

'Cheating bastard,' John punches his cupped hand like Batman and Robin. Kirk may be too big for John to clump but when has this ever stopped him?

Soppy crouches down to let Little slide over his head to ground. He takes one of the two bottles from Soppy's fist and hands it to me. I hesitate.

'Go on, you'd have won if Kirk hadn't cheated.' He turns to John. 'Crying like a baby, he was.'

I like the Woods brothers. Even without a dad to insist that they do the right thing, they give away lemonade they can't afford to buy. We unscrew the tops and start swigging. Losing doesn't feel quite so bad.

Sarah is with her parents on the other side of the road. Her dad tilts his head to one side and his smile says, 'never mind eh, Fish boy'. Sarah gives me a 'bad luck' shrug but makes it clear that it's best if she doesn't come over. I don't mind. Gunfight or road race, what hero likes being second?

## DROWNING AND DENYING

Rooksy and I are walking beside the dry channel that runs through the Peabody Estate. It was once the course of the River Tachbrook, which is now a sewer flowing inside a giant rusting pipe, ringed every ten yards with nut-and-bolt collars. Before reaching the Thames, the pipe enters the 'hydraulic'. The Hydraulic Pumping Works contains several large tanks of deep water. When its drains open, surface pressure forces the water down through a network of pipes with enough force to raise lifts in high buildings for miles around. It's 'working water' that doesn't have to be too clean. When the levels drop, the tanks' sides become green-slimed cliffs.

'Fancy climbing over?' says Rooksy.

No, I don't. In nightmares, I'm drowning in one of these tanks, searching the snotweed walls for handholds as the gurgling drains suck me down.

At the swimming pool, I'm a creature of the shallow end. Every time I steel myself to dip my head under water, the blurred light and the burbling distortion tell me that this is not the beginning of swimming, but of drowning.

I was once pushed into the deep end. Down I went, not to the bottom but far enough to believe I'd never get back up. In a terrifying few seconds, I clawed ineffectively at the water as divers arrowed down around me, trailing streams of bubbles and others rowed themselves silently along the bottom before turning to rise in balletic slow motion. My treacherous lungs were trying to force open my mouth and inhale water. I was beginning to think that this wasn't such a bad thing when a thud in my back propelled me towards the surface. John had spotted me in time.

On the poolside, I coughed and puked chlorine spume while he thumped my back in the mistaken belief that he was helping. Once he knew I was OK, he fell into hysterics at how my arms and legs had whirred like a cartoon character's to get out of the water. Next minute he was up, hands on hips, defending me to the frowning pool attendant who was squeegeeing away my vomit. 'He can't help it, someone pushed him in.'

So, no, I don't want to go in the hydraulic.

'No thanks Rooksy. Not bothered.'

Close by, Griggsy is climbing over the spiked railings embedded on top of the hydraulic wall. He shouts at Rooksy, 'Ya won't get 'im in 'ere without 'is rubber ring ... no fucking shallow end. Try the paddlin' pool in the kiddies' playground.'

A lidded jam jar hangs on string from his belt. He's after water fleas for his terrapins. In summer, the tanks teem with all sorts of crawlies loved by his tiny, scrawny-necked turtles. Weird pets, but Griggsy isn't the kind of kid who'd keep kittens.

'Chicken are ya?'

Well yes, shit scared actually.

'No, don't fancy it.'

'Chicken,' he says, keeping to the point.

With his back to Griggsy, Rooksy is mouthing 'wanker'.

I smile but it's not funny that both my friend and my enemy know I'm scared. This spurs me to climb the railings after all. 'Come on then, no big deal.'

'You sure?' whispers Rooksy. 'Don't do it because of him, he's related to what lives in here.'

I keep climbing despite Griggsy's contempt for how tightly I'm holding the bars. I reach the inside ledge and sit back in relief against the railings, but worrying that the dark water is relishing the arrival of a non-swimmer. In Pimlico, the hydraulic is the nearest thing we have to a haunted house and what bottle I have left is rapidly disappearing.

Rooksy drops down beside me and Griggsy sets off with sickening bravado along a narrow wall that divides two tanks. He even crouches on the way to trawl the jam jar through the water's scummy surface. Disappointed with his catch, he empties the jar and lopes off to forage in the other tanks.

Rooksy pats me on the back. 'Now what?'

Trouble is, unless you own terrapins, there's nothing to do. With Griggsy here, leaving straight-away might look sissy, so I make my way round to the far side, where a large metal cistern is set on a raised concrete platform.

We sit down in its shade. Below us, on the other side of the railings, is Yorath's furniture ware-house. Four pantechnicons are parked in the yard, which is extra quiet in the way only normally busy places can be when there's no one around.

I'm idly fingernailing rusty flakes off the cistern when Rooksy jogs me. A big man in a Fred Perry shirt has appeared on top of Yorath's big wooden gates. He drops to the ground inside and rubs the dirt from his hands. Another man lands beside him; it's Siddy Smith. A ladder is shoved up and over from the other side. Siddy props it against the wall while his eyes flit nervously between the yard and his accomplice.

Although we're thirty feet above them and safe behind the hydraulic's railings, we're trapped. The men have only to look up to see us and any move-ment will catch their eye. What to do? Sit it out? Or scarper and risk being seen? I'm for getting out before becoming a witness to a crime by the kind of men I wouldn't want to testify against.

I go to leave but Rooksy grips my arm and puts a finger to his lips. I sit back, imagining the men's faces snarling at me across the courtroom as I stand in what their kind call the 'grass' box.

The big man lumbers out of sight down the side of the building. He takes too much time for the anxious Siddy who strums his fingers on his chest while scanning the yard. His head whips around at the splintering crack of a door being kicked in. The big man reappears with two large cardboard boxes. He sets them down and sends Siddy back for more. Soon a dozen boxes are stacked ready. A third man appears on a ladder on the other side of the wall to receive the boxes. I hold my breath each time one of them pauses or lifts his head. Then I close my eyes and keep them shut. When I open them, the boxes and the big man have gone and Siddy is straddling the top of the wall. Rooksy grins and gives me his 'OK' sign.

'Oy, where've you cunts got to?' Griggsy has decided to locate us.

We freeze. Siddy's eyes narrow. He glances down at the other men but says nothing, and seems relieved that they don't know we're here. He pulls the ladder out of the yard. Before he drops out of sight, he looks up, puts a finger to his lips, draws it across his throat and points it at us.

Siddy's message is clear enough but once again, he has pressed Rooksy's crazy button. He jumps to his feet, waving V-signs with both hands and wiggling his hips. Siddy pauses long enough to let us know he'll remember this.

'Rooksy, what are you doing?'

'That bastard really gets to me.'

'But why make it worse?'

He thinks for a moment. 'Not sure it can get any worse.'

It can for me.

'Where are ya then?' shouts Griggsy.

He's patrolling the railings on the far side. We come out from behind the cistern. 'What you two bin up to? Touchin' each uvver up?'

'Oh fuck off,' says Rooksy.

Griggsy eyes him, considering violence. 'Ooh, upset ya, av I? Diddums.'

Rooksy puts a hand behind his back and makes a wanker sign. I wipe my nose to hide a grin.

Griggsy picks up the jam jar, screws on the lid and examines what look like shoals of commas wriggling in diluted Swarfega, but he keeps an eye on Rooksy. I shake my head, urging him to shut up. A fight is scary enough, but in the hydraulic it could be life threatening. Griggsy waits for Rooksy to say something, anything that will allow him to start the scrap. Rooksy doesn't oblige and Griggsy assumes that he has bottled it. He ties the jam jar to his belt, climbs over and slides down the railings like a fireman on a pole. Impressive, except that he lands with a deep knees-bend that allows the hanging jar to reach and smash on the concrete ledge.

'Oh dear,' says Rooksy from the corner of his mouth.

Like Guy the Gorilla, Griggsy glowers at us through the bars, as if thinking about climbing over to pull our arms off. He decides against it and kicks the glass debris off the ledge.

'Fuck you two.' He grabs the railings and jerks himself towards us to launch a farewell gob that lands far out in the middle of the tank. He jumps down and strides off with the lid and neck of the broken jar dangling on the string.

'Fuck you too,' I say loud enough for only Rooksy to hear.

'I swear one day I'm going to do Griggsy, in the dark, with something very heavy,' says Rooksy, as if he's playing *Cluedo*.

Relief at Griggsy's departure lasts until I remember Siddy's farewell gestures. 'What about Siddy?'

He grins. 'Fond of me, isn't he? Look, he won't do anything, not to you anyway. He'll be scared we'll grass him up.' He smiles. 'He did look miffed though, didn't he?'

'Are you surprised?'

He puts a hand on my shoulder. 'It'll be all right. Let's go.'

The direct way back is between the tanks along the narrow wall that Griggsy swaggered across earlier. I wonder if I could do it too and for a moment my fear is being matched by the excitement of trying. I step forward.

Rooksy holds up a hand. 'You sure? You don't have to, you know. If you want, I'll say you did it anyway...'

He would too. 'No, thanks Rooksy.'

'Suit yourself, blowed if I would. Wait a minute.' He scoots around the tanks and takes up position at the far end of the wall. He holds out his arms to me. 'Don't look down, just look at me.'

The first steps go well and I make steady progress. Rooksy gives me the OK sign. However, half way across, my confidence evaporates and I begin to sense that the hydraulic is alive and aware of what I'm doing.

'Go slowly, don't look down,' shouts Rooksy. But

I do, if only to reassure myself that the water isn't rising to get me. In the resulting giddiness, I take a few faltering steps that become a desperate dash for the end. When I realize I'm not to going to make it, I come to a swaying stop. The remaining ten feet of wall may as well be ten miles. My head spins, the tank seems to shift like a jogged basin and the dark water swells towards me. I crouch to grab the wall but miss and tumble in. The impact slaps open my eyes and water fills my mouth. I get to the surface choking and thrashing close to a slimy wall. There are no handholds.

'Billy, Billy, over there.'

Above me, Rooksy is pointing into the corner where a rusting metal ladder rises from the water. I bob higher for a better look but coming down takes me under and the dragging weight of my jeans and shoes holds me there. Then there is a booming in my ears and thousands of tiny bubbles boil around me in green light. Flailing arms are shoving and hitting me. When I resurface, I'm close enough to the ladder to grab it. I hang on to its bottom rung, coughing and retching. Six feet away, I catch sight of Rooksy's head going under.

He comes up spluttering with his arms scrabbling around uselessly in front of him.

'Towards me, Rooksy!' Holding on to the ladder, I swing my body back out into the tank. 'Grab my legs!'

He lunges for me but falls inches short and sinks out of sight. He reappears only to plunge straight back down. I swing out again and this time my foot thumps into him. He catches hold and pulls himself along my legs until he can grasp

176

my belt and finally the ladder. We hang on the rusty rungs with our legs locked together below the water, spluttering and grinning. Rooksy, eyes closed, is shaking uncontrollably.

'Fucking hell Rooksy.'

He opens his eyes. 'Fucking hell is right.'

'You can't swim.'

'You can fucking talk.'

'No, I mean, you can't swim but...'

'Well, I can now ... a bit. And we're the first ones to do it in the hydraulic. How about that then?' Yes, how about that. 'Once is enough though, eh? Thought I'd had it.' He starts shaking again.

'Come on Rooksy, let's get out of here.'

He forces a smile and gestures like a butler to usher me first up the ladder. 'After you.'

At the top, we strip to our underwear and lie back on the warm concrete with our outstretched arms across each other's chest. We laugh at the sour steam that's rising from our clothes. Relief is making everything funny.

'At this rate we'll have tans like Kirk Douglas,' says Rooksy.

An appealing thought but I've had enough of the empty fish tank stench and the drying scum that is tightening my skin.

'We stink,' I say.

'We certainly do.'

'Let's go then.' I lift his arm from my chest and get up. We put on our jeans, shoes and socks. Our shirts are almost dry but stiff as if they've been starched. We tie them around our waists and climb out. On the other side, Rooksy holds up one of the dangling sleeves and sniffs. 'Yeuch, Eau de Terrapin. Time for a bath. See you later then?'

'Yeah, see you later and thanks ... you know.'

'Right, and thanks too, you know...'

He saunters off shaking his legs like Charlie Chaplin trying to get a fish out of his trousers. I set off at a jog and I'm almost home when I run into Griggsy. He's holding his hand out to a terrified Derek McCloud. Derek rummages in his pockets, finds a coin and hands it over. Griggsy pats him on the cheek.

When he sees me, he moves quickly to block my way. 'Hello, shitbag, got any money on ya?'

'No, skint.'

Seeing me shirtless and with dried slime on my skin he bursts into laughter. 'Don't tell me you fell in, what a prick.'

I shrug and try to move past him. He thrusts an open hand into my chest like a traffic policeman.

'Sure you've got no money to borrow me?'

I turn my empty pockets inside out.

'Fuck me, you stink.' He wipes his hand on Derek. 'Where's Rooksy then?'

'Gone home.'

'He fall in too?'

'No, he jumped in...'

'Not to save ya?'

'No.'

'Must fancy ya.'

'No he doesn't.'

'Calling me a liar?'

The answer has to be 'no'. But no what? No, I'm not calling you a liar? No, Rooksy doesn't fancy me? Or, no, Rooksy doesn't fancy me and I *am* calling you a liar, you fucking moron?

178

I opt for safety. 'No, I got out on my own...'

'You mean your best bum-boy-friend didn't help you?'

'He's not my best friend.'

I hate Griggsy for frightening me like this but no more than I now hate myself.

'He is a bum boy though, isn't he?' This is the second time he's made Rooksy out to be queer. Does he mean it? Or is it what he calls everyone he doesn't like?

'No, he's not.'

He frowns, grabs the back of my neck and pulls me close to his face, 'So you *are* calling me a liar.'

'No.'

'Well I say he *is* a bum boy.' He gives me a light head butt for emphasis.

My voice is a squeak. 'OK, he is...'

'That's better.'

He pushes me away, spits at my feet and bounces down the road sniffing his hands in disgust.

Derek gives me a pathetic grin, as if we're somehow closer mates because Griggsy has picked on both of us. I ignore him and run home.

How does jumping in to help me make Rooksy a bum boy? Isn't it what a best mate would do? Even if he can't swim? But what if Rooksy is queer? He knows about bummers all right, and what they do in the dark at the Biograph. But Rooksy? Who risks being murdered by Siddy Smith for a look at Madge's tits? Who has all those pictures of naked women? Perhaps you can like women and be a queer? But he joked about wanting to kiss me. But it was a joke?

# BODYLINE CRICKET

John and I are making our way down the Play Street for a game of 'twosy' cricket. I'm carrying the wicket: a cardboard box containing two bricks for ballast. He's practising Peter May on-drives, raising the bat to eye level on the follow-through. We're about to cross the end of the alley when we're stopped by a rattling of mudguards and the sound of shoes scraping the ground in the absence of brakes. Bike and rider, metal and muscle whoosh towards us.

'Out the fucking way, shitbags.'

Griggsy swerves out of the alley into the street. At the same time, he leans over to barge John to the ground. His cricket bat clatters across the road. Whooping like a Comanche, Griggsy pedals furiously to the end of the street and turns out of sight.

I pick up the bat. John gets to his feet rubbing his shoulder. 'Bastard.'

On our 'pitch', I place the wicket over the dimpled manhole cover in the middle of the road. I'm about to take guard when John throws me the ball and holds out his other hand.

'Can I bat first?'

When we're on our own, he asks, when others are playing with us, he doesn't.

'OK.'

He takes the bat and I walk back beyond the

180

bowling crease: a strip of tarmac covering an old road repair. John stands ready, tapping the bat on the ground. I start my run up.

'I said out of my way shitbags.' Griggsy roars up behind me, clouts the back of my head and flashes down the pitch. John jumps aside but can't stop Griggsy's swinging leg wrecking the cardboard box and spilling the bricks across the road.

'Howzat, cunts!'

He thinks he's Reg Harris, doing a wild cycling circuit that takes in the Play Street, Moreton Hill, our street and the alley. Our game can't survive, and there's no point waiting till later because although Griggsy has no brain, he has loads of stamina. Few things make him happier than ruining games that others won't play with him.

John tries to restore the wicket but it's leaning irretrievably to 'off'. He gives up and decides to complete its destruction with violent front and back swings of the bat. He walks towards me.

'John?'

He isn't going to stop. I try to hold him up by tossing him the ball, which he lets bounce off his chest. He continues past me, holding the bat with both hands in a distinctly non-cricketing grip. He's taking deep breaths.

'John, please, it's not worth it.' I grab his arm but he rips it away and breaks into a jog until he gets to the entrance to the alley. He waits, pressing down with open palms on the bat's handle, like Gene Kelly does on his umbrella in *Singing in the Rain*. But John isn't smiling.

I cover my ears, wanting to 'La, la' everything away and praying that Griggsy won't do another lap. I make a last attempt to pull John away. He won't budge. His face is harder, older. If we survive what's about to happen, I know that I'm bound to see this look again. There'll always be a 'Griggsy' to deal with and John will never let things go.

He lifts the cricket bat and shakes it the way men do to get their shirt cuffs to show. The bike rattles into the far end of the alley, my stomach churns and I feel light enough to be blown away.

John takes up a stance that's more baseball player than Surrey cricketer. By the time the bike's front wheel appears, he's swinging. It's partly Ken Barrington hook, but it's mainly Babe Ruth. The bat cracks into Griggsy's face and his arms fly up like an Indian shot from his horse. He lands on his back and his head squish-cracks on the alley wall. The riderless bike shoots across the street and crashes against the kerb. Griggsy curls up, moaning and gurgling. His eyes are closed. I grab John and silently beg him to leg it. He isn't finished. He produces an on-drive into Griggsy's back, a flat thump that brings blood spraying through his teeth. John waits, watching and shrugging me away. When Griggsy comes to and tries to get to his knees, John bats the side of his head, less violently this time, more of a clip to square leg. Griggsy rolls on to his back and deep treacly coughs shake his body.

'Enough, John!'

He relents and backs away without taking his eyes off Griggsy, who he decides can take a bit more. Although Griggsy probably can't hear, John tells him why. 'Bastard, gobbing in my hat...' The

182

kick thuds into Griggsy's ribs. 'Busting our ball...'
A second kick, which is more of a toe-poke.
'Hitting Jojo...' He joggles Griggsy's body back
and forth with the sole of his foot.

'John, please, please!'

Griggsy's eyes flicker. John crouches down and
whispers to him. When he stands up, his face has
softened.

'OK,' he says and lets me pull him away. At the
street corner, he stops to look back. Griggsy isn't
moving.

Josie comes up behind us.

'Watcha Billy, watcha John.'

John walks off.

'What's up?'

I can't speak. She looks past me to see Griggsy
lying by the alley.

'David?' She hobbles over to him, stopping
once to raise and lower her arms, silently asking,
'what's happened?' I shake my head.

My little brother. A year ago, he was playing
cowboys; now he could be going to borstal, maybe
as a murderer. I have a talent for avoiding fights
although I've seen lots, but I'm sickened by what
John has done. Even when really riled, Audie
Murphy doesn't kick a man who's down. Is my
brother turning out to be a baddie? I love him but
will I always be able to like him? Consequences
rampage through my head: what Griggsy's old
man will do; what Mum and Dad will say; what
will happen to John. I lean giddily against the wall
and puke.

When I next look around the corner, Josie is
helping Griggsy to sit up but she fails to hold him

183

when he rolls forward to the ground. He needs an ambulance but the nearest phone is at Swole's, which means I'll have to go back past Griggsy and Josie. As I wobble towards them, Griggsy comes to life and turns on to his side. He mumbles something and puts a hand to his bleeding mouth to check his teeth. Josie is rubbing his back and talking to him between angry glances at me.

Griggsy struggles to his knees. I wait, praying he'll get up. Then, with Josie's help, he does! Once on his feet, he staggers around, eyes down, looking for his bike. I jog back to the corner before he sees me. When he finds his bike, he stands it up, rests a forearm along the handlebars and limps towards the end of the street. Josie walks beside him, keeping her hand on his back until she's sure he won't fall again.

Griggsy may be a bastard but I thank god that he's a such *hard* bastard.

Josie comes towards me but because I don't know what I can say to her, I back around the street corner and run away.

When I get home, John is sitting at the top of our steps. 'Did he get up?'

'Sort of, with Josie's help ... you've really hurt him.'

He shrugs. 'Don't think he knew what happened.'

'But what if he did?'

'Don't think so. Anyway...'

I remember him crouching beside Griggsy. 'What did you say to him?'

He looks away.

'What?' I scream.

184

'I said, "It's me, John Driscoll".'

'Are you nuts? It's Griggsy, mental fucking Griggsy, and you nearly killed him. Now he's going to kill you and me!'

'He couldn't hear me.'

'How do you know? And what if Josie tells him what happened?'

'Think she will?'

'She might.'

He thinks about this for a second, shrugs again and goes indoors.

## HEADLONG

Rooksy and I are outside Plummer's. It's nearly five o'clock but the heat is still oppressive. Rooksy tugs his damp shirt away from his chest and flaps it to cool himself. 'I could almost go swimming again. How about you?'

'No thanks.'

'Not even in our private pool?'

'No!'

'Jubblies then?'

'Not for me, I don't have enough.'

Once when Mum asked Dad why he always had to buy the first round, he said that if you can't afford to be first to the bar you should stay out of the pub altogether. She wasn't convinced but I was impressed; it's the kind of thing Audie Murphy would say when he's playing an honest homesteader.

'Sure? I've got plenty...'

'Sure, thanks.' If he asks again, I'm going to say yes.

He shrugs and goes into the shop. When he comes out, he's holding two Jubblies. He offers one to me. 'There you are.'

'Thanks, you shouldn't have.' I take it from him but his 'knew you would' smile tells me that Dad is probably right.

Sarah and Josie come around the corner.

'Well, hello,' he says, giving me the public nudge reserved for friends in the presence of someone they fancy.

'Like a Jubbly girls?'

Josie doesn't stop. 'No thanks Peter, late for my tea.'

Sarah shakes her head and pauses long enough for Rooksy to say, 'Have a seat, I'm sure Billy would like you to stay.'

Yes, he would. The three of us sit down.

'Like a suck of mine?' says Rooksy, holding out the Jubbly.

'No thanks,' says Sarah. She misses his lewd smirk. He winks at me but I refuse to smile. His raised eyebrows ask, 'What?'

'Sorry you didn't win the race, Billy,' says Sarah.

I want to tell her what really happened but I've already told Rooksy, in some detail, and he stopped listening before I'd finished. 'Thanks, it was no big deal.'

This seems to be all she needs to know because she changes the subject. 'What have you been up to today?'

'Not much.'

'That's because there's sod all to do around here,' says Rooksy.

She shrugs and nods agreement.

'We should go somewhere,' he says.

'Where?' says Sarah. I love her 'wheurr'.

'Anywhere away from here, somewhere with grass but no dog shit. How about tomorrow?'

Fast work, Rooksy. And tomorrow would be fine. I'd also like to be as scarce as possible after what John did to Griggsy.

Sarah stands up. 'I don't know ... maybe.'

She's considering it! I dive into planning mode. 'We could get Red Rovers.'

Red Rover tickets allow you to travel as far as you like on red buses. John and I have used them to go all over London, visiting depots to jot down the bus numbers and underline them in a spotters' book – something we stopped doing the day after Rooksy asked, 'Why? How different is one bus from another?'

There *are* differences, which I tried to explain but he said, 'I mean, what *is* the fucking point?'

None really, just as there's little point in arranging your coins face-side up or trying to see ten Ford Anglias before a Morris Minor comes along. I do it all the time. John grinned at my embarrassment because it was like me telling him it was time to stop playing cowboys.

'What about Hillswood?' I say.

'Where's that then?' says Sarah.

'Surrey, near a huge slope. From the top, you can see for miles and there are woods at the bottom. It's quite a way but it takes only two buses: 68 and 60a...' Rooksy's eyes close. Who but a pathetic bus spotter would know the numbers?

Rooksy stands up and says to Sarah, 'Sounds good, shall we?'

Please God let her say, 'yes'.

'OK, but I'll have to tell my mum.' She's not only saying yes, she's looking at me as she says it. 'I'll have to say I'm going to Battersea Park for a picnic or something ... maybe with Christine.'

'Christine!' we say together. Not busty Christine Cassidy, who now has a gobby flauntiness she didn't have when only her face was plump.

'Look, I'm not even thirteen yet. And ... well I can't say I'm going with you two ... you know, just boys.'

We know.

I'm smiling. Rooksy notices and shoves his grinning face into mine.

I blush, searching for something to say. I hold up my Jubbly to Sarah. 'Would you like some?'

'Oh thanks Billy, I would.'

I tear back the top seam with my teeth to expose a ridge of orange ice for her – and wonder if tomorrow will ever come.

In the morning, at Victoria Station, there's no sign of Sarah.

'Maybe we should go on our own,' says Rooksy.

No. We've had some great days out, including a riverboat trip to Richmond, and a day at Hampstead Heath where we drank lemonade outside Dick Turpin's pub. Not today, though, it would feel like losing a bob and finding a tanner.

On the far side of the station, a bus moves off to reveal Sarah standing on the kerb, with Josie.

188

'Oh fucking marvellous,' says Rooksy.

They cross towards us hand-in-hand.

'Hello,' says Josie, with her hand to her face and dismay in her eyes at our reaction.

'I've asked Josie to come too … that's all right isn't it?' Sarah isn't asking.

I avoid looking at Rooksy and smile at Josie. When I see how pleased this makes her, my smile becomes genuine.

'No, yes, fine, isn't it Rooksy?'

He gives Josie his Errol Flynn smile. 'Course it is.'

'Where do we get the tickets then?' says Sarah. Josie takes hold of her arm with both hands and pulls her close.

In the queue for tickets, I notice the duffel bag on Rooksy's shoulder. I've brought nothing for the trip.

'It's not much,' he says, loosening the cord at the bag's neck. 'Not much' is a bottle of Tizer, loads of ham sandwiches in greaseproof paper and some Kit Kats. Sarah has a bag too, which she opens to reveal cheese-and-pickle baps and a bottle of diluted orange squash.

Josie has also brought nothing. 'Didn't know I was coming until this morning.' Rooksy and Sarah swap smiles and I feel a pang of jealousy.

'This'll do for all of us,' says Sarah.

As we make for our bus, Josie touches my arm and stops walking. 'I won't say anything Billy … about what happened with David.'

I don't reply.

'It was John wasn't it… I mean, you didn't?'

Well, no. I'm pleased she thinks I couldn't have

done such a brutal thing, then again, I'm not; she clearly doesn't think I'm tough enough.

'He asked for it, you know, he really did.'

'Maybe ... but don't you feel sorry for him? He must feel so lonely ... everyone's either horrible to him or scared of him.'

I'm about to say that this might be because *he* is horrible and scary, when she says, 'Poor old David.' Josie Costello is kind.

We take the two front seats on the top deck. The girls sit on the right, with Josie by the window so we get her good side. 'On top, up front' is the only way to travel on double-deckers. As a small boy, I 'steered' the bus with the handle that winds the top third of the window up and down. If I sat low enough in the seat, the window became a bright screen on which building tops and church steeples slid across the sky each time the bus turned a corner.

We're soon talking and laughing too easily. The girls shove each other and giggle at everything, especially at what Rooksy is saying.

'What a fine head of skin,' about a bald man at the bus stop below. 'God, have you ever seen tits as big as that,' about a woman leaning over a green-grocer's stall. Then he whistles the Laurel and Hardy tune to accompany a fat man waddling to his seat but he can't keep it up and his cross-eyed attempts to purse his lips have us choking with suppressed laughter.

The bus trundles through Stockwell, Clapham and Balham, past crowded pavements and shop fronts shaded under stained and faded awnings. Above them, the dark windows of dingy flats reflect the dull red of our passing bus.

From Tooting Broadway, another bus takes us south through fewer high streets and longer stretches of open land where the stops are further apart. Not many red buses came so far out of London. This is the territory of Greenline single-deckers on which we used to take day-trips with Mum and Dad. Their closing doors make them stuffier than red buses and they retain a faint smell of lavender from the ladies who travel to London on shopping trips; it reminds me of Aunt Winnie before she gets through too many of her du Mauriers.

We rattle past fields and roadside pubs at speeds that aren't possible in London. Before long, we're rolling into Hillswood, with its newly built parade of shops behind wide pavements and flowerbeds bounded by low walls. In the station, and the bus takes a few seconds to shudder to silence. He climbs down from his cab, slams shut the little sliding door and, with the conductor, crosses the road to a pub. We follow them and as we pass the front of the bus, I stop to listen to the engine plinking as it cools down, and to savour the smell of hot metal and evaporating diesel.

Rooksy bumps into my back. 'What is it with you and buses?'

He wouldn't understand.

Wooden tables, benches and Double Diamond umbrellas spread across the pavement in front of the pub. We're weaving our way through when the Beatles' *She Loves You* blasts through the open doors and brings us to a tingling halt. Josie starts singing it too and we all join in. The song has just come out and we could listen to it all day; so could someone in the pub because the jukebox plays it again, and again. The girls sit on a bench and rock side-to-side as they sing along. Rooksy moves behind Sarah to do his John Lennon knees-bends and mouths 'sheee loves yoooooo' at me while embracing himself with his own arms. Josie catches him and bends forward laughing. When the record stops, we wait to hear it a fourth time but Elvis starts singing *You're the Devil in Disguise* so we head for the sweetshop next door where we all buy a Neilson's ice cream and I get a couple of Mars Bars to add to our provisions.

Once we're outside, Rooksy hands me another two. 'Here you are, now there'll be one each.' He hasn't paid for them.

'Bloody hell, Rooksy.'

He bites off the bottom of his cone to suck out the ice cream. 'Think we should be going, don't you?'

The girls have noticed nothing. 'Where now?' says Sarah.

'Follow me.' That's 'me' the expedition leader.

I take them along a path through nettles, whitened by dust scuffed-up from the dry clay. After half a mile, the path turns out of the sun into the shade of a wood. In the cool chlorophyll air, Sarah and Josie pull their cardigans around them without doing up the buttons. I wonder why girls do this.

Rooksy and I push on and the girls dawdle behind, arms linked and walking close enough for it to look as if they both have a limp. Rooksy and I reach a small clearing in front of a brick water

192

tower that's covered in ivy, except where a rusted metal door stands ajar. A man in maroon overalls emerges and bangs the door shut. He pushes his fingers through dark slicked-back hair, picks up his bag and leaves the way we've come.

At the next bend in the path, we stop to check on the girls. They're about fifty yards back. The man is standing in front of them. We run back down the path. 'Come on you two, we'll be late!' I shout, hoping he'll move on. It seems to work because he looks back and starts walking. Sarah pulls Josie to one side as he passes.

'All right?' asks Rooksy.

'He said we should be careful, being on our own, that there are men who take advantage of girls,' says Josie.

Rooksy kicks at some nettles. 'Oh yeah? Maybe he knows *who* exactly?'

The girls exchange glances. 'Maybe,' says Sarah. 'Anyway, let's go. I want to see this view Billy's promised us.'

We set off again, at Josie's pace.

As we get deeper into the wood, even the dappled light grows dim and it no longer feels like a summer's day.

Josie gives a pretend shiver. 'Scary isn't it? Those trees look like they could turn nasty.'

Cue Rooksy singing 'We're off to see the wizard', interspersed with ghostly 'whoo hoos'.

Before long, it gets brighter ahead, not just daylight, more the big, wide light you get when you're close to the sea but can't see it yet. At the edge of the wood, the path peters out in a broad swathe of grass. We emerge into dazzling sunshine and a warm breeze blows in our faces. Ahead, the sky reaches down to the ground and we're looking out into miles of thin air.

Josie takes Rooksy's hand. 'Blimey, look at that. I've never, ever, seen so far.'

He looks at me, eyebrows arched. I wonder if he's going to be unkind but when he turns to Josie, it's with his big-screen smile. She lowers her eyes and tries to let go, but Rooksy holds on. Sarah looks at him, then me, shrugs and holds Josie's other hand.

Dear Josie, who usually waits for others to take the lead, has gone and held Rooksy's hand. We exchange glances. Something is changing, shifting us closer and the silence becomes thrilling when Sarah clasps my hand to make the chain complete. 'You were right about the view, Billy.'

'Here we go then,' says Rooksy. '*Famous Five* out for the day minus the bloody dog.' Four abreast, we set off to the lip of the great slope to survey the Surrey countryside.

At the top of the slope, we sprawl on hands and knees, flattening the long dry grass to a warm mesh. Hidden inside our bower, we lie on our backs and watch white smoke-signal clouds scudding overhead. Insects are ticking around us and one or two tired birds sing out sporadically. From the wood, only an unseen dove is giving of its best.

Josie shifts on to her knees and cocks an ear to the sky. 'Is that a cuckoo?'

The dove *has* sounded a little like a cuckoo. The only birds Josie knows are sparrows and pigeons, the ducks on Battersea Park Lake and the flocks of starlings that swarm above our street every evening on their way to roost in Trafalgar Square.

Because Sarah is from the country, Josie looks to her, bright-eyed.

Sarah starts to tell her that it isn't a cuckoo. 'I don't...' But it *has* to be a cuckoo for Josie. I catch Sarah's eye in time. 'I don't know, wait a mo,' she says. When the dove calls again, she smiles. 'Yes, that's a cuckoo, all right.'

Josie claps her hands: 'A cuckoo, I've heard a cuckoo! Blimey, wait till I tell Mum.'

'Blow me, a cuckoo,' says Rooksy with a wink.

'I know a rhyme my mum told me,' says Josie.

*'Sit and hear the cuckoo cry*
*Stand and see the swallow fly*
*See the foal before the mare*
*And you'll have luck through all the year'*

'Well, there are plenty of swallows, look!' says Sarah.

Genuine swallows have arrived, screeching around us like fighter planes breaking formation. Josie struggles to her feet and spins round to follow them.

'Now all I need to do is "see a foal before the mare".'

'Even two out of three must be lucky,' I say.

She eases herself back down on to the grass, 'Do you think so Billy? Blimey, a cuckoo.' Sarah hands out her rolls and we take turns to swig her orange squash.

Below us, the slope plunges into trees that fill the valley bottom. Disembodied shouts and laughter drift up to us and, occasionally, the muffled growl of a car travelling along a hidden road. I peer down through the haze, trying to match what I can hear to what I can see; it's like searching the sky for a singing lark.

'Why don't we go down there?' says Rooksy.

Josie isn't so sure. 'But it's so nice up here. Do we have to?'

Rooksy gets up. 'Why not, I've had enough of the view.'

Josie will find it hard to get down the hill, but we keep the pressure on by saying nothing. She palms her hands in prayer and blows between them as if trying to separate two sheets of paper. 'OK, but I might need a hand.' She stretches her bad leg down the slope, swivels and pushes herself to her feet.

'We can take our time,' says Sarah.

The slippery dry grass lies flat down the hill as if it's been combed by a vanished river. Before long, we're slipping on to our backsides and up again as grasshoppers arc out of our way like the tips of invisible bow waves. Sarah is ahead of me and Rooksy is further down. We're in free fall.

Above me, Josie shrieks. I slide to a halt and look up. She's on her back, out of control, trying to stop herself by thrusting out her good leg as if she's stabbing a footbrake. Her dress is rucked up around her waist and the more she tries to pull it back down, the more she slips. I move to help her but I'm stopped by the sight of her white knickers – and how tightly they're pulled against her. A fleshy catch forms at the top of my windpipe. I look away.

Rooksy's windpipe is OK; he gives Josie a full,

four-fingers-in-the mouth, wolf whistle.

'Peter, stop it,' says Sarah.

He laughs and climbs towards Josie. She has managed to stop by turning on to her stomach. Her tucked-up knickers cover nothing and her thighs and bum are blotched red with grass burns. She yanks her dress back down and lies with her head buried in the crook of her arm. Sarah calls to her but gets no answer.

I'm closer than Rooksy and should be helping, but I'm just standing there, taking in what I've seen.

'Billy ... really!' says Sarah. My face flushes, not least with the shock of feeling so groiny out in the open air.

Rooksy arrives alongside Josie and gets her to sit up. She adjusts her dress and stares down the hill.

He puts a hand on her shoulder. 'Good job you've got clean knickers on.' Her head drops. He waits a moment and puts his arm around her. 'Come on, come on, I'll give you a hand.' He throws his duffel bag to me and, standing below her on the slope, pulls her to her feet.

He presents his back to her. 'On you get.'

She hesitates and looks at Sarah, who raises her hands and lets them fall to her sides. Josie climbs aboard and Rooksy hoists her further up with his hands on her bum. She doesn't complain and wraps her arms around his neck. Then he's off, piggybacking her down the slope, speeding up into barely controlled leaps, while Josie's joggled-doll voice shrieks at him to slow down.

I offer Sarah my hand. She looks at me without smiling, shrugs and takes it.

'You don't want a piggyback then?'

'Not funny, Billy.'

I'm smiling stupidly, embarrassed by what I've seen, yet strangely excited that Sarah has been here at the same time. And, now I'm wondering about the colour of *her* knickers. We start down and our pace quickens into long, risky bounds until falling seems the only way to stop. I hope we will because I'd enjoy helping her up, if not in quite the same way Rooksy helped Josie. Unfortunately, Sarah is as nimble as a bloody goat all the way down.

At the bottom, Rooksy and Josie are waiting with their arms out to help us stop. We could avoid them but we collide anyway.

Josie slips her arm through Rooksy's. 'Blimey, I don't want to do that again. How will I ever get back up?'

Rooksy winks at me. 'I can always lend you a hand Josie ... or two.'

Head down, she goes over to Sarah, who brushes a smile from her mouth with the back of her hand. Rooksy feigns upset. 'Oh, OK then.'

What *is* he doing? I mean, Josie? But why not Josie? She's the nicest of our friends – and now we know she has quite a figure. Rooksy winks and gives me his OK sign. He may not fancy Josie but he's enjoying making her happy.

Flushed from our exertions, we stand facing each other, exchanging self-conscious smiles. For a few seconds, it's like we're once again in headlong descent, wondering how we'll stop. Josie's cuckoo calls. Warm, sappy air rises between us as we breath in whatever is making this day special.

Sarah breaks the spell. 'Where now, Billy?'

'There are fields on the other side of these trees, and a little caravan park.'

'OK then, let's have a look.'

Sarah starts walking but Josie hesitates, wondering whether to wait for Rooksy, but she chooses Sarah and off they go, arm-in-arm, in synchronized limping.

Rooksy mocks my mouth-open look and grips his crotch.

I whisper, 'Josie? Really?'

'Well, you know.' He looks into the distance and pulls his comb through his hair. 'I liked the cuckoo. Let's hope one doesn't call while she can see it.'

We laugh and, arms around each other's shoulders, we follow the girls.

Ahead of us, a small field contains a cluster of caravans whose wheels have been replaced by bricks. Each one stands in its personal garden, bounded by a low white fence. There are pots of flowers outside each door as well as short, untidy lines of washing – and gnomes, lots of gnomes.

Small children wave, wondering whether to approach us. We wave back but deter them by carrying on through a clump of trees to another clearing that is half in shade. At the far side, bathed in sunshine, a large wooden hut sits with its back to more woods.

'It's a chalet,' says Rooksy. 'My uncle's got one at Camber Sands.'

# TRUTH

Rooksy leaps on to the wooden veranda to peer through one of two dusty windows. Next, he runs his fingers along the top of the doorframe and feels under the stubby window ledges.

'What are you looking for, Peter?' says Josie.

'A way in.' She's puzzled. 'A key, a key to the bloody door. There's usually one hidden nearby.'

He could be right. Ada Holt keeps one under her doormat and half the kids in our street let themselves in with a key on a string they pull from the letterbox.

'I'm not going in there. Not on your Nelly, I don't like the look of it,' says Josie.

Nor do I, not one bit.

Rooksy goes over to a water butt standing on breeze-blocks down one side of the chalet. He drops to his haunches to feel about underneath. A few seconds later, he straightens up waving a key. Oh god, here we go.

With no hesitation, he unlocks the door and pushes it open. 'There we are.'

Josie calls to him, 'Peter, don't ... we shouldn't.' I couldn't agree more.

'It's the afternoon. The owners won't be coming now, will they?'

Josie takes a step back. 'I don't know, Peter.'

Rooksy looks to me for support. I'm not offering any. Please Rooksy, don't ask me in front of

200

the girls.

'Billy? You coming in or not?'

Bastard. In every frightening film I've seen, the first rule that always gets broken is, 'stay out of the scary-house'.

'Don't think so Rooksy, it's all a bit *Hansel and Gretel.*'

The girls laugh and I take it as a cue to leave. But Rooksy steps inside, turns around and waits with his arms spread as if it's a hotel. His dare works on Josie, who shrugs and loyally limps inside. In vain, I search Sarah's face for a clue to what she'd prefer to do. So I opt for what I hope will impress her, 'Come on then.' I jump up on to the veranda and wait for her. I'm not sure whether I'm being brave, or weak.

Once we're inside, Rooksy closes the bloody door. Another scary-house rule you shouldn't break. The girls swap anxious glances. He strides past us to an old Formica topped table, plonks down his duffel bag, pulls out one of two wooden chairs and sits down.

We're in the bigger side of the chalet, which is divided in two by a partition containing a door-less doorway. Opposite the front door, on the far wall, a Belfast sink and a single gas ring sit on top of a small cupboard. Above the sink, a tap hangs skew-whiff from the end of a pipe that pokes out of the wall. On our left, a faded red leather couch faces the doorway to the other room. By the sink and around the table, the brown linoed floor is worn through to the beige webbing.

'Who's ready to eat?' says Rooksy.

The rest of us are more nervous than hungry.

What's more, a baking, stuffy smell, like months-old fart is rising from the floor.

'What *is* that?' says Josie.

'Smells like the squashed rats you find on bombdies,' I say.

Sarah shivers her shoulders.

'No, it's creosote, and Calor gas, it gets into everything,' says Rooksy.

'Gas?' says Josie. She gets up and opens the door.

'It's OK, it's not like gas at home, not dangerous.'

'Yeah, but it's managed to kill something in here,' I say.

They all laugh.

'You are funny,' says Sarah. For a moment I forget how much I don't want to be here.

Fresher air comes in through the door. The girls go over to the couch and sit down and I join Rooksy at the table. We pass round his Tizer, wiping the top of the bottle with our dirty hands before drinking. Rooksy's ham sandwiches are soon gone and we eat the Kit Kats after picking the foil from the melted chocolate – a must if you have fillings. I pull out my Mars Bars but they've mushed and warped in my pocket. I lay them by the sink to firm up. When I turn on the tap, it bounces around as water coughs into a chipped enamel bowl. I rinse my sticky hands and cup them to drink the cool water; warm Tizer isn't a thirst quencher.

'Well, now what?' says Rooksy.

I'm for leaving. 'Perhaps we should go now.'

'No, let's stay for a bit. What do you say, girls?'

'To do what?' says Sarah.

We all look at each other. Back comes the silence that surrounded us at the bottom of the slope, the same sense of this being a special day and of there being more to come. I wonder if their hearts are beating like mine?

'How about the truth game?' says Rooksy.

'Truth game?' says Josie.

'We ask each other questions and, no matter what, you must tell the truth.' He looks at me, and seems to be reading my mind, 'Unless you tell the truth, there's no bloody point.'

Josie leans forward, stretching her frock over her knees like a tablecloth. 'What do you think, Sarah?'

'Don't know.'

Rooksy winks at me, 'Right then, the truth game. Are you in girls?'

'Yes, let's,' says Josie.

Sarah smiles at Josie's enthusiasm. 'OK then.'

Rooksy gets up, closes the door again and comes back to squeeze between the girls on the couch. I turn my chair round and face them.

'Now, does everyone swear on their mother's life to tell the truth?' says Rooksy.

None of us answers.

'Well?' He puts an arm around both girls to jolly them along. Sarah pulls away; Josie moves closer.

'Bit much, isn't it?' I say. 'I mean, what if we say something that isn't completely true?'

'Then your mum will probably just get sick. Now, do you swear on her life that your answers will be the whole truth and nothing but the truth? Or not?'

They're all smiling. I push my hands into my pockets and cross my fingers. 'I swear.'

He says, 'I too swear that I will tell only the truth.' Then he gets the girls to promise too.

'Now, who's going first?'

Josie sits forward. 'Go on then, I will.'

'OK Josie, are you a virgin?'

'Peter!' says Sarah, slapping at his leg.

He spreads his hands. 'Truth game.'

Josie locks her fingers to make a visor over her eyes and stares into her lap. 'Course, what kind of girl do you think I am?'

'See, not so difficult is it? Now, Billy?'

Panic. 'What me?'

'No, not are *you* a virgin, what do you want to ask Josie?'

I trawl my head for a safe question. 'What do you want most in the world?'

I get a 'for goodness sake' look from Sarah. She's right, what else could Josie want most?

Josie isn't offended. 'Oh to get rid of ... you know.' She lifts a hand to her face.

Silence follows. Sarah chases it away with what I think is an unkind question. 'Who do you love?'

We wait. Watching Josie's bowed head, I realize how stupid I've been to assume that her birthmark could somehow stop her loving someone, or wanting to have a boyfriend. She turns away from Rooksy and the clear side of her face reddens.

Sarah reaches past him to touch her knee, 'Josie.'

'Blimey, well, I think I could, sort of ... love Peter.' She covers her face with both hands but she's not unhappy. Sarah's question wasn't unkind at all.

204

Rooksy waves like a king to his subjects. 'Who doesn't?' He puts his arm around her. She hunches up with pleasure but won't look at him. We wait for him to remove his arm and sit back but he doesn't.

'OK Billy, now you. Questions please girls?'

Josie is in first. 'Who do you love, Billy?'

'Look, shouldn't both the girls go first?'

Why are we doing this? At any other time, it would be easy to stop or to walk away. Yet here we're accepting stupid rules, asking more about each other and being prepared to reveal more, than we would dream of doing normally.

'No. Come on, what have you got to say?' says Rooksy.

If I had the nerve, I'd say a lot: that I think about Sarah all the time; that I dream of her being my girlfriend, or being married, like Roy Rogers and Dale Evans; that I gallop into Indian camps to rescue her; and that I've felt like this for ages.

Rooksy is staring at something on the ceiling. Blood thumps in my ears. But Sarah is smiling like she used to when I put my hand up in class. *Go on then*.

'It's Sarah.'

Her head drops. Josie claps her hands. 'I knew it, I knew it ... everyone knew it. There you are Sarah, told you.'

Everyone?

Rooksy takes his arm from around Josie's shoulders. 'Well, now we know.'

'Yes, but it's a secret Pete; we can't tell anyone else,' says Josie.

'Yeah,' I say, remembering how he kept Swole's

secret. He holds up his hands and finger-zips his mouth.

'OK Sarah, what's your question for lover boy here?'

'Oh, I don't know. Let's see ... have you ever farted?'

Josie splutters, 'Blimey.'

'What sort of bloody question is that?' says Rooksy.

'It's *my* question,' says Sarah.

I want to hug her.

'Doesn't everyone?' I say. We both grin and the lie is cancelled.

Rooksy and Josie exchange puzzled looks.

'OK Pete; what do you want to ask Billy?' says Sarah.

'Well it won't be, "have you ever had a shit?"' Josie rocks forward laughing.

'Let me think.' He sits further back on the couch and rubs his palms along his thighs. 'Do you love anyone else? Family and pets not included.' He swallows and it jerks the smile from his face. He looks away. With a jolt, I realise what he wants me to say.

Sarah is wondering why I'm taking so long to say, 'no one' and Josie is worried that there might actually *be* someone else. Rooksy won't look at me. I could say what I think he wants to hear, and add 'only joking', like he did after saying he'd sooner kiss me than Madge. But no, I will not, because it's the *truth* game and he shouldn't have bloody well asked.

Sarah speaks up. 'Truth game.'

I say, 'No, no one else.'

He sits back on the couch. 'Well, Sarah, you're in the clear.'

'What do you mean?'

'It means, Sarah, that you're the only one. What else?'

It's getting hot. Sweat trickles from my temples, Sarah raises an arm to dab her forehead with the short sleeve of her dress and Josie flaps her frock, revealing the insides of her thighs. Rooksy goes to the sink and splashes water in his face.

The game feels over but Josie says, 'What about you, Peter?'

'Yeah, what about you,' I say.

He comes back and sits down between the girls. 'OK, fire away.'

I try a Rooksy question. 'Have you seen naked women? In the flesh?'

Sarah frowns.

'Family excluded?' he says.

'Family excluded.'

'No, never have.'

'And who do *you* love, Peter?' says Sarah. Josie covers her birthmark as if it will put him off saying what she wants to hear.

'Who do I love?' We wait. He glances at me, then at the ceiling. He struggles to smile. 'Well, there's Billy.'

Josie slaps the tops of her thighs. 'No, love, Peter, you know, loving someone, the question wasn't "who's your best mate?"'

Rooksy looks at me with what little bravado he has left. 'Why shouldn't it be Billy?' He puts his hands over his eyes.

I breathe out. Josie looks at Sarah, who is staring

at Rooksy. My head whirls. I need to say something funny, to make what he's said sound less serious. Sarah puts her hand on his knee and Josie starts rubbing his back as if he's been injured. Saying something funny now would be a mistake.

'Blimey, it's suffocating in here,' says Josie.

Sarah moves closer to Rooksy. 'Oh Peter ... Peter?'

Josie gets up to open the door again.

Rooksy keeps his hands over his eyes. 'Don't be stupid, it's just that, well, if you haven't got a girlfriend, there's only your mates, and Billy's...'

'I see,' says Sarah.

'No you don't.'

Josie returns and gives a little laugh of embarrassment. 'You're not ... Peter, you're not, not like ... are you?'

He shakes his head and pulls his hands down his cheeks. His eyes are full of tears.

She sits down beside him. 'What's it like?'

'Josie ... please,' says Sarah.

'Sorry Peter, I didn't mean...'

Saying the wrong thing can sometimes be the right thing. It makes Rooksy smile and he sits up straight and rubs his eyes. 'Look, let's not get carried away. Remind me never to suggest truth games again.'

From both sides, the girls lean closer to him. I don't share their sympathy. The truth game was his idea, because he wanted something to be true that isn't true, but he still went on to say what he did. Serves him right.

Josie puts her arm around him. 'This doesn't mean though ... it doesn't mean you don't like girls, does it?'

'No, of course it doesn't mean that,' he says.

Sarah puts her arm around him too. 'And it doesn't mean that girls won't like you.'

He rubs his knees. 'Hope not.'

But it *does* mean that he could be queer. Sarah and Josie's tenderness for him surprises me. If we were still in the truth game, I'd tell him he shouldn't have said such a thing, that it was embarrassing, that it changes things. Bloody hell, Rooksy.

The girls are waiting for me to speak. The truth would hurt him. I want to be older, to have the right words, kind words to get us through this. When they come to me, they're not kind or unkind but what a boy of thirteen says in the middle of children's game. 'Sarah hasn't had her go yet.'

'Yeah, your turn Sarah,' says Josie.

'Maybe we should stop now,' says Sarah.

Rooksy cocks his head and wipes his face with his shirtsleeve. 'Why stop now?'

Josie shifts back in her seat. 'Oh Sarah, take your turn, please. Billy? Go on, ask her.'

I dare not ask what I want to know, in case I get the wrong answer. 'What do you want to be when you grow up?'

Rooksy shakes his head at my cowardice. Sarah clamps her lips in between her teeth. She's disappointed and I'm ashamed.

'I think I'd like to be a nurse.'

Josie clasps her hands around her knees and rocks back. 'My turn, who do *you* love then?'

Rooksy stands up. I want to get up too, to run from the room ... and to stay. Sarah squeezes

Josie's hand. 'Billy, Billy's the one.'

'Oh Billy,' says Josie.

'Who's a popular boy then?' says Rooksy.

I should say something, but it's all too much. Sarah stares at her clasped hands in her lap. Audie Murphy would take action: sit beside her; hold her hand; kiss her or even punch Rooksy. I stay put.

'OK, now my question,' says Rooksy.

'Well?' says Sarah.

'Will you always love him?'

She takes a deep breath and tells the bloody truth. 'Always? I don't know, Peter.'

You don't know?

'You don't know?' says Rooksy.

She looks at me as if I must agree. 'I can't say I know if I don't, can I?'

Why not?

Rooksy thrusts his face closer to hers. 'Why not?'

She glares at him. 'I've had enough of this. Why are you asking this?'

'Because, *I'd* know.'

'Blimey,' says Josie.

Sarah gets to her feet. 'Well, good for you.'

I give him a weak 'girls eh?' grin.

He ignores it and turns, unsmiling, to Josie. 'Fancy coming for a walk?'

Josie gets up with a half hop on her good leg and holds out her hand. Rooksy sees it but strides to the door as if he hasn't. She limps out after him.

# PROMISES

I stand by the opening into the other room. Against the opposite wall, sunlight is streaming on to a canvas camp bed. It's covered by a brown blanket, with a flap of white sheet showing at the top. A rolled-up sleeping bag sits in place of a pillow. Next to the bed is a small side table and a dark, scratched chest of drawers.

Sarah comes up behind me. 'Are you OK?'

'Yeah.'

'He's very upset.'

So am I. 'I know ... but what can I do? I don't know what to say to him.'

'You must have known how much he likes you.'

'I didn't. Well, yes, a bit, he said some things...'

'Oh?'

'Once he said he'd sooner kiss me than Madge Smith.'

'Who wouldn't?'

Is she being nice to me, or rotten to Madge? She's not smiling – rotten to Madge then.

'He said he was joking. But the way he looked at me, I could tell he sort of meant it, and then that he wished he hadn't said it. I think he was hoping I'd say that I feel the same way. But I couldn't, because ... well, I don't. I mean, I *do* like him, but not... You know. Anyway, afterwards he seemed OK about it.'

She says nothing and I keep going. 'I mean, best

mates *do* like each other a lot, don't they? When I fell into the hydraulic, he jumped in to help me, even though he can't swim. He could've drowned.'

'Not sure I could have done that.'

Maybe, but I'd like to hear what you *would* do, for me. We're alone, after declaring our love for each other, but we're talking about Rooksy. Anyway, boys don't, or shouldn't talk about loving each other. I love John but it would not be a good idea to tell him.

'Will this make a difference? Now that he...'

She means, 'now that Rooksy could be queer'. He has changed everything by saying what he did. Now we'll be thinking about it whenever we see him.

'No. Well, yes, it does make a difference, and if everyone thinks... Griggsy said I'm best mate to a bum boy.'

'What did you say?'

The truth game is over and I wonder if I should tell her. But today has a become a day when nothing else will do. 'I said that Rooksy wasn't my best mate, and that he wasn't even a mate really, and right after he'd risked his life for me... I was frightened.'

Her eyebrows rise but she says, 'Look, it's OK.'

'I wish I was braver.' She shrugs as if it doesn't matter. But it does. 'Rooksy and John don't seem to be afraid of anything; they never think about how others are reacting to them. I do, I can't help it. When things get dangerous, I can't stop myself imagining what might happen next. Sometimes I panic and if I can't change the subject I often tell lies.'

She squeezes my hand and smiles. 'I said it's OK, Billy. Anyway, Griggsy's a pig.'

I should tell the truth more often, and sooner.

'Let's not say anything to anyone about Peter,' she says.

'No, of course not.' Fine by me, I've had enough of talking about Peter. Now, about us. 'Sarah, did you mean it?'

'What?'

'Saying you loved me?'

'Yes. Did you?'

'Oh yes. It made me feel wonderful. I mean, saying it did ... but hearing *you* saying it to me, that was even better.'

She pulls her hand through her hair and tugs it before letting go. 'Let's sit down.'

We sit on the side of the camp bed. She props her head on her hands. The air has become heavy, soft, as if it will absorb anything I say. She smiles and my awkwardness soaks away into cotton-wool calm. I can barely hear myself saying, 'I would like to kiss you.'

'Would you?'

'If you don't mind.'

'No, I don't.'

I want this to be a big screen kiss. I put my arm around her but, because we're sitting side-by-side, I can't get the angle right. Our faces come together but our mouths barely touch. I expect her lips to feel something like mine but they're softer, thicker. Now we're nose-to-nose and finally kissing but still not able to get close enough. The only way to do this properly is for her to lie back and allow me to lift and hold her, like Audie

213

Murphy would.

She shifts and plumps the sleeping-bag pillow and stretches out. I put an arm under her back and lift. However, I'm perched with only half my bum on the bed and as I take her weight, my legs swing up and we thump back down. I bury my head in the sleeping bag, waiting for her laughter. Instead, she eases my face around in her hands and kisses me. Her mouth is slightly open, our teeth touch and then, briefly, the tips of our tongues.

She's making a lovely 'mmm' sound that buzzes on my lips. I wonder what to do next or, rather, if I should be doing *anything* next. Her eyes don't help me, except to hint that she, too, isn't sure. This could be the beginning of sex and it has me shaking.

The top two buttons on her frock are undone. With my fingers trembling with the effort to be gentle, I undo the next button. She looks away. Is that a frown? I lift the unbuttoned flap and see first the lovely little hollow behind her collarbone. Her white bra is little more than two loose triangles, and it has slipped to one side. An uncovered breast, small with a surprisingly large nipple is nestling in tent-light. I've never seen anything so beautiful. She turns on her side to face me, pulls her dress to and does up the button. Would she have let me touch if I had tried? I doubt it but I hadn't wanted to. Looking had been enough.

I reach down to her stomach and marvel at its softness. Years of knowing girls, playing with them, talking to them, talking about them, hasn't prepared me for the shock of how different they are.

She takes my hand and pulls it up between our faces. We alternate between kissing and pulling back to see each other more clearly. And all the time I can feel myself growing stronger, strong enough to pick her up, something that, like Audie, I should be able to do for my girl. I squeeze her to me and start to move on top of her. Then I remember I have an erection and that it could spoil everything. I ease away but she clings to me. I pull back again.

'Sorry.'

'It's OK, Billy.'

'Is it?'

She nods but I think we're both embarrassed and we settle for just lying face-to-face and taking kisses when we want to. After a time, she eases up on to an elbow. 'Do you think you'd like to be married? One day?'

'Oh yes, I think so.'

'Think so?' she says.

'No, I would. I would, if it was you.'

'Really?'

Audie Murphy takes off his hat and looks into her eyes.

'Will you marry me, Sarah? One day?'

'You can't ask me now, I'm only thirteen.'

'Oh.'

'Will you ask me again, though, when we're older?'

'Yes. Yes, I will.'

'Good.'

'What will you say if I do ask?'

She looks past me as if checking something, then she smiles. 'I will say, "Yes, Billy Driscoll, I will marry you.'"

I'm not sure if this is a very childish or a very grown-up conversation.

*Yes, Billy Driscoll, I will marry you.* Her promise shrinks the intervening years and doubts fade. But not all of them; what Rooksy said comes back to me. 'Sarah, you said, earlier, that you couldn't be sure if you would always love...'

'Because, Billy, it was the truth game. I mean, I don't *know*. And how can *he* know? He might *want* to love always but he can't *know*, can he?'

'No, I suppose not.'

But I know, with all my heart, that Rooksy is right: you *can* know.

I settle for next best. 'But you do want to?'

'Oh yes, Billy, I do want to.'

We lie down again and shift around to get closer. In the warmth of our mingled breath, there is a faint scent of new chewing gum. Behind Sarah's face, dust is drifting along shafts of sunlight, the wooden walls crack in the heat, flies drone, my thoughts thicken and slow.


# TEAMWORK

'Wakey, wakey, you two. Talk about babes in the bloody wood.'

Rooksy and Josie are standing over us. We sit up and swing our legs to the floor. I don't like Rooksy's smile because he's assuming what we've been up to. Sarah gets up and goes into the next

216

room with Josie.

As soon as we hear water splashing into the sink, Rooksy says, 'Well?'

'Well what?'

'How'd it go?'

'Oh, fine'

'Fine?'

'Yes.'

'Did you?'

'What?'

His eyes widen, 'You know...'

'No Rooksy, I didn't do anything.'

'Not even a bit of tit?'

'No.'

'No?'

'They'll hear you,' I hiss.

'Whisper it then.'

'Nothing, nothing bloody happened.'

'And the colour of her knickers?'

'I don't know.'

'Love is blind, eh? Anyway, we saw while you were asleep. Would you like to know?'

'No.'

'Suit yourself.'

'Fine.'

'They're white.'

'You bastard.'

He grins while nodding agreement. I don't find it funny.

'Anyway, where've you two been?' I ask.

'Oh just walking. Have you noticed how curvy Josie is?'

Oh yes. 'Yes.'

'I know, but she really is, you know...'

'But you didn't do anything?'

'We had a bit of a cuddle. If it's tit you're after Billy, she...'

'I'm not. You didn't?'

'Didn't I?'

'She let you?'

'Maybe.'

He sits beside me on the bed. 'But you, you sure you didn't get any...?'

'I didn't want any.' I hate his 'any'.

'No?'

'No.'

He smiles. 'Not queer are you?'

'No, no I'm bloody not.'

'Maybe you two should have gone for a walk and let Josie and me stay here.'

'But Josie? I thought you didn't...'

'What?'

'I don't know ... girls?'

'Never said I didn't like them, did I?'

Sarah and Josie come back in.

'Shouldn't we be going home now?' says Sarah.

No, not now, please.

Josie puts one hand in front of her mouth and the other on Rooksy's shoulder, 'Oh not yet, this has been one of the best days ever.'

He pulls away from her touch. Josie tucks her hand under her arm. Sarah sees the hurt and hooks her arm through Josie's. Rooksy stares at the floor. Josie's blue eyes glisten and she folds her arms to clamp Sarah closer to her. How easy it is to be blind to others' feelings. I haven't understood until today that Josie is so much more than the 'poor' girl with a birthmark and a limp. And that years of living with these handicaps doesn't toughen you against pain and disappointment.

Rooksy touches her gently on the back. 'OK, Josie.' He goes into the other room and returns with two chairs that he places side-by-side opposite the bed. 'Go on Sarah, sit down with Billy.' Sarah hesitates. 'It's all right, you can be boyfriend and girlfriend in front of us.'

Josie likes the 'us' bit and pushes Sarah to sit on the bed beside me.

Rooksy holds out an arm to show Josie to her seat and sits beside her. He pats his thighs. 'Well, what shall we talk about now?'

'How about what we'll do when we grow up?' says Josie.

Rooksy and Sarah aren't keen, but now the future is exactly what I want to talk about. 'It would be lovely if we could stay friends until then, you know, like this ... don't you think?'

Lovely is a girl's word and Rooksy launches into exaggerated Cockney to sing, 'Oh woodern it be luvverly...'

Josie reaches forward to put her hands on Sarah's knees. 'Yes, it would, wouldn't it? What do you think we'll be doing?'

'Brains here will probably go to some poncey university,' says Rooksy.

Here it is again, mention my being clever and even he takes the piss.

I'm about to say 'so what?'

'So what?' says Sarah. 'Why shouldn't he? If he's bright enough?'

Rooksy's face hardens as if he's going to tell her why, but he decides not to. 'Well, I think I'm going

219

to do what my old man does: work for Cunard. You get to go all over the world on liners and in the nice weather, you wear white uniforms. I'd like to be a purser.'

'A purser?' says Sarah.

'You're in charge of the people on board who aren't sailors, and you're responsible for all the money and things.'

'Sounds wonderful,' says Josie.

'What about you Billy?' says Sarah.

'I don't know. Lots of boys go to university from my school but I'm not sure if I want to.'

'If you can, then you should,' she says.

'If you do go, then what?' says Rooksy

'Not sure ... think I'd like to write stories, maybe work on papers, be a journalist...'

I've read the newspapers regularly in our school library since Miss Birkett suggested it. 'A different kind of reading, Billy, less to get through, but a little each day will keep you abreast of what is going on in the world.'

It has, but it's a mixed blessing. Last year, I was terrified by the Cuban missile crisis and had nightmares about atomic bombs hitting London, and faces melting in the radiation. My friends knew things were serious but they didn't get the detail that was in the newspapers. When I warned John that there might be a nuclear war, all he said was, 'who do you think will win?' Then the Russians backed down and, not for the first time, I had been shitting myself about something that could have happened, but didn't.

'Sounds like a great job,' says Josie 'and you wouldn't have to leave Sarah to go abroad, like

Peter.' She glances at Rooksy, who looks away in time.

Then Josie asks my question, 'What do you want to do Sarah?'

'Well, even if even if I do become a nurse, I think I'd like to live in Somerset. Mum and Dad are going back to live there one day.'

Somerset may not be abroad but right now it feels like it.

Sarah takes Josie's hands. 'And what about you?'

Josie sits up straight. 'Well, I'd like to get rid of this first.' She lifts a hand to her face. We say nothing and she pushes on. 'There's a good chance, you know. And there are new ways of making it lighter, a sort of bleaching. And Mum wants me to visit places where you can get cured, like Lourdes, where miracles happen all the time. Anyway, one day I'd like to be a secretary like my Auntie Bridget. She wears such nice clothes, and a different nail varnish every day. And in her office, they bring tea and coffee and biscuits on a trolley, mornings *and* afternoons.'

Rooksy says, 'If we make money, maybe one day we could buy a chalet, you know ... between us, better than this...' He runs out of steam, thinking he's said something dumb, but we surprise him with nods and smiles. Nevertheless, I give him a fingers-down-the-throat vomit sign that goes some way to restoring normality between us.

Josie swivels round to Rooksy. 'That would be lovely, Peter, let's promise.'

'Our *one-day* chalet,' says Sarah. 'Why not?'

'We might have children by then,' says Josie.

'Not me,' says Rooksy, too quickly.

'No, s'pose not,' says Josie, too quickly.

We fall silent.

Rooksy raises his hands. 'Look, let's not overdo this … things change. I mean, today … has been really nice.' He hesitates. We must be staring at him. 'Look, I don't know. Billy's a good … my best, mate. I mean when you ask a question like that... What I meant to say was...'

Josie clasps her hands and pushes them out over her knees. Rooksy wraps an arm round her. 'Oh I don't know, Josie, I think I'll be a bachelor.'

'My dad's always saying he'd sooner be a bachelor. Whatever happens, there's no reason why we shouldn't stay friends though … is there?' says Sarah.

Rooksy stands up. 'But it can. Our friends, even Billy, call people "queer" to insult them.'

We do, but only people we think *aren't* queer. I mean, we'd never call a real spastic a 'spaz'.

'I won't do it again Rooksy, ever.'

He gives me his big smile. 'I'm thirsty.' He goes through to the next room. The pipe thuds in the wall and water hisses into the basin.

'What the fucking hell do you think you're doing?' The voice is calm, deep and chilling.

Rooksy stands frozen to the spot.

'Nothing, just getting a drink of water...'

'Trespassing little bastard.'

With his next steps, the man will see us too. There is panic in Sarah's eyes and her hands come together in front of her mouth. However, seeing Sarah so frightened slows my usual plunge into shit-myself panic. Instead, I have this Audie Murphy moment; I know what to do! My heart is racing as if I've taken lots of asthma pills, but so is my brain. I pull Sarah to her feet, then I grab Josie and push her down on the bed. Her legs swing up and we both know she's shown her knickers. She tugs her dress down and starts resisting me. I grab her shoulders and whisper, 'You're sick, OK? OK?'

She relaxes, gives a little nod and closes her eyes. I sit down beside her and put my hand on her forehead. The man is in the doorway.

'Oh, so you're *all* here.'

He's changed out of his overalls into trousers and a white shirt with the sleeves rolled up. Black hair covers his forearms.

'Well now...' He looks angry, but pleased at what he's going to do about it. He goes to the front door, locks it and strolls back, making sure we see him put the key in his pocket.

'Please, we need that water Rooksy, we must cool her down.' I'm trying to remember if fever was part of having a fit? What did it say in *Common Ailments*?

The man comes to the bedside and put his fists on his hips. 'Oh yeah?'

'Rooksy, bring the basin, quick.'

'What's been going on? What have you dirty little buggers been up to then?'

No one speaks, but Josie gives a believable groan.

'Been playing with each other, have we?' He smiles as if he's already doing something dirty.

'Rooksy, she must have some water, now!'

The man scowls at me. 'What's the matter with her then?'

'She's sick ... it's serious. She's had a fit. We

have to keep her cool ... and get help.'

He nods as if he understands but his eyes tell me that he doesn't. Forget *Common Ailments*, I can make it up!

At the end of the camp bed, Sarah stands with her arms crossed over her chest. When the man takes a step towards me, I shout, 'Rooksy, please, get the water!'

Josie is getting into the part: groaning and rolling her eyes. When she rolls on to her side and reveals her birthmark, the man frowns and seems more convinced. Rooksy brings in the basin, sets it down by the bed. I get out my hanky and, like the old doctors in dark suits in cowboy films, I fold it to an oblong, soak it in the basin and lay it across Josie's forehead.

'We need help ... an ambulance.' I'm calm, in charge like the old doc ordering others to boil water or to ride to town for help.

The man makes an irritated 'tch tch' sound behind his front teeth. He goes up to Sarah. 'What have these boys been doing then? Have they been touching you? In private places? Eh? Was it horrible? Or was it nice?' She backs away and plops down on the bed by Josie's feet.

He stands in front of Sarah with his crotch close to her face. 'Didn't get you to take your knickers off, did they?'

Eyes shut tight, Sarah shakes her head.

'Have you still got them on?'

She starts crying and nodding.

'Let me have a look then.'

Josie groans.

I shout at him. 'Look, this girl hasn't got her pills

and if we don't get her to hospital soon, she could die.'

'What kind of pills?'

I can't think of a name. Rooksy tries to be helpful. 'Er ... yellow ones.'

My asthma pills will do. 'Ephedrine, she's left them at home.'

He believes me. 'Ephedrine, oh OK. Right then, what's her name?'

'Josie.'

He comes to Josie's end of the bed and prods her arm. 'Josie, Josie ... you're going to be all right, understand?'

She curls up and moans.

Rooksy is getting the hang of things too. 'Look if she dies, it'll be your fault.'

The man shoots out a hand to lift Josie's dress. 'Just want to be sure these girls haven't been assaulted.'

I snatch her dress down again. He raises a hand but doesn't hit me. Saliva glistens on his bottom lip. 'So, you've put them back on again have you?' He moves back to Sarah and lifts the hem of her frock. She screams.

I dive forward to grab his arm. 'Leave her alone, you bastard.'

He pulls away and shoves me to the other side of the room. I rush at him, kicking out and punching until he gets a grip and clamps my arms to my sides. 'Stop, it. Stop or I'll beat the shit out of...'

The man pitches forward. Rooksy has jumped on his back and seems to be trying to bite his ear. With a roar, the man pulls Rooksy around, staggers across the room and slams us both into the wall. Josie gives a deeper cry of pain. He glances at her, then glares at us while he gets his breath back.

Rooksy gets into his stride. 'Let us out of here, you bastard. Open the fucking cunting door you fucking bastard fucker.' Josie's groan is one of pure admiration. The man stands open-mouthed and uncertain. Rooksy gets his words under control. 'Filthy bastard, interfering with girls ... what's wrong with women your own age? Too much for you are they? You bastard, open that fucking door and let us out of here.'

The man takes a step towards us.

Rooksy points at Josie. 'If anything happens to her, it'll be your fucking fault ... murder even.' Even in the cinema, he wasn't this good.

'Interfering? I was only checking that you hadn't...'

'Checking? Checking? You fucking pervert.'

The man looks about him, rubbing the sides of his head. 'Now you just wait a minute.' He looks over at the girls. 'OK, you can get her out of here.'

He's had enough! He goes to the door, opens it and looks around outside before standing back to wave us out. 'Go on, go.'

Sarah rushes past him. Rooksy and I get Josie to her feet and take an arm each to help her walk. She lets our necks take her full weight and starts coughing.

Once we're outside Rooksy shouts over his shoulder, 'If anything happens to her, so help me...'

The man flinches and raises a hand. 'Look, the blokes with the caravans have cars ... they could give her a lift to hospital.'

Rooksy scents blood. 'You dirty bastard.'

'Rooksy, please,' I whisper.

He isn't finished. 'And ... we want our bags... and ... and our Mars Bars.'

The man is puzzled. 'Mars Bars?'

'They're by the sink, bags are on the table.'

The man glowers at Rooksy, but goes into the chalet.

'Mars Bars?' I hiss. 'For Christ's sake Rooksy, let's go!'

Josie carries on sagging heavily between us and her groaning is close to giggling. The man returns and throws the Mars Bars on the ground. He waits while Sarah picks them up and hands her the bags. Rooksy wants more. 'And, she's going to need things ... other things ... like, like a blanket, get her a blanket.'

'A blanket? It's seventy degrees,' says the man.

Rooksy falters. 'She needs a blanket because ... because she fucking needs one.'

I provide the detail. 'If her temperature falls, she could go into a coma. We have to keep her head cool and her body warm.' Complete bollocks, but we've got him on the run. He shakes his head and goes back in.

'A blanket?' I mouth at Rooksy. He shrugs and grins.

The man returns and goes to put the blanket over Josie's shoulders.

Sarah snatches it from him and screams, 'Don't you dare touch her!'

'Look, I didn't mean any harm, I was worried about you girls.'

'Worried my arse,' says Rooksy.

The man walks back to the chalet and puts a hand on the doorpost for support. I'm beginning to feel sorry for him, like I sometimes do for Audie's beaten opponents.

Rooksy is showing no mercy. 'Look why don't you fuck off inside your poxy little shed before we call the police.'

This latest insult revives the man's anger. 'Look, big mouth, button it. No one was hurt. Nothing happened, OK?'

Rooksy lets go of Josie and moves forward, let-me-at-him style; Josie sinks to the ground, pulling me down with her. I wonder if she's really sick after all, until she opens one eye to check what's going on.

'Nothing happened? Call that nothing? Just, fucking … fucking fuck off, will you.' The man's face darkens and he steps forward, fists clenched. This scares Rooksy but he remains defiant. 'Go on then.'

I hold my breath. Is he daring the man to hit him or telling him to fuck off? The man grabs Rooksy's shirt. Saying anything now could be fatal; for once, Rooksy shuts up.

The man takes a long look at Josie sprawled on the ground, shoves Rooksy back towards her and returns to the chalet. In the doorway, he stops to look back. Please Rooksy, don't say any more.

He can't help himself, 'Go on, fuck off in, go on!' The man closes his eyes as he fights to control his temper. He goes inside and shuts the door.

We help Josie to her feet and move off. As soon as the chalet is out of sight, we stop and I lift Josie's arm from my shoulder. 'That'll do Josie, you're better now.'

She takes her own weight and stands back. With a hand in front of her face, she gives a nervous laugh. 'Blimey, I've never been so scared.'

Rooksy sniffs his hands and makes a face. 'Not only a pervert, he uses brilliantine.'

Sarah clutches the scrunched up blanket to her stomach, shaking but trying to smile. Josie limps over and gives her the kind of hug I want to give her.

We make our way past the caravans. Two men are smoking beside a Hillman Minx. Rooksy whispers to me. 'Let's see if we can get the gnome growers involved.' He goes up to them. 'Excuse me, but that bloke through there was asking these girls what colour knickers they were wearing.'

'Please, Peter,' says Sarah.

'What, him with the chalet?'

'Think so. We just ran,' says Rooksy.

'You all right, girls?'

'Yes,' says Sarah.

'We are now,' says Josie.

The two men throw down their cigarettes and head towards the chalet.

## FRIENDS

Josie stands at the bottom of the slope, considering the daunting climb. Rooksy comes alongside and puts an arm around her. She looks over her shoulder at Sarah and me. She's glowing at the idea of us being two couples. So am I.

'You'll say if you need a piggyback, won't you,' says Rooksy.

She giggles and clasps his arm as they set off. I take the bags from Sarah and hold her hand. We climb steadily to the top half of the slope, which is still bathed in sunlight. We lay the blanket on the ground and get down to spread it out. Rooksy fumbles in his duffle bag. 'Mars Bar time?'

Josie crosses over to me on her knees and gives me a hug. I'm surprised by the soft pressure of her breasts and how solid she feels compared to Sarah. I've never held a girl close before; now I've done it twice in one day.

She sits back on her heels. 'Thanks Billy.'

Rooksy squeezes my arm. 'Quick thinking, Billy, bloody quick. And what a temper, I'd never have thought...'

Sarah sits down on my other side and leans over to kiss me on the cheek. 'Yes, Billy you were wonderful.'

I trawl my head for something modest to say, like Gary Cooper at the end of *High Noon*, but I manage only an immodest grin. I've done some clever things before but this is the first time I've been really frightened and *not* bottled it. Audie Murphy has rescued his girlfriend from the Comanches. There should be music.

Rooksy squeezes Josie. 'And you, miss, you want to forget about that secretary lark, you should be an actress.'

'You were terrific, Josie,' says Sarah.

'Oh Peter, his face when you were using those swear words,' says Josie.

'Billy's not the only one with a vocabulary you know.'

I shove him and he falls back on the blanket. 'Maybe, but what about the "yellow" tablets ... and who asked for the blanket for a girl who needed to be kept cool?' We all lie on our backs laughing.

'I wonder what he'll say to those men?' says Josie. 'Do you think they'll bash him?'

'Hope so,' says Rooksy.

'Me too,' says Sarah.

Now that we're safe, I hope they don't.

As we're finishing off our misshapen Mars Bars, black clouds roll over the lip of the slope above and the grass below darkens as the shade rises towards us. We start climbing before it reaches our blanket.

The first crack of thunder comes while we're in the woods and when we emerge, large scouting raindrops are exploding on the dusty path. The girls lower their heads and hurry on. I hold back and lift my face to the sky.

'What are you doing?' says Rooksy.

'What my Dad does. He says you should keep your head up to the rain because it's better to get it on your face than the back of your head.'

'Oh yeah?'

'Yeah.'

'Like this?' He arches his head back as far as it will go. The rain gets heavier. The girls hoist the blanket over their heads and scoot for the bus stop. We stroll after them, faces up, getting drenched but grinning like Gene Kelly.

On the bus, Sarah and I sit behind Rooksy and

Josie. The first stop is by a field. Four horses are ranged along the fence, facing the road. A watchful brown foal with a white blaze is standing further back. The sound of the bus clunking into gear spooks it to canter across the field on stiff-skinny legs.

I tap Josie on the shoulder. 'Quick, look, in the field!'

Josie looks up in time to see the foal coming to a splay-legged halt under its mother. 'A foal, I saw the foal. Look!'

Rooksy winks at me. 'But did you see it first, Josie?'

'I did, I did, it was running and I saw it before I saw its mum.'

We break into smiles. Josie bounces up and down in her seat. 'Now we'll have good luck, all the year.'

I don't believe this for a minute – and there never was a cuckoo – but I've never felt luckier.

Rooksy and Josie pass the blanket back to us and we sit low with it stretched over our heads. Under our damp canopy, we whisper and laugh for the rest of the journey.

From Victoria Station, we walk home hand-in-hand. At the Peabody Estate, we linger, facing each other in the fading light. In the day's final silence, our smiles weaken and the magic begins to drain away. One by one, we hug each other.

Josie is the first to leave. 'Bye, it was smashing wasn't it? Thanks for a lovely day.'

When she reaches the estate entrance, she doesn't wave but stands, looking back at us as if she's forgotten something. She comes limping

232

back and stops in front of Rooksy. Her head drops for a moment and then she puts her hands on his shoulders and kisses him on the cheek. Josie's wonderful encore. I want to applaud.

She takes a step back. 'I didn't ask my question.'

We don't get it.

She looks at the ground. 'The truth game. I never got to ask Peter my question. I'm glad really because it wouldn't have been the one I want to ask now.'

Sarah puts out a hand to her. 'What is it, Josie?'

'Peter, I just want to ask if you'll be my friend anyway, you know, even though...'

Even though? Even though she has a birthmark? Even though Rooksy might not like girls? Even though there may never be another day like today? It doesn't matter; Josie loves Rooksy 'even though'. And we love Josie.

Rooksy hasn't taken his eyes off her. He takes her face gently in his hands. She tries to pull away and clutches weakly at his fingers. He holds firm, pulls her close and kisses her birthmark. 'Just try and stop me.'

Josie's arms drop to her sides and before she can leave, Sarah steps forward to kiss the purple skin. By the time I lean in to kiss her too, Josie has started crying. I expect the skin to feel hard or lumpy but it's so smooth and soft, I wonder how her 'good' side could be any better. Josie only has good sides.

'Blimey,' she whispers and goes to cover her birthmark. But she lets her hand drop and she lifts her head high to smile through tears at her friends.

Rooksy plunges his hands into his pockets.

Josie touches him lightly on the arm and limps away. At the entrance to her yard, she gives her little wave and goes in. We stand without speaking, taking in what all that has happened on a day when amazing things have seemed normal. And nothing has felt more normal than kissing Josie's untouchable birthmark.

'Bye Sarah,' says Rooksy.

She takes both his hands. 'You're all right, Peter Rooker.'

He starts to make his 'thank you fans' face but can't keep it up. He gives her a grateful smile and cups his hand around the back of my neck.

'Great day, Billy. See you tomorrow?'

'Yeah, see you Rooksy.'

He puts his arms around our shoulders and squeezes Sarah and me together before strolling away. Sarah and I walk until we reach the corner of her street; far enough, as her parents might be out looking for her. She lets go of my hand. 'Bye, it was lovely, wasn't it ... and scary.'

Don't go.

She gives me a quick kiss on the lips. I hug her and hold on as long as I can to the last of the day's magic. She steps back. 'See you tomorrow, maybe?'

'Oh yes, tomorrow.'

Before turning the corner, she stops, clutches her hair with one hand and waves with the other. I run home churning with a mix of sorrow and elation. When I reach my house, I can't bear to go in. So I run around the block a couple of times until I'm ready.

# SHAKING HANDS

The handles of the two string bags of shopping have etched white weals into my hands. I've made it back from the market after helping Mum with the usual load: potatoes, onions, braising steak, 2lb bags of Tate and Lyle, a jar of Golden Shred, a tin of Golden Syrup, Danish bacon, Crosse & Blackwell salad cream, Anchor butter, Stork marge, a bottle of Camp coffee, eggs, tomatoes, a pack of PG Tips – the ones with fag-cards inside – and a split-tin loaf.

Aunt Winnie is waiting at the top of our stairs. 'Glad you've turned up Maureen, I was about to go to the afternoon matinee at the Biograph.'

Mum hopes that this means she won't be stopping. 'Never mind, perhaps we'll see you later.'

'No matter, I can go tonight.'

Mum gives a resigned nod, no doubt contemplating what it might be like to have the time to go to the pictures in the afternoon. 'Oh, OK, you'd better come in then.'

'Whoa there!' A cart pulled by a chunky skew-bald draws up sharply beside us. The pony's shuddering breath flaps its lips in protest and a tangle of copper immersion tanks and several toilet cisterns with the pipes still attached clatter forward and back across the cart's flat bed. Griggsy's dad jumps down nimbly for a big man and his hobnailed boots crack on the pavement.

His brown corduroys are held up with braces and a rope tied around his waist. A large red hanky is knotted around his neck and his open shirt has no collar. The bags are suddenly too heavy. I plonk them on the pavement.

'Excuse me darlin', I'd like a word with you.'

He's standing too close. Mum steps back, 'Yes?'

'Yeah, about your boys and my David.'

'Oh?'

'He's bin hurt bad. And at the 'ospital they said he couldn't 'av done it by falling off his bike.'

'Oh dear, is he going to be all right?'

'Maybe. Anyway, he thinks your boys were there, when it 'appened.'

Like his son, he snorts phlegm up into his head with the same 'fuck you' rudeness that goes with trying to be frightening. Mum looks at me.

'Well, I'm sure ... Billy?'

He pushes past her. His face comes close enough for me to smell stale tobacco breath and to see that three or four teeth have his mouth to themselves. 'D'you 'av anything to do with 'urting my boy?'

Mum moves between us. 'Just a minute.'

I'm close to choking on what feels like cotton wool. They're all looking at me, waiting. I shake my head, which must make me look guilty, so I follow up with a squeaky, 'No. Nothing.'

Aunt Winnie prods Griggs's arm. 'What? Billy? The size of him? Hurting your boy? Do be brief. Do you know that this lad suffers from a weak chest and that he's going to have to go to a sanatorium in South Africa? Do you?' She purses her lips and lifts her big chin.

Mum closes her eyes. Griggs closes his eyes too

236

and hisses exasperation. 'I couldn't care less darlin', he can go to fucking Timbuktu for all I care. I wanna know if 'e 'ad anything to do with 'urting my David.'

'Well, really! What kind of language is that?' says Aunt Winnie.

He ignores her and leans around Mum to ask me, 'Well? Did ya, eh?'

Mum edges back in front of me. 'He's just told you he hasn't.'

'Yes, he has,' says Aunt Winnie.

Griggs scowls at her, scraping the back of his hand across the stubble on his chin. 'Who the fuck *are* you, anyway?'

'I'm, I'm...' She looks at Mum and me as if she's forgotten and wants us to tell him.

'I've had about enough of this,' says Mum.

'What about 'is brother then?'

Aunt Winnie splutters, 'His brother? His little brother? John is barely twelve years old, for God's sake. The very idea, you'll be accusing girls next.'

'Look, why don't you shut your trap, you interfering old cow.'

'How dare you,' she says, clutching her handbag to her stomach.

Griggs has just joined the boy who asked for a light in the Biograph, and the convent school nuns in Aunt Winnie's rogues' gallery.

'If you was a bloke...' he says.

She's dying to reply, but he's succeeded in frightening her. She fingers her hatpin.

He turns to me again. Thanks to good old Aunt Winnie butting in, I haven't had to lie, but Griggs isn't giving up. 'Well? He's got a nasty temper

237

your brother, hasn't he?'

I nod and try to swallow.

'Oh? Who says so?' says Mum. She knows all about John's temper but doesn't like the idea of it being general knowledge. When Griggs tries to take me by the arm, she pulls me behind her.

Griggs leans down to look in my face and is about to pull Mum out of his way when there is whistling and the thwack of a rolled-up newspaper. Dad is turning up like the 7th Cavalry. Griggs straightens up and smiles. My initial relief drains away. Things will get nastier now that Griggs has a man to deal with.

'Afternoon,' says Dad.

Aunt Winnie rides out to meet him. 'Ah Dan...' Dad doesn't answer; he can see from Mum's face that something is up. Griggs dives in.

'My David's in 'ospital and I was askin' if your boy knows anything about what 'appened to him.'

'Hurt is he? I'm sorry to hear it.'

'Are you now? Well I wanna know if your boy,' he jabs a finger at me, ''ad anything to do with it.'

'A strapping lad, your David. A little bigger than Billy now, wouldn't you say?'

'I ain't talking about size Paddy, I'm talking about someone 'urting my boy and when I find out who did, there's gonna be a sorting out.'

'*Dan*, Mr Griggs, my name isn't Paddy, it's Dan. Look, I hope your David is going to be OK. What has Billy to say?'

I shake my head.

'There now,' says Dad.

'And you believe 'im, do ya?'

'I do.' Dad switches the *Evening Star* to his left

238

hand and his speech slows. 'He does, now … *your* son, Mr Griggs, he does, I hear, occasionally, be a little hard on the smaller lads.'

'Who says?'

'Well, it's what I hear.'

Griggs takes a deep breath.

'Then again, boys get up to all sorts, don't they? And us parents would do well not to … should maybe think twice before getting too involved. Do you not think so? Mind, no lad should get badly hurt. I think we agree there.'

'Oh yeah, Paddy?'

'I say to you now that if my boys were to be hurt, I might be looking to do some sorting myself.'

I plunge my trembling hands in my pockets.

Griggs shakes his arms down like a boxer. 'Oh, really?'

Dad doesn't take his eyes off him, like Audie Murphy before he draws his guns. 'So I think the best way, the best way altogether, is for us to look after our own boys, keep a good eye on them and not go rarin' up too soon on their behalf. How's that now? What do you say?'

He takes Griggs's hand to shake it. Griggs raises his left arm, fist clenched. Mum gives a little cry. I grab her around the waist.

Griggs doesn't throw the punch. His face tightens and his lips suck back in a gasp. Dad moves closer. Griggs returns his stare while trying to pull back. Dad's grip tightens. Griggs's free hand drops to his side. He looks around at us and forces a smile. 'OK Paddy... OK, let's do that.'

Dad holds on for a few more seconds. 'Grand. And the name is Dan, Mr Griggs.'

He lets go.

Griggs steps back, flexing his fingers. 'Dan, yes, OK Dan.' Aunt Winnie folds her arms under her bosom and lifts it in triumph. Griggs glares at her. He gives Mum and Dad a weak smile that disappears when he turns to me. He climbs on to his cart, grabs the reins and lashes the pony forward.

'Shall we go in, so?' says Dad. He stands aside to let Mum and Aunt Winnie go first.

As she passes, Aunt Winnie ruffles my hair, 'What did I tell you?' she whispers.

Dad puts a hand on my shoulder. 'Mind yourself now.'

I nod and he picks up the shopping bags to carry them down the stairs.

I take hold of the railings to stop my hands shaking. How has it been possible to come so close to a fight yet manage to avoid it? Dad has never had to hit John or me to get us to do what he wants, and he hasn't had to hit Griggs either. It's a matter of being determined not to start the hitting, while not being afraid to be hit. This is something I'm not up to. Neither is John, but for different reasons.

## REVENGE DEFERRED

It had to happen eventually. John and I are heading for the play street when we see Griggsy lurching straight for us. I put a hand out to John. He stops, takes a deep breath and clenches his

240

fists. It's too late to run for it.

'Keep walking,' I say, from the corner of my mouth, stopping will make us look guilty. Us? What have I done? Nothing. Well, nothing *to* Griggsy. But there are other nothings: nothing to stop John nearly killing him; nothing to help Griggsy when he was badly hurt; nothing, except worry about what might now happen to John, and to me.

John smiles, a sure sign that I look shit-scared. However, this shouldn't make Griggsy suspicious; it's how he likes you to look. He comes up to us with less of his stupid bounce and although he's rising and falling as usual, there's a pronounced dip to one side, like a spring has broken. A bruise is turning yellow on one cheek and a front tooth is missing.

'Hello shitbags.' The 's' hisses through the gap in his teeth. He aims a clouting swing in our direction to make sure we stay where we are.

'You was there, weren't ya, when I came off me bike?'

We say nothing.

'You was, I remember...'

'We saw you but we didn't see you fall off,' I say.

'Oh yeah?'

If we're going to get bashed, John wants Griggsy to know our side of it. 'Yeah, we left after you knocked over our bloody wicket.'

I wince. This will only irritate Griggsy and it could jog his memory. His head drops and he scowls at John from under his eyebrows.

'Oh I did, did I? Shame.' He gives John a more than playful push on the chin with his fist.

'Yeah, you did.'

Griggsy's body tenses. John stares back at him, ready to take the punch. The space between them is hard enough to touch.

'Are you OK now?' I ask.

I'm not sure which of them shows most contempt for my creep question. Anyway, it works. Instead of clumping John, Griggsy sticks his face close to mine and gives me a stinging slap on the cheek.

'Your little brother's got a big mouth.'

I smile as neutrally as I can, but I nod too. John's look of disbelief has my face burning more from shame than the slap. Griggsy cuffs me again. John moves forward. I put my arm out to stop him. If Griggsy's going to clump anyone now, it must be me. As my legs start giving way, he gobs on the ground. With half an eye on me he looks at the phlegm as if he's comparing me to it, or about to tell me to pick it up. His eyes flit between John and me. He steps closer. His jaw muscles twitch and his fingers flex, but he doesn't hit me. Instead, he stands with his chest heaving. He's struggling to control himself and an angry, frustrated glance tells me that although he *does* know we were the ones who hurt him, he's pretending he doesn't because he's been warned off by his father. He hurls me out of his way and lopes off. The sneering threat on his face makes his leaving every bit as scary as his arrival, but for now, that's it: nasty enough, but on the Griggsy persecution scale, not much worse than usual.

'He doesn't know,' says John.

'Oh yeah?'

'Yeah. See, if you do someone, you've got to do them properly.'

'Oh really?'

'Yeah, really.'

'You're a jammy bastard.'

He shrugs, agreeing with me for the wrong reason.

We head for Plummer's and sit down on the Big Step. He stares at the tiles for a while then bangs his fist down, 'Bastard.'

'What?'

'Griggsy, he doesn't know.'

I'm not going to put him right. 'No. As I said, you're a jammy bastard.'

He stands up. 'But I *want* him to know. I want him to know he didn't fall off his bike ... that it was for what he did to Jojo and the cowboy hat.'

'The fucking cowboy hat that wasn't even yours!'

'But he'd know, he'd know what he got done for.'

I give up. He's just turned twelve. He'd still like to play cowboys and send toy soldiers into battle, and it's not long since he used to beg me to tell him stories in bed at night or to provide a commentary to our games, like Michael does when we're playing football. But sometimes, my 'little' brother is more like my older brother.

He punches his chest. 'Wish I was big enough to tell him that it was me ... me! See what he could do about it then ... if I was bigger.' He shrugs again, calmed by the thought that has struck him. 'But I will be, one day.'

I've always been scared of Griggsy. I still am but

243

now I'm also a bit scared *for* him.

There was a time when I was bigger than John but I can't remember it. The evidence is a black-and-white photo on our sideboard. I was six and he was five. We're standing in front of a Cumberland stream, wearing cotton shirts and khaki shorts. My dark hair is neatly combed and parted on the right – the girls' side. There was no forcing a parting into John's blond thatch. He's gripping the bamboo shank of a tiddler net as if it's a spear. I have a skinny arm around his shoulders. His head is cocked in complaint and his body is leaning away from my embrace. If it were a moving picture, he'd be missing from the next frame.

He's shorter but not smaller. His legs are firmly fleshed and ready to harden into muscle; mine descend, stork-like, from shorts to my buckled sandals.

Whoever held the Kodak Brownie, probably Mum, has asked for a smile and I'm grinning. Meeting others' expectations was already a speciality – a natural skill if you care a lot about what others might be thinking of you. John didn't consider what anyone was thinking until he had to and he didn't smile to order. He was already stronger than I was and accepted his ranking as younger brother only because I could tell him stories, even make him laugh – sometimes. Adults were always expecting replies to their tiresome questions and he was happy for his talkative brother to provide the answers.

Once the picture was taken, John would have gone back to the stream and I would have looked to our mother to see what was wanted next.

I find it hard to recognize *me* in that small boy, apart from his willing smile for the camera. And it's even harder to remember how it was to *be* him. In always trying to see myself through the lenses of others, I think I must have buried who I am under layers of who I want to be.

John liked me then. I think he still does, but he never says so. He doesn't speak much anyway and when he does, it's usually to ask, 'what shall we do?' or, 'what shall we play?' Once, not so long ago, under Aunt Winnie's relentless questioning about what he liked, he gave in and said, 'Billy's stories, like the one about our bed being able to fly.' Until recently, I could hold him in thrall by inventing worlds and scary adventures in which he wanted to take the lead but deferred to me because I was the one providing the next part of the story. Not any more.

Our Irish uncles call him 'The Quiet Man' and Mum worries about his shyness. When he's asked or told to do something, he has this stiff, chinny look that makes it clear he doesn't have to comply, but that he will, only on this occasion. Mum, teachers and Griggsy, know this look. Only Dad hasn't seen it.

And he can fight. Lately, he's become my protector against the aggression that the things I say – along with my bash-able physique – seem to inspire in other boys. He's ferocious in battle and doesn't stop even when he's hurt or crying. Being protected by my younger brother is embarrassing but better than being bashed up.

'So, you'll be as big as Griggsy one day. What is it with you? It's over. Why do you want to keep it going?'

He's in no mood for criticism. 'And why do you always bottle it? Eh?'

'I don't.'

He gives me that look of his. OK I do, I do bottle it.

'You're like bloody Kim in that story; the "little friend of all the world", that's who you are. Why be nice to that bastard?'

Because if I'm not, he might bash me up.

'I'm not nice to him, what's the point of making him mad?'

'Bottler.'

I shake my head to show that he's too dumb to understand what I'm saying. He rams me against the wall.

'Bloody clever clogs aren't you? Eh? Bloody show off. Rooksy and that Sarah might think you're clever but they don't know you're a bottler – and that you talk bollocks.'

No point telling him that *he's* talking bollocks because Sarah and Rooksy *do* know. I push him away but he shoves me back harder. 'And when your big mouth gets you in trouble, then what, eh?' – I edge away but he grabs me by the throat, shouting, 'Then I step in or clump someone, and it's *me* – not you – they end up not liking. You're just a bottler who talks a lot ... can't see why they like you so much.' His face is an inch from mine and there are tears in his eyes. 'But not as much as I do ... and I know what you're really like!'

He lets go of me and storms off.

# HAIRCUTS AND MALTESERS

When I turn up outside Plummer's, Josie shouts out to me as if I've been hiding. 'Billy!'

She gets up from the Big Step and gives me a hug. I flinch and she lets go. I haven't meant to react like this but we're not at Hillswood now. She dips her head, puts out her callipered shoe and swivels it, toes up.

I take her arm. 'Sorry.'

Christine and Shirley are standing in the shop doorway behind her. 'Don't look now Cinderella, but your ugly sisters are here.'

'I know.' She laughs but doesn't look at them. 'They've been taking the mickey out of me because my Mum still uses Rinso powder instead of Squezy to do the dishes.'

So does mine but I decide not to let on. 'So what?'

Christine and Shirley link arms and their mouths become tight circles of 'ooh look at you two'. Josie knows what they're doing but all she does is shrug. She accepts so much and, even now, she's taking no offence. But I am. I can't bear the undeserved power they wield over her because she needs them more than they need her, because a birthmark reduces her value as a friend.

Josie gives me a small sad smile that catches me unawares and I find myself close to tears. I put my arms around her and give the girls V-signs

247

from behind her back. They go into the shop, noses in the air.

I stand back and point to her birthmark. 'Do you know what this is Josie?'

She covers it with her hand. She knows all right but still shakes her head, waiting to hear.

I've heard the description often enough in church but only now do I see what it means. 'This, Josie, is an outward and visible sign of an inward and spiritual grace.'

'Is it?' She doesn't understand but she's taken it kindly. 'Thanks Billy, you make it sound almost nice.'

I can think of nothing to say.

With the hand that has been covering her face she touches my arm. 'Seen Rooksy?'

'No.' And I'm glad. The longer we go without meeting, the less real what he said at Hillswood might become. I wonder if he's keeping away for the same reason.

Josie's head drops, because, she *would* like to see Rooksy. I've been thinking only about myself, again.

She lets me off by changing the subject. 'What about Sarah?'

'Not today.'

However, I know I won't have to wait long, and I love knowing. We've got into a routine since our long day out. Each evening we say something vague like, 'See you tomorrow', and the next day, we're on the Big Step within five minutes of each other.

Josie and others are usually there too and we all wander the streets, talking in a way that I never do with my mates. John is scathing about me for hanging around with a bunch of girls instead of playing cricket.

At first, the girls, too, took the mickey but they've got used to me being with them. Now I think they even approve a little – in the same way that I like seeing Rooksy's parents holding hands. It's nice to see people being happy.

We don't stay with the others long. At some point we quicken our pace to pull ahead, slow down to fall behind, turn corners when they go straight on, carry on when they turn, whatever it takes to detach. Time and distance unspool easily until we're alone and we go through delicious clumsy moments when she catches me looking at her, or when I catch her.

Our conversations have a rhythm that deepens with nods and touches while we swap stories that seem to have been lined up in our heads, waiting to be shared with someone special. And because she's so special, my stories are mostly true.

While Sarah talks, I study her face: the tiny blonde hairs above her mouth, the lighter strands of hair where it's brushed back near her ears, the little tug on one cheek when she's about to smile – and how, when she does, it widens her brown eyes and brings her face nearer to mine.

I grow lighter in her company and I want to run all the time.

Christine and Shirley come out and linger on the Big Step, exchanging smirks. 'You coming Josie, we're going now?'

'Not yet.'

'Good for you Josie. Let them go to the ball,

who'll want to dance with them anyway?'

Josie lowers her head and bites her lip.

'Suit yourself,' shouts Christine. They huff off.

Josie calls after them, 'See you later, maybe?'
They ignore her. 'Blimey Billy, I think they're
upset.'

'Good, sod them.'

'Yeah,' she says with little conviction. I squeeze
her hand but she pulls it away and raises her eyebrows to let me know there's someone behind me.

'Watcha Josie, 'allo shitbag.'

Griggsy is standing uncomfortably close.

'Please David, why can't you be nice?'

'It's 'im, 'e gives me the shits.'

Entirely mutual, Griggsy.

He carries on speaking to her as if I'm not here,
'Whatcha doin?'

'Just talking to Billy about...' she catches my
eye, 'oh about nothing.'

'About all 'e's good for.'

'David, please.'

'It's true. Anyway, 'ere...' He holds out a packet
of Maltesers.

'What's this for?'

Griggsy looks down and shakes his shoulders,
'For 'elpin me when I was hurt, when I came off
me bike.'

He hates me for being here to witness this. I
would have waited until Josie was on her own
but, like John and Rooksy, Griggsy doesn't hold
back once he's decided to do something.

He fixes his eyes on me and I look away. 'You
'elped me when no one else did.

'Blimey, thank you David,' says Josie.

He rises on to his toes and down again, struggling to find something else to say.

'Anyway, fanks Josie.'

Hearing him say her name so gently lifts him out of my 'right bastard' category.

Josie puts a hand on his shoulder. 'Thank you, David.'

He waits and I begin to feel sympathy for him as he tries to think of something nice to say to her. He gives up and yanks me violently out of his way and bounces off down the street – straight back into the 'right bastard' box.

Josie shakes her head. 'Blimey, who'd have thought...'

Not me. You've never really got anyone's number, not their whole number. Mental Griggsy has shown gratitude to a girl in public and, even worse, in front of me. Maybe he could keep kittens after all.

Josie opens the Maltesers and offers me one. I wait until Griggsy is out of sight before accepting.

'He's a funny one isn't he?' says Josie.

'Yeah.'

She catches me looking past her and guesses that it's to see if Sarah is coming.

'I'll be off now Billy. I think I'll go to the ball after all. There might be a prince looking for a girl in a brown boot. Say hello to Sarah when you see her.'

Moments later, Sarah comes around the corner. 'What's up with David Griggs? He just said hello to me ... and smiled!'

I don't answer. I'm taking in how different she looks.

She twirls to let me see.

'Well?'

Her hair is shorter, much shorter. It's clumpier too and cut into the nape of her neck, which is now there for all to see. No less beautiful but I'll miss the special glimpses I used to get when she pushed her hand through her hair.

'It's lovely...'

'You don't like it.'

'I do, it's just that...'

'What?'

'I liked your neck being covered.'

'You don't like my neck?'

'No, no I love it, I really do. But...'

'What?'

'I liked seeing it when you lifted your hair.'

'You are a strange boy, Billy.'

'I like the pointy sideburns.'

'Do you? The style's called *Italian Boy*,' she says, as if this explains everything.

Surely, Italian boys don't have their hair cut like this? In our barber's window, under the Vaseline Hair Cream adverts, there are photos of men with Italian hairstyles, trying to look like Tony Curtis. They're old fashioned now, as most boys are imitating Beatle Cuts and leaving hair cream to 'greasers'.

Mr Harold Byrne, the barber, is a cheery Northern Irishman with strong views on long hair and the abolition of National Service. When I was small, visits to *Maison Harold* were an ordeal, thanks to Mum's notions of what a small boy's haircut should look like. But Mr Byrne always tried to cheer me up with his unchanging jokes that I did my best to find funny.

'Now there's a hard job, Billy boy.'

'What's that, Mr Byrne?'

'Mending broken biscuits.'

I had to clamber on to a board laid across the arms of the chair. Mr Byrne swirled the barber's white bib in front of me like a matador and snapped the metal stud to fix it around my neck. In the large Brylcreem mirror, I watched him pump me higher with the foot pedal while holding his arms aloft, 'Look, no hands.'

Mum's standing orders were, 'I don't want to have to bring this boy back for three months'.

'Three months! Mrs Driscoll, I could be out of business in three months and I'll not recognise this boy then, so I won't.'

'I'll remind you. Now, can we please get on with it?'

He gave me a wink in the mirror and some whispered consolation, 'Let's see now if I can reduce your sentence to ten weeks.' Then he'd cut and clip while talking about Manchester United and their 'great' goalkeeper, Harry Gregg, and commiserate with me for being an Arsenal supporter.

Once the job was done, he'd release the stud of the bib and whip it away with a loud 'Olé'. For years, I thought this meant 'finished'. Before I slipped off the wooden board, he'd say, 'Shall we leave the shave till next time?' Then he'd lean closer and whisper, 'And would you be wanting anything for the weekend, sir?'

I always answered, 'No thank you,' and he'd roar with laughter.

'Time enough lad, time enough.'

The price of a haircut, and no tip, was all Mum would run to, so I never asked why, on Tuesdays – reduced prices for boys – he was offering stuff for the weekend.

I know now because Rooksy told me but Mr Byrne stopped asking the question as soon as he suspected I'd know what he was talking about.

There's nothing Tony Curtis about Sarah's *Italian Boy*, she's prettier than ever and I wonder why until I realise it's because I can see more of her face. But her hair is so short!

'You won't be able to wear ribbons anymore.'

'Don't want to, they're a bit babyish.'

'Oh.'

'Disappointed?'

'No. Well yes ... a bit. But I do like it, your haircut ... it shows more of your face.'

'And is that a good thing?'

'Oh yes.' Her eyes seem larger, and there's more room for her smile.

'It's supposed to give me an elfin look.'

It does. She's a beautiful elf.

'You are so pretty.'

'Do you think so?'

'Yes, I do. When I think about you, you know, when you're not here... I'm not being rude or anything, but all I can really remember is your face.'

She looks puzzled.

'I don't mean I see only your head...' I blush at having said something so stupid. 'But your face...'

'You don't think it makes me look like a boy?' She glances down at her chest. 'You wouldn't prefer me to be more like Christine or Shirley?'

'No, I wouldn't. Anyway, you'll have them too, you know, one day ... probably.'

Will I ever get this right?

She frowns. 'Probably? Well, I sincerely hope so Billy, as I'm a *girl*.'

'No, what I mean is, what I meant to say was ... well, you can look forward to having bigger, you know ... but Christine and Shirley can't look forward to being pretty.'

For once my words have matched what I want to say. Her mouth stays closed while she smiles and lowers her eyes. She holds my hand. This is another thing I think about when I'm not with her.


## BARGAINS AND CASUALTIES

Mum and I are on the bus from Brixton. We've been to get me some new trousers: light grey and more fashionable than regulation charcoal grey but concerning for Mum, as they'll show the dirt more easily and, because they're a good fit, I'll get less wear from them as I grow.

'We'll keep the receipt, just in case,' she says, as if this was something she doesn't always do.

Buying the trousers took twenty minutes but afterwards we trailed around the stalls and arcade shops of Brixton Market. Worse still, Mum was drawn into a crowd around a costermonger selling crockery, pans and towels from the flat back of a lorry.

First up was a tea service; pale green with

grooves scored around each piece, like those used by WRVS ladies at bazaars.

'I'm not asking for a dollar, I'm not asking four bob. I don't even want three and six.' He prodded the air with three fingers. 'Three shillings. Now who wants one? Come on darlings, don't miss out. Only half-a-crown to the first taker.' Up went the hands and he picked a pretty blonde who was among the last to respond.

All quite entertaining, once. However, he hooked Mum into staying with, 'If you think they were a bargain, look what I've got for you now.' This time he waved and flapped the same kind of towels that Jojo uses at the swimming baths. Mum bought two before I could get her to leave.

As our bus approaches the stop, we overtake Rooksy. I think about staying on to the next stop after Mum gets off but he sees us standing on the rear platform.

'Hello Mrs Driscoll.' It's his best 'he's such a nice boy' manner. Suitably charmed, Mum heads home. I get the smile reserved for those seen out with 'mummy'. You can't avoid shopping with your mum but you'd rather your mates didn't see you. This is tricky for John and me because Dad insists that Mum shouldn't have to do 'heavy work'. We're not asked to help with cooking, cleaning or doing the dishes. However, we do have to help with bringing in coal, carrying shopping, fetching paraffin for the Tilley heater, taking the laundry to the bag wash, clearing cinders and mangling the water out of washed clothes.

'Watcha Rooksy.'

'Watcha. Nice shopping trip?'

'Trousers.'

'Long ones, I hope.'

It'll be some time before he stops referring to my humiliation when I started grammar school. Because I'd what Mum deemed perfectly serviceable short trousers, I'd been forced to wear them for a whole term. Everyone else was in long trousers – except a boy with three French Christian names and a lisp. He was proud of his names and blissfully unaware that they made him a dick. When asked, he gave you the poofy trilogy in haughty tones, as if he were saying, 'Prince Charles actually.' If it hadn't been for Jean, Jules, Yves 'Thaunders', I'd have been the official 'school pune'.

Thanks to the embarrassing exposure of my skinny legs and the resulting chapped knees, I acquired the nickname of 'Matches'. But ridicule at school was nothing to the scorn of local friends. Worst of all, was being seen by the girls because short trousers confirmed me as a boy, and someone who couldn't possibly be a *boyfriend*.

'Seen Sarah?' Rooksy asks.

I nod.

'Our long day out last week, good, wasn't it, the Hillswood place?'

'Yeah.'

An uncomfortable silence sets in. The longer it lasts, the more likely it feels that one of us will say something he'll wish he hadn't.

He isn't just Rooksy any more. He's the boy who said he loved me, for god's sake. At Hillswood, what mattered most was that he's my best friend. Here in Pimlico, what matters is that my best friend could be queer – and what it could mean if anyone finds out.

Rooksy speaks just in time. 'We should go again before the end of the holidays.'

'Yeah.'

'What do you fancy doing?' He's acting as if nothing has changed. I want to head for Plummer's where Sarah and Josie will be on the Big Step. When I don't answer straightaway, he says, 'Seeing Sarah again today then?'

Sod his 'again'. 'Maybe.'

'Thought we could go the pictures, that's all. Not that I'm bothered, it's fucking cavalry and Indians, again.'

So what? This one stars Jeff Chandler, whose grey hair makes him look older than he is, unlike Randolph Scott, who has blond hair but looks too old to fight and kiss young women. I'm hoping to go with Sarah. Not that I can afford to pay for her but I've enough to buy her an ice cream, or a Kia-Ora.

'Yes, but I thought I might take ... go with Sarah.'

'Oh.' His face tightens. 'Right, well, I don't fancy playing gooseberry.'

'Fine.' But it isn't fine. It feels as if we've fallen out. I should tell him that I don't want to knock about together so much, but all I say is, 'Maybe we could do something later?'

'Yeah maybe, maybe not.'

'All right then.'

'But don't put yourself out for me will you.'

I'm about to tell him I won't, when a screech of brakes jerks our heads around. A white Ford Zodiac nosedives to a halt beside us. Two big men fill the front seats; the passenger is Siddy's partner from the Yorath's break-in. The back door flies open and Siddy dashes towards us. Rooksy grabs my arm to run.

'Don't you fucking move,' screams Siddy.

He rushes past me, thuds into Rooksy and drives him hard against the railings, where he pins him by the throat and rams his fist repeatedly up under his chin.

'Don't ... don't ... you ... ev ... er ... fuck ... ing ... cheek ... me ... a ... gain.'

Each shove sends Rooksy's eyes up into his head. His face turns a choking red and deep white marks are visible on his neck each time Siddy releases his grip.

He cuffs Rooksy across the face. 'Little mister fucking big mouth, what have you got to say now then?' Rooksy has nothing to say.

The men in the car are jeering but not at Rooksy's come-uppance, they're taking the piss out of Siddy! The man in the passenger seat opens his door. 'Mind yourself Siddy, these kids can pack a punch.'

Siddy makes the mistake of trying to explain. 'If you'd heard what he said about my Madge, dirty toe-rag. He's got it coming.'

He says nothing about us seeing what happened at Yorath's yard and can't have told the men we were there.

The passenger closes his door. 'All right, sort him then. We've got to go.'

Siddy thrusts his face within an inch of Rooksy's. 'Do it again and I swear it'll be the last thing you ever fucking do. Understand?' Rooksy moves his head left and right and blood wriggles out of his nose. 'Well?' He bangs Rooksy's head against the railings.

I grab Siddy's arm. 'Leave him alone!'

The passenger waves from the car. 'Yeah, leave him, we're off.'

Siddy lets him go, shoves me away and swaggers towards the car. This is too much for Rooksy who lunges forward screaming, 'You fucking bastard, you haven't hurt me...'

Siddy performs a surprisingly nimble sidestep and gives Rooksy a backhanded clout that propels him onwards into the road.

Another screech of brakes signals the start of a slow-motion film. Rooksy tumbles over and rises to his knees with his hands in front of his face. A Jaguar slides in from the right and its low snout flips him up and on to his back. His head bounces off the road. When he tries to get up, his legs give way and he tumbles headfirst against the kerb. He curls up on his side. His eyes are closed and although he's not moving, he isn't quiet. 'You bastard, you fucking bastard.'

The driver of the Jaguar jumps out and kneels beside him to cradle his head. The Zodiac driver opens the door. 'Siddy, get in, NOW!'

The Jaguar driver also shouts at Siddy in a posh voice, 'What is going on here? I say, you... You there, do you know this boy?' Siddy stands with his mouth open. 'Look, go and call for an ambulance, while I see to him.' Siddy doesn't move. The man waves an arm to shoo him into action, 'Go on man, what's the matter with you.'

The Zodiac revs up and starts pulling away.

260

Siddy looks at me. 'Look, he ran at me ... he ran at me. You saw it. I didn't push him, I didn't...' Siddy Smith is frightened! He spins around and sprints to catch the Zodiac, pulls open the back door and jumps in. Rooksy gets to his feet and staggers to the pavement, 'bastard bastard bastard.'

I grab hold of him, 'He's gone, Rooksy.'

I get him to sit on a doorstep. A woman opens the front door and the posh man asks her if she has a phone. She has. While she goes to call an ambulance, he squats down. 'I'm very sorry about this lad but there was no time to stop. Anyway, don't you chaps worry, everything's going to be OK. Who was that man?' I tell him it was Siddy Smith. 'Well, Mr Smith has some explaining to do.' He talks like 'Lockhart of the Yard' in *No Hiding Place*.

Rooksy holds his head. The hair sticking out between his fingers is matted with blood and a swollen cheekbone is closing one eye.

'What happened there then? Billy? What's going on? Jesus my fucking head...' The posh man frowns.

'You went for Siddy and ended up in the road and the car ... Jesus, you did it *again* Rooksy! Why can't you let things go? What *is* wrong with you?'

'I feel sick, that's what's wrong with me.' He lies down on the doorstep and rests his head on his arm. There's another gash behind his ear.

'Rooksy?' He doesn't answer. Only the whites of his eyeballs are visible under flickering eyelids.

'Rooksy?'

The posh man puts his hand on my shoulder, 'Don't worry; we'll soon have him shipshape. Where do you boys live?'

'Not far, by Peabody.'

'My head, Billy, my fucking head. Jeff Chandler's on at the Biograph, suppose you want to see it. Fucking cavalry and Indians...' His voice trails away.

'Rooksy, Rooksy, wake up!'

A crowd has gathered around us.

'It's a young boy ... he's been run over...'

'Has someone called an ambulance?'

'Poor kid. Is his friend hurt too?'

The posh man barks at them. 'Give the lad a bit of air, will you?' The faces in the crowd turn as the ambulance men push their way though. One of them starts talking loudly to Rooksy. He opens his eyes but doesn't answer.

They lift him on to a stretcher and carry him into the ambulance, where they cover him with a bright red blanket. A policeman arrives and takes the posh man to one side. Then he comes over and asks me for Rooksy's name, age and address. Behind him, the doors of the ambulance are closing. I rush forward. The man inside holds up his hand, 'Sorry son, not allowed.'

'Billy? You coming with me Billy? Billy!' Rooksy twists and turns on the metal bed.

'Billy, where are you?'

'Here, I'm here Rooksy.'

'Come with me, please!'

The ambulance men look at each other, 'OK, in you get then.'

'Go on son,' says the policeman, 'I'll see you at the hospital.'

The posh man waves, 'Chin up, young chap.'

I sit on the stretcher bed opposite Rooksy. The

ambulance man is wiping blood off his face while he asks him the same questions, over and over, 'What's your name son? How old are you? Where do you live? What's the name of the Queen?'

Rooksy murmurs answers but soon gets annoyed. 'I've already told you. You fucking deaf?'

The ambulance man winks at me. 'Good sign.'

Rooksy gasps and puts his hand to his head. 'Billy? Stay with me, won't you?'

'Yes, Rooksy.'

He closes his eyes and whispers, 'Stay with me, Billy.'

He holds out his hand and I take it.

'So you're his mate then son?'

'Yes ... his best mate.'

'I reckon you must be.'

At the hospital, I follow him through casualty until the trolley reaches the heavy swing-doors. A nurse bars my way. 'You'd better wait here young man.'

The trolley barges the doors open. Rooksy wriggles around but doesn't open his eyes. 'You there, Billy?'

'Here, Rooksy!'

The doors swing back and he's gone. I wait, trying to glimpse inside each time they open. The ambulance man comes out. 'Why don't you have a seat, son.' He leads me over to a long wooden bench. 'Don't worry.'

I sit down, wondering if Rooksy could die. I think a lot about dying and, in particular, what it would be like for *me*. I've even thought of it happening to Mum and Dad, or John. It's quite enjoyable at first: imagining how sorry everyone will feel for me. I also think of the nice things people might say about me if *I* died.

I'd get loads of sympathy if Rooksy dies. But I'd miss him. This is the closest I can get to what death means: missing someone, or being missed. The difference between imagining death and death really happening dawns on me, and my eyes fill with tears.

The policeman comes over with Rooksy's mum.

She touches my cheek. 'Oh Billy, don't cry love.'

A nurse takes her arm and leads her through the swing doors.

The policeman sits down beside me. 'Don't be upset son, he'll be OK. Do you feel up to telling me what happened?'

I wipe my face with my hanky, blow my nose and nod.

## MAKING AUDIE PROUD

'Is Rooksy going to be OK?' says Sarah.

'They're keeping him in for observation. They do that if you've been unconscious, even for a minute.'

We're walking along the Play Street hand-in-hand. I've told her what happened and added bits about helping Rooksy – but not about crying like a baby in the casualty department.

'Are you going to see him?'

'Yeah, meeting his mum at visiting time tomorrow.'

She seems more concerned about Rooksy than listening to my story about him. Part of me wishes it was me who got injured and that she could come and visit me.

As we pass the wood yard, we hear Swole screaming from behind the gates, 'I didn't mean to, I didn't mean to.'

Mr Dunn shouts, 'Do you know how long it'll take me? Do you? Eh? Eh? EH?' Each 'eh?' is followed by a thud. The small door in the big wooden gate swings open and Swole tumbles through. He scrambles to his feet and when he sees us, he brushes at the tears in his eyes and tries to smile.

Sarah rushes towards him. 'Raymond?'

He looks back, wild-eyed, into the wood yard and gives a cry. Dunn pushes open the little door. Swole tries to run but his legs give way and he sinks to his knees.

'Back in here!' Dunn thrusts one leg out through the gates, grabs Swole by his collar and yanks him back into the yard. The little door slams and bounces open again. More blows, more screams.

Sarah grasps my arm and gives me the 'what shall we do?' look that Audie Murphy gets from women in moments of danger. But there's no Audie reaction from me. All I can manage is a helpless shrug. What's happening to Swole is horrible, but it's how some fathers behave and there's nothing we can do – we should keep walking. She bursts into tears at our helplessness and stamps her foot. There's more scuffling on the other side of the gates, and another thud. Swole lets out a dull groan, followed by the whimper of someone expecting more blows.

Sarah rushes to the door, calling, 'Raymond? Raymond!' as if our being here might save him from more punishment. She may be right, most families stop laughing, arguing or fighting, when strangers arrive. Not the Dunns. Swole gets another clump.

She steps through the door, pushing her fingers through her short hair, 'Stop it, stop it!'

I follow. Swole is on his knees, hanging by the scruff of his neck from Dunn's fist. In his other hand, Dunn holds a thick leather belt.

He swings around to face us. 'Get out of here.'

Sarah whimpers, 'Stop it, stop it please.'

'Mind your own business. Out of it. Now!' He lets go of Swole and comes towards us. I pull Sarah back. At first, I think he intends only to shoo us away but he keeps coming and I remember that he hit Michael when he was nowhere near as angry as this.

'Arthur, no … don't, don't, don't!' We haven't noticed Mrs Dunn who is standing with her back against a wall and, with each plea, bends forward, as if trying to relieve a violent stomach-ache. Dunn glares at her and she jams the scrunched hanky against her mouth to stop herself saying any more. To show how little notice he takes of her, Dunn lashes Swole again with the belt. This time Mrs Dunn screams as if the blow were on her own back. Swole curls into a ball.

'Leave him, leave him you … you…' Sarah's voice is gurgling with tears. I pull her away but notice that Dunn has stopped moving, as if her words have switched off his anger. His mouth opens, he drops the belt and staggers away, pressing the insides of his wrists over his ears as if he's hearing some unbearable noise. He spins around blindly. Sarah runs to Swole to help him up. He resists, trembling and eyeing Dunn for his next move. After a few seconds, Dunn regains his senses. He snatches up the belt and raises it above Sarah. I step in front of her. Brave move, but my words don't match, 'Please Mr Dunn ... don't.'

Mrs Dunn screams, 'Arthur...'

He shouts at her. 'I told him! I told him ... not to touch, but he did. I told him. The glue wasn't set, but he had to lift it.'

'It's only a cabinet, for God's sake, a bloody cabinet.'

He roars at her. 'Only a cabinet? Do you know how long...?'

'No more, Arthur, stop!'

He ignores her and stands in front of us with the belt trailing on the ground.

'Can't chastise my own son?'

'Chastise,' she screams, 'what you do to him?' She swallows hard, 'Anyway, he's not your son.'

Dunn gasps, 'Don't you...'

'That's why, isn't it? That's why ... why you beat him. No man would treat his own blood like you do.'

Swole has heard what his mother said. He looks at Dunn, shaking his head in terror, as if trying to let Dunn know that it doesn't matter.

Dunn speaks in a whisper, 'We agreed we'd never say.' His voice grows to a shout, 'Never... We said, never.' He walks towards her. 'Never! Why did you have to say?'

She sobs and bends double to force out her

reply. 'Because it's true.'

Dunn pulls her up by her hair and she shrieks. Swole gets to his feet and runs to her, 'Mum...' He pulls at Dunn's sleeve and gets another lash with the belt. Mrs Dunn wraps her arms around him and they collapse together on to the ground.

'Leave him alone, you fucking bastard, you pathetic bastard.' I can't believe I've said this, especially 'pathetic', which from the look on his face, is worse than 'bastard'.

Dunn's head drops. 'Right, you little...'

Time to run. He's blocking our way to the gate. Behind us, rising twenty feet against the high back wall, is a huge pile of scrap wood: off-cuts, flat bits of plywood, and half-sawn or broken timber.

Sarah is unable to move. Dunn comes forward with a low growl that rises to a roar. For a mad moment I try to work out what he's saying instead of running. Sarah's scream gets me going. I shove her towards the woodpile and with another 'pathetic bastard!' I run from him in the opposite direction. Behind me, boards crack and timbers shift as Sarah starts climbing.

With Dunn close behind, I stumble into a large sawdust mound and drop to all fours to scrabble through. Beneath the biscuit mash, splinters jab my hands but I'm soon up again, making for the gates. Once through, I'll be clear. Sarah screams my name. She is high on the woodpile crouching a few feet from the back wall. I have to go back for her and surprise myself by actually doing it straightaway. I duck back into the yard and air flaps in my ear from Dunn's hand swinging inches from my head.

Mrs Dunn is taking her chance to usher Swole indoors. She looks at me over her shoulder, wild-eyed like a mad woman.

Sarah hasn't moved. I run towards her shouting, 'keep going.'

I get a few feet up the pile but it's like climbing up a down escalator as boards slide and planks rise or sink beneath me. One piece sticks to my shoe. My next step brings a sharp pain as the nail works in. Standing on one leg, I yank at the wood until it comes away but lose balance and crash on to my back. Dunn is almost on me. I hurl the wood at him and it cracks into his head. He barely notices and comes on more aggressively, but the pile is giving way under him and he makes little progress. I make it up to the back wall. Dunn stands below, getting his balance, legs apart like he's on a rolling ship. He starts climbing again.

Further along the wall, Sarah's light blue summer frock and white ankle socks stand out bright against the sooty bricks. She looks down at the alley below. Because the wood yard lies up Moreton Hill, from this side it's a drop of only ten feet but it's too much for her. Her eyes close and she shrugs her shoulders in surrender.

I belly across the top of the wall and swivel my legs over the drop. 'Sarah, like this!'

Small sobs burst from her lips but, gingerly, she gets down on to her stomach and her legs dangle over the edge. She can't let go. I smile, like I think Audie Murphy would, to reassure her.

Dunn surges forward to grasp the wall between us. 'Go Sarah.'

Dunn pulls himself up beside us, Sarah shrieks

and drops. He watches her sprawling below in the alley. When he turns to me, there are lines of dried froth ringing his mouth. He seems more puzzled than angry. He puts out a hand. 'Look, wait don't...' As I let go, I realize that he isn't trying to grab me.

The landing snaps teeth through my tongue, my head spins and iron saliva fills my mouth. Sarah is sweeping in and out of view as if I'm watching her from a playground roundabout. Her image steadies and I spit out some red foam. Above us, Dunn is leaning straight-armed on the wall, shoulders up around his ears as his head rocks from side to side. He gives a huge sigh, lifts his hands from the wall and leans back out of sight.

Sarah and I sit on opposite sides of the alley. She takes a hanky from the sleeve of her dress and dabs her eyes. I help her to her feet.

'Now what the bloody hell is going on here?' Beryl Street is standing, hands on hips, at the entrance to the alley. 'Are you all right, Sarah? Now what've you done to upset that miserable bugger?'

Sarah lifts her arms and lets them fall.

'And what will your mam say about you being in that place?' Her eyes narrow. 'You've been crying cariad. Come on, what's happened then?' She notices we're holding hands. I let go and instantly hate myself.

'Well?'

'Oh, nothing Mrs Street,' I say.

'Didn't ask you clever clogs, now did I?'

'Really, nothing,' says Sarah.

'Oh yes? You in tears and him with a bloody mouth: there's "nothing", for you.'

270

Sarah turns her back to her and walks off. Beryl frowns so I give her an apologetic wave. She scurries up to me and grabs my arm. 'Look, are you sure you two are all right? Nothing bad happened did it? Because if he needs reporting, I'll bloody well do it.'

She would too. 'No, thank you Mrs Street. We're OK.'

I run to catch up with Sarah and take her hand.

## BLOOD

When we reach the turn for Sarah's street, I say, 'It's OK now.' At this point in Audie Murphy films, he tells the girl he's saved that everything is all right. Then the music swells and everyone starts smiling.

Instead of smiling, Sarah is crying. I put my arms around her, gauging how tightly to hold. But gauging isn't what's needed and she doesn't respond to my feeble embrace. If there is a next time, I'll try to give her the powerful hug of someone who can look after her.

I stand back, awkward. She rubs away tears with the heel of her hand and reaches for the hanky in her sleeve. I kiss her cheek – and taste the salt on her skin and catch again the scent of her hair, of cotton frock and girl. She tries to smile and in this moment I know that whatever Rooksy says about fabulous flesh, love starts with a face.

'I was so frightened,' she says.

271

'Me too.'

'You didn't look scared.'

'Oh, I was … but, when you care about some-one. I think…'

'What?'

'I think it makes you braver.'

She shakes her head. 'You do go on about being brave, don't you.'

'Do I? I'm not boasting, it's because…'

'I know. Look, if being brave and tough was so important, girls would prefer boys like Griggsy, wouldn't they?'

Mum said as much when I admitted wanting to be like Dad and John. 'There's more to being a man than that, Billy. Do you know that John is always asking where you are? He needs your company and your stories. And he loves your Norman Wisdom impression. Dad couldn't be more proud that you're at grammar school and might go to university one day.' Then she laughed, 'I think you're all right too. No one has everything Billy, but you have more than most.'

Kind of her, but it didn't help. I'd much sooner be like Dad and John.

I smile gratefully and Sarah takes my hand. We reach the shallow bombdie, which you don't have to climb down into, because the houses that were blitzed had no basements. In the ruins of the one remaining house, chimney sweeps dump their soot, which is collected in lorries for farmers who spread it on their fields of sprouts. All over the surrounding open space, tiny shards of glass that were once bottles sparkle in the sun, and the blistering tar releases small stones that stick to our shoes. Behind the soot house, we sit on a low broken wall. I put my arm around her and she tugs it down around her neck to bring us closer and rests her head on my shoulder.

The bombsite isn't quite the location of my movie dreams. There are no cheering crowds, no *Big Country* music and no sunsets behind the buttes. It's only Pimlico but it's who you're with that matters.

A sharp pain is pulsing in the sole of my foot. I pull off my shoe. There's a dark red stain on my sock. I peel it off to find blood seeping from a black puncture.

'Does it hurt?'

Yes, but what would Audie Murphy say?

'No, not much. It's just hot … and a bit wet.' I put the sock and shoe back on.

We sit, elbows on knees, hands under chins. My bitten tongue is swelling and my mouth tastes of metal. I hope some blood is showing, like it does at the corner of cowboys' mouths during fistfights.

'What do you think he'll do?' she says.

'I don't know, but I'm going to tell what we saw.'

'Who?'

'Well, my dad for one.'

But will I? With any luck, everything will settle down, Swole will be OK and Dunn will let things drop.

'Poor Raymond, he was so frightened.'

'Yeah.' But I also saw shame on his puffed face, at what his father was doing and at what we heard his mum say. Does it mean he's adopted? That Mrs Dunn has been married before? Maybe Swole is a bastard? So what? If Swole's a proper bastard, I'm going to tell him that it's much better than just being a bastard like Dunn.

She hunches up, holding her stomach. 'I've got to go.'

When she gets up, I notice a bead of blood rolling down the inside of her ankle. Her eyes follow mine and she sees it too. She spins away from me. 'Oh no.'

'I got some blood on you too. Sorry.'

She shakes her head.

'Sarah?'

'I must...'

I've remembered my hanky and as it's clean, I give it to her. She grips and stares at it.

'Please don't go, not yet.' I say.

'I have to.' She dips her head and I realize it's not my blood she's looking at. I turn away. Rooksy talks with distaste about how girls bleed every month and how lucky we are to be boys. My face burns. You idiot Billy Driscoll, let her go.

'Yes, yes, of course.' She gets up to leave and I take her hand. 'It doesn't matter Sarah, really...'

She bends down to wipe away the blood and through my embarrassment comes the memory of the 'Indian promise'.

'Billy?' I must have been staring.

'I'm sorry. I was thinking about the Indian promise. You know, what they do in cowboy films, you mix your blood with someone else's ... someone you care for. It's a promise, for life, that you'll always be friends, blood brothers.'

'Brothers?'

'I mean...'

'I know.' She takes a deep breath. 'I've spoiled

274

your hanky.'

'It's nothing, really.'

'I've got to go.'

Not yet, please. Stay with me. Be my girlfriend. 'I know.'

'Compadré, señorita, buenos dias. If it isn't Ry Rogers and Dale Evans. Fine pair yiz are.'

Michael ambles up and stops to shake one foot then the other to rid his boots of prairie dust.

I lift a hand in greeting. Sarah starts to leave. 'Yiv been croyin, Sarah. What's happened?'

I answer for her. 'We were at Swole's; his dad's a nutter.'

'Pure Comanche. Sure, wasn't he after hittin' me for nott'n at all and a barely-sucked gobstopper destroyed? Lucky for him me ould fellah didn't find out.'

I tell him what happened at the wood yard and it brings Sarah close to tears. I take her hand and say what Audie Murphy would say, 'Don't worry, I'm going back to make sure Swole's all right.' There's nothing I'd rather do less.

When I look to Michael for support, he heads me off at the pass. 'Not me, I'm not after another slap in de kisser. What d'ya tink ye can do?'

Good question. 'Anyway, I suppose it's all over now; they're probably having their tea.'

Sarah believes this no more than I do. 'I'm coming with you.'

What? 'But you're going home, aren't you?'

'I won't be long, I want to know if he's OK. Will you wait for me ... at Raymond's?'

'Yes, but I don't think...'

'I can't let you to go on your own, Billy. I'm

275

coming with you!'

But I wasn't really going to go. Oh god, me and my big mouth! 'Yes, OK.'

'See you there, then.'

After she leaves, Michael points at the hanky on the ground. 'Yours?'

'Yes.' I pick it up. It's still folded and inside it's smeared with blood.

'See yiz later muchacho, mind yourself wid dat bastard Donn. If ever a renegade needed drivin' back to de reservation, 'tis him.'

He strolls off.

I sit down to remove my sock. I dab the seeping wound with the blood-stained hanky, hoping that the Indian promise will hold good even if one of us isn't here.

## AFTERMATH

I'm waiting outside Swole's apartment. The half-open front door is more forbidding than if it were closed.

Sarah comes running up to me; she's wearing a different dress. 'Have you seen anyone?' We're outdoors, in broad daylight, yet she's whispering.

I shake my head. 'Look, it's all very quiet, why don't we leave it?'

She reaches for the doorbell but I stop her before she can press it.

This irritates her. 'I think we should find out.'

'OK, let's see.' It's hard being like Audie.

I push the door wider and call out as softly and inoffensively as I can. 'Raymond? Mrs Dunn?'

From the wood yard at the end of the passage comes a cool draught, smelling of glue and sawdust. I step inside to the kind of quiet that you know you're sharing with others although you can't see them. Sarah takes my arm. The entrance to the kitchen is halfway down the passage. Smashed glass from the top half of the kitchen door covers the floor. I signal that we should leave but she takes a deep breath and tiptoes down the passage, reaching back for my hand. I move alongside her and ready myself for Dunn to burst out in front of us.

Through the kitchen door comes the sound of sniffing and whimpering. Our feet crunch on the broken glass and we stop to look through the shattered window.

Mr and Mrs Dunn are sitting opposite each other at the table. Dunn's head is face-down on his folded arms. The muscles in his back twitch and beneath the table one knee bounces up and down. Mrs Dunn stares at him while her fists squeeze the sides of her face.

Dunn groans. This startles her into putting out a hand towards his head, but she pulls back before touching him. From her pinny, she takes a hanky, which she holds in both hands, scrunching and twisting it while watching him. He mumbles something and she dips her head slowly as if she's listening to a confession. Swole is on the floor beside her, quiet now, with his arms clamped around his knees. Snotdribble glistens on his face. His eyes are fixed on his mother but now and then

277

they flit to Dunn.

Dunn lets out a deep sigh. Beneath the table, his knee comes to rest. Mrs Dunn's hands stop moving. There is just stillness, stillness and breathing. We could be looking at a photograph.

Dunn's back begins to shake. I've never seen a man cry before and Swole's dad is the last man on earth I expect to see in tears. He has grown smaller.

How can they say nothing for so long? Now Mrs Dunn is crying too, but not moving. It's like seeing tears on a statue. Dunn lifts his head an inch and stops. He knows she's looking at him.

She locks her fingers together, as if she's about to do 'here's the church, here's the steeple...' The tendons stand out on her hands as she pushes them towards him. She looks so fragile, she could shatter if Dunn shouted at her again. He stretches out his arms and takes her clasped hands in his. The knuckles of his hands are cut and bloody.

She lifts her chin. She no longer looks frightened, just sad. Still he will not look at her and his big rising and falling shoulders seem to lack the strength for him to sit up and face her.

They haven't noticed us. We know we shouldn't be here. But we daren't move.

She allows him no comfort from touching her. He uncups his hands, presses down on the table and stands. She refuses to look at him. Her brow crinkles, and her lips move silently as if she's reading something to herself. He sighs and looks down at Swole, who shuts his eyes tight. Dunn trudges towards the door.

Swole jumps up crying, 'Mum, mum, mum,' like

a baby. She notices him only when he throws his arms around her neck. She holds him close, stroking his face, shooshing into his ear. Dunn stops beside us in the doorway to look back at them, but their eyes are closed. He nods as if he's agreeing to something. When he finally notices us, it is with dead eyes and all we get is a puzzled tilt of his head. After a final look at Mrs Dunn and Swole, he makes his way along the passage, feeling for the walls like a drunk. The passage darkens as he closes the door to the wood yard behind him.

Swole is sobbing into Mrs Dunn's chest. She looks over his shoulder and calls us to her.

'You must have been so frightened, I'm sorry. He's sorry too. He can't help it. He's not well. He gets so angry ... sometimes it makes him much worse, he doesn't know what he's... Oh, I don't know what to say to you.'

We don't know what to say either and wait beside her for Swole to stop crying.

From the wood yard, a metallic rumble rises to a scream as the circular saw picks up speed. Next comes the sound of wood being fed to the spinning teeth; not the smooth, satisfying buzz of timber being sliced but the short, splintering snaps of something harder, more brittle being destroyed.

Mrs Dunn's mouth drops open and she stares at the wall as if it's a window to the wood yard. 'Arthur, no ... don't, please!'

She gets up and tries to ease Swole away from her but he clings on, pressing his face to her bosom, like a small child confronted with strangers.

'You two must go home now. Go home, please.

I'm so sorry. Nothing like this will happen again. I'll speak to your parents later.' She steers us towards the door. 'Home ... please.'

The saw has stopped cutting and calms to a shrill whine. Then a thudding change of pace brings panic to Mrs Dunn's face. She rips herself free from Swole and rushes down the passage. She opens the door to the wood yard to the shriek of the whirring saw. Her scream is louder. She stands framed in the doorway with her back to us and her hands pressed over her ears. Swole runs to her. Without turning around, she throws out an arm and pulls him in to face her. He has seen something, 'Mum, mum, mum.'

When we reach her, she stretches out her other arm to hold us back. Behind her, Dunn lies on his side in the sawdust pile, shifting and curling as if trying to get comfortable. A dark red patch spreads through the sawdust beneath him. Flecked jam-like lumps have rolled down from the stain. One hand is clamped over his forearm, trying to staunch the blood that seeps between his fingers. He lets go for a moment as if to reveal what he has done. Blood is oozing from what looks like a tar-filled gash. Small puffs of sawdust erupt near his mouth with each breath. On the floor around the saw-wheel deck, the cabinet lies dismembered, its delicate doors sliced and strewn about like ruined triangles. The saw whines as if it's hungry.

A shudder runs through Dunn's body. His white lips open and close but we can hear nothing above the noise of the saw. His head lifts and falls back into the sawdust.

Mrs Dunn pulls Sarah and Swole closer to stop them looking.

I shout at her. 'I'll get help, Mrs Dunn. An ambulance, I'll call an ambulance!'

'No.' She lets go of Sarah and her fingers dig into my arm.

'But we must!'

She closes her eyes and shakes her head. Her grip tightens but I break away and dash past Dunn to punch the big red button on the wall. The saw groans to a stop. Below its rim of teeth, there is a perfect brown circle of drying blood.

Mrs Dunn pushes Sarah and Swole back into the passage. He starts 'mum, mumming' again, this time with a burping catch in his throat each time he draws breath.

'Please Mrs Dunn...' I'm shouting as if the saw were still spinning. I feel pangs of excitement, and shame. I'm not thinking about saving Dunn's life but about how *I'm* doing the saving. It's my chance to be the man of action, to make the dramatic call, to use the big black phone in the wood yard office. Audie Murphy would hold Mrs Dunn by the shoulders, look her in the eye and tell her to be calm, and to wait while he gallops for help.

'Mrs Dunn...'

She won't look me in the eye. 'No, Billy ... please, wait.'

I run past her to the office and dial 999. The operator puts me through. The man's voice is infuriatingly calm and he doesn't think it's at all remarkable for a boy to be making this life-saving call. 'Yes, young man this may well be an emergency. Now, what has happened? What's your

281

name? What's the address? What number are you calling from? OK, please stand by, an ambulance is on its way.'

Back in the wood yard, Mrs Dunn is still holding Swole and Sarah in the crook of each arm. She stares at Dunn. Tears are spilling over her cheekbones and she's reaching for them with her tongue. Dunn bends and straightens his legs, and pushes his head further into the sawdust as if it's a pillow.

'They're coming, Mrs Dunn.'

She isn't listening. Without letting go of Swole and Sarah, she sinks to her knees. Sarah eases herself free and comes over to me. Swole clings to his mother. She sits back on her heels and Swole kneels beside her. She begins rocking back and forth, watching her husband and kissing the top of her son's head. She doesn't stop, even when we hear the bell of the approaching ambulance.

I meet the ambulance men outside and show them through to the wood yard. They rush straight past Swole and his mum to deal with Dunn. One talks to Dunn while he straps his arm and the other runs for a stretcher. When he returns he tries to engage Mrs Dunn but she won't answer.

He turns to me. 'How long ago did this happen?'

'About fifteen minutes ago.'

'Is this lady his wife?'

Mrs Dunn surprises him by getting up. 'Yes, I'm his wife.'

'What happened?'

'I don't know, an accident, we found him like this.'

'Are you coming with him to the hospital?'

'No, I have my son to look after.'

One look at Swole curled up on the floor and the ambulance men accept this.

'Are you going to be all right, love?'

'Yes.'

'You know where he'll be: at Westminster Hosp...'

'Yes. Fine.'

'There are some neighbours outside, perhaps one of them can come in to help.'

'Perhaps.'

As Dunn is lifted into the ambulance on the stretcher, his head lolls towards me. His eyes are closed and his face looks like it's made of candle wax.

The second ambulance man says to me over his shoulder, 'Will you find a lady who can come in and sit with her.'

I tell him that I will but first I go back in to see if Sarah is all right.

Mrs Dunn is coaxing Swole back into the kitchen. She sits him down at the table. And clears her throat.

She says, 'Sarah, are you all right? Can you go home now or shall I ask Billy to fetch your mum?'

Sarah can't bring herself to answer.

'I'll take her home, Mrs Dunn.'

'Thank you Billy. Please tell her mother and yours that I'll be coming to see them.'

'Yes, Mrs Dunn.'

She sees us to the end of the passage and before she closes the door says, 'I'm so sorry. Home now.'

All the way to her house, I can't get Sarah to say anything and she only nods when I ask her if she's OK.

I rehearse in my head what I can say to Mrs Richards. However, when she opens the door and takes one look at Sarah there's no chance to say anything. She pushes me aside and wraps her arms around Sarah, who starts sobbing.

Still holding Sarah, Mrs Richards asks me what happened. While I'm telling her, she shakes her head and anger reddens her face.

She screams at me, 'What were you doing in that place? What was she doing there with you?'

'We were... Mrs Dunn is coming to see you, to explain...'

'She better had. And I'm going to see your parents Billy Driscoll. Now go on, go home. And you stay away from my Sarah.'

Sarah finally finds her voice. 'Please Mum ... it wasn't his fault.'

Mrs Richards isn't listening. She pulls Sarah even closer and tells her, while looking at me, 'We've had enough of living here, my lovely. It was a mistake ever to have left our Somerset.'

She eases Sarah behind her into the passage and slams the door.

## REVELATION

The stuffy hospital lobby is crowded with people waiting, hurrying or wandering around, unsure where to go. It's like Victoria Station with central heating. Rooksy's mum hasn't seen me. Her bright red lips are pursed to one side as she nibbles the inside of her cheek. She's making her way to the staircase, reaching inside her sleeveless dress to pull up a bra strap. Other men and women turn to look at her as she passes. I step in front of her.

'Hello Billy.'

'Mrs Rooker.'

'Come to see Peter?'

'If it's OK.'

'You may have to wait a bit.'

'I don't mind.'

'Come on then.'

We climb the stairs.

'He's very poorly Billy, under observation, the bang on his head gave him concussion.'

She says no more and we make our way up to the second floor. In the long corridor, I spot Madge Smith standing to one side. Without make-up and wearing a long-sleeved blouse with a dark skirt, she looks like a mum and much less glamorous than Mrs Rooker. Madge shakes her head, pleading with me not to let on who she is.

To distract Mrs Rooker, I ask, 'Is this the ward?'

She's forgotten I'm with her. 'Oh Billy, yes, yes it is. He's in his own room at the end. Do you mind waiting here? You can keep him company when I go back to work.'

I sit on the varnished wooden bench and look back along the corridor. Madge has gone.

Nurses come and go, with the starchy rub-rustle noise that makes them sound so busy. I spent some time in this hospital last year – in the pulmonary ward. 'Pulmonary' is a word I use when talking about my asthma; pulmonary difficulties sound much more serious. Once they had my breathing under control, it was quite nice to be looked after and to have others worrying about me.

I shared the ward with old men who could spit more phlegm in a night than Griggsy could manage in a week. The worst gobber was an old geezer who insisted on being useful by helping with meals and handing out Horlicks in the evening and generally being a pain in the arse. He had cancer. None of your asthma, bronchitis or emphysema rubbish. He thought cancer made him top dog: Mr 'seriously sick bloke', making the best of it. 'Cancer,' he whispered to me with a wink, 'keep it to yourself.' He'd said the same to the other men. We felt sorry for him but the way he milked his illness got on everyone's nerves. However, it did make me wonder if, like John, others notice when I make too much of being asthmatic.

Mrs Rooker comes out of the ward and puts a hanky in her handbag. Her eyes are dabbed-red.

'I must get back to work now, Billy. He's glad you're here but remember he needs rest and quiet. Here, buy yourself a lemonade or something.' She gives me two shillings.

'Thank you Mrs Rooker, I won't stay long.'

Rooksy grins at me from his bed. He lifts his plastered left arm in greeting. A bandage circles his head as if he's an injured *Bash Street Kid* and there's a dark bruise under one eye.

'Watcha Rooksy, how are you feeling?'

'OK, but my bloody head hasn't half been aching.' He points to the biro on the bedside cabinet, 'Want to be the first to sign my plaster?' I scrawl my name on it and add Chad's long-nosed face peeping over a wall.

'Mum's upset, did you see? She wants to know what really happened, and who Siddy Smith is.'

'What did you tell her?'

'Nothing, told her my head was starting to hurt. According to the copper who came yesterday, we could press charges. Grievous bodily harm, manslaughter even, if I'd been killed … if he deliberately pushed me.'

'But he didn't.'

'No, I suppose not. Maybe I'll tell Mum later. Everything worries her when dad's away, and this lot's doing her in. Anyway, what's going on outside?'

I tell him about Dunn and the circular saw.

'Bastard deserves it,' he says.

'He's in here somewhere. Beryl Street told Mum he's lost pints of blood, and will probably lose his hand.'

'Nasty.'

'There's talk of him going to a mental hospital.'

'Sounds about right.'

'If I hadn't called the ambulance he'd have died.'

'Yeah?' he says, as if it was nothing special.

'Well, what do you think of this then? Mrs Dunn didn't want me to do it. She wanted him to die!'

'Don't blame her.'

OK, Dunn may be a bastard, but I saved his life and the only credit I've had is a, 'Well done son,' from the ambulance man.

'What about Sarah and Swole?'

'She was very upset, couldn't speak. When I took

her home, her mum got angry with me because she thought it was all my fault ... in a way it was.'

This is enough about Sarah for Rooksy. 'And Swole?'

'His mum's taken him to stay at his aunt's. I think he's gone mad, it was like he'd turned into a baby.'

He grins. 'Not *all* of him, I bet.'

'Blimey Rooksy, it's been scary.'

'Yeah.'

'So, what about Siddy Smith?'

'That bastard. The coppers are going to be feeling his collar.'

'He didn't mean to do it, you ran at him and sort of missed.'

'Maybe. Anyway, fuck Siddy Smith!'

'Hello boys.' Madge Smith is looking around the door.

Has she heard? We wait for her to blast us. But this isn't scary Madge and it's definitely not sexy Madge. She tries to smile and clutches her handbag tightly to her chest as she comes over to the bed.

'Look, I shouldn't be here but ... Peter, I'd like to talk to you, please.'

'What about?' says Rooksy.

'I think you know, Peter. Anyway, how are you? You're going to be OK now, aren't you?'

'Suppose so ... eventually.'

'I'm so sorry about what happened. But you know what Siddy's like ... what a temper he's got. What is it about you that gets to him so much?'

'Don't have a go at me. I'm the one who's in hospital.'

'I know, I'm sorry. Look, we've had the rozzers around twice. One lot saying they might charge him for GBH and another pair, plain clothes, who reckon he nicked stuff from Yorath's.'

'They've been here too,' he says.

Madge closes her eyes. 'Oh no.'

Rooksy winks at me.

I move away from the bed. She comes over to me. 'Oh Billy, how are you love?' For the second time today, I've been temporarily invisible. 'I heard about Arthur Dunn ... shocking thing for you kids to see. Are you OK?'

'Yes, Mrs Smith, fine.'

She goes back to Rooksy. That's enough about me then.

'Look Peter, Siddy's not a bad man and going to jail would do for him ... and me. Don't know how I'd manage. And now you've been hurt, he thinks you're going to tell the police you saw him, you know...'

'Nicking the stuff? Billy, do you think we should tell the police if we saw anything, you know, about those big boxes?'

Madge looks at me.

'Boxes? I don't know ... we didn't see much anyway.'

'But we did see *something*,' he says.

'Please Peter, Billy. Think of Jojo? What good will it do him to have his dad in the nick? Don't tell, please. I'll do anything if you promise not to.'

Rooksy drops his head back on the pillow and closes his eyes. There's a hint of a smile. Madge glances back and forth between us.

'Please boys, I'd be...'

No problem for me. 'Well, we didn't really see...'

Rooksy cuts across me, 'What if we don't say anything?'

'Oh Peter, thank you.'

'Would you really do anything for us?'

Her face grows taut. 'Yes, I...'

He winks at me. 'Madge, you don't mind if I call you Madge, do you?'

She shakes her head, but she minds all right.

'Well, you know how attractive I, we think you are.'

'Don't be ridiculous.'

'Well, if you can do one thing for us Madge, we won't say anything, promise.'

The way he's using her name feels like bullying. I want to shout, 'it doesn't matter, Mrs Smith, you don't have to do anything,' but I can't squeeze a single word past the lump in my throat. Please Rooksy don't ... don't be a bastard.

'Well? What?' says Madge.

'Your breasts, Madge, Billy would ... like to see them.'

Oh no! Block my ears, la-la-la.

'What?'

'Your breasts, he, we would like to see them properly.'

I wait for her to explode but she just stares at the floor.

'You'd what? You dirty bleeders. I wouldn't dream...'

Rooksy toughens up. 'Well then, we can't promise.'

Her face freezes. 'If you think that I'd...'

Rooksy says nothing. She knows he means it.

She drops her bag on the bed and grips the end rail, taking deep breaths. Her eyes close and I wonder if she's going to faint. The fight has gone from her voice, 'What, here?'

'It is ... private,' he says.

Her shoulders slump and she stands, shaking her head. 'You may not be a bad boy, Peter Rooker, but you do bad things, and this ... you don't know how bad this is. You should be ashamed, both of you should be ashamed.'

We should.

'You'll say nothing about...?'

'Not a thing Madge.'

'Billy?'

I shake my head.

'And the other thing? That...' she points at his plaster cast, 'the accident.'

'That's what it was Madge, an accident. Billy was there, he saw it.'

I'm nodding.

She goes to the door to check the corridor. She closes the door and as she crosses to the bed, she's pulling her blouse out of her skirt. Facing Rooksy, she undoes her bra from behind, lifts up blouse and bra together, and looks away. A deep blush spreads up her neck to her face. There they are, in profile: Madge Smith's tits. The first bare breasts I have ever seen. White, with their curved weight resting against the top of her brown stomach. Fabulous, maybe, but my only urge is to run away.

Rooksy clears his throat, 'Lovely, Madge but...' He nods towards me.

I lean back against the windowsill, giddy with

291

embarrassment. Madge turns full on to me, eyes closed, head up. I only half see her breasts because I can't take my eyes from her face. Tears are streaming down her cheeks.

I look away. 'I'm sorry, Mrs Smith.'

'You'll keep your promise?'

I turn back to her. She's tucking her blouse back in her skirt. 'Yes.'

'We will Mrs Smith, honest,' says Rooksy.

She goes to the door. 'You'll never mention this to anyone ... ever?'

I keep nodding. It's all I can do, nod my head.

'I'm so ashamed,' she whispers. 'I hope you are too.' She picks up her bag from the bed and leaves.

I am ashamed and I always will be. I've seen Madge's breasts after all but what I'll remember is Jojo's mum crying because we made her do a terrible thing.

'There you are Billy, at last. Didn't think she'd do it. What'd you reckon?'

His smile gets to me. I scream at him, 'She was crying, Rooksy, crying! It was a horrible, rotten thing to do. You ... we shouldn't have made her. It was like attacking her.'

'Sshh, you'll get the Sister in here. Look, maybe we shouldn't have. But at least she got what she wanted too.'

'Want? I didn't want that.'

'Oh yeah?'

'Well, I might have said I did, but I didn't mean...'

He's gazing at the ceiling. 'I'm a bit tired now.'

'It was wrong Rooksy.'

'Said I'm tired and I've got a bit of headache.'

292

'Yeah, OK.'

His closes his eyes and I leave. Before the door swings closed behind me, he says, 'Fabulous flesh, Billy, always worth a look.'

I push the door open to look back. His eyes are closed.

## FORGIVENESS

I'm running through the market, walking is too slow when churning thoughts keep bringing me to the point of saying 'oh no' out loud. The crowds around the fruit-and-veg stalls are slowing me down. I duck between two barrows to cross the road but the reason I'm running is blocking my way. Madge Smith is holding open a string bag for a barrow boy to tip in apples from his weighing scoop. She yanks Jojo's hand away from the rows of strawberry punnets. Then she sees me. Her face hardens and she pulls Jojo closer. He wrestles free to come up to me; her frown follows him.

'Watcha, Billy.'

'Hello, Jojo.'

'Coming down our street later?'

I move around him. 'Yeah, maybe.'

Madge pays the barrow boy, comes over and puts a hand on Jojo's shoulder.

'Hello, Billy.'

'Mrs Smith.'

I wait, unable to look at the woman who is Jojo's mum, who lives around the corner, who knows

Mum and Dad, who Rooksy and I made cry, who's standing too close. Has she, like me, been wondering what she'll do the first time we meet? What she'll say to the kid to whom she's shown her naked breasts? Her son's friend, whose parents she knows? I'm about to leave but I can see she's going to speak.

She releases Jojo, who goes go back to the strawberries. She sighs and puts down her shopping bag. 'How's Peter?'

'I think he's OK, I'll see him later.'

She inhales deeply. 'It was a rotten thing Billy, but I think you know that, don't you?'

I steel myself to look at her and nod. She checks that Jojo isn't paying attention.

'You're very young, and Peter is ... well, he's a strange boy. I know it was probably his idea.'

I resist the urge to agree with her.

'I hope you'll never do that sort of thing to anyone, ever again.'

I shake my head. She takes another deep breath and her frown begins to fade.

'Anyway.' She pauses. 'I think the best thing that we can do now is to put it behind us and never speak of it again. Understand?'

No, I don't understand but I want to. 'Yes, yes, Mrs Smith.'

Relief is opening me up to tears. Madge Smith *is* doing something about what we did to her, yet it doesn't involve revenge. Why? Because she's the only one who can, because she's the grown-up, because she knows that when kids do bad things, it's adults who have the most power to put those things right – and because she's a good mum.

'Thanks, Mrs Smith.'

She rubs her palm over the top of my head.

'Maybe we'll see you later then, Billy love?'

I nod. What a big thing it is to forgive someone, and to be forgiven. I can't hold back the tears. She puts an arm around my shoulders and hugs me before ushering me on my way.

'What's up with Billy, mum?'

'Nothing love, Billy's all right.'

In my street, Christine Cassidy comes skipping up beside me, all smug face and tits.

'Billy Driscoll, you've been crying!'

'No I haven't, got some dirt in my eye.'

'Yeah, my eye.' She's pleased with this. God I hate Christine Cassidy.

She tucks her forearms under her breasts and shuffles them higher. 'I've got some news for you, Billy Driscoll ... lover boy!'

'Oh yeah?'

'Yeah, Sarah Richards is leaving, going back to Somerset. With her mum and dad.'

'What?' I say, even though I've never heard anything more clearly. She gives me a hateful smirk. I grab her arm. 'When?'

'At the end of the holidays, I suppose. Her dad's going down first to sort things out. Let go of me will you?'

'How do you know?'

She yanks her arm away. 'Her mum told my mum.'

'So?'

'So no more Sarah.'

I've never sworn at a girl before but I'm about to tell her to 'fuck off' when Michael turns up.

'Billy, how are yiz? And señorita Cassidy, is your dad's limp any better?' Christine scowls at him for relating her, yet again, to Hopalong.

'I was just telling him that Sarah's family are going back to Somerset.'

He sighs. 'Headin' west is it? Like de settlers in *Wagon Train*. Jez Billy, dat's a shame.'

'Yeah, he won't have his "ooh arr" girlfriend any more.'

'Is dat a fact? Tis a sad day Kid, isn't she de only pretty gorl we have around here?'

'What would you know?' says Christine.

'Sure don't I only have to compare her to de likes of ye.'

'Sod you fatso. I'm glad she's going, glad, do you hear?' She storms off.

He aims a finger at her back and pulls the trigger. 'Away wid ye, ya Comanche squaw.' He flips the brim of an imaginary cowboy hat. 'Now isn't dat one enough to turn a fellah homisexshil.' His hands make the shape of breasts, 'Even wid her big girly tings an all.'

'I have to get home, Michael.'

He squeezes my arm. 'Steady Kid.'


## LOSING AND FINDING

Outside our house, John is bouncing a football off the pavement, two-handed, like a goalie who's about to boot it up field.

'Fancy a game?'

'No, I'm going in, feel sick.'

'Just for half an hour, come on.'

Josie crosses the street towards us. 'Billy? Can I talk to you for a minute?'

John shakes his head, clasps the ball to the back of his neck and walks off.

Josie puts a hand on my arm. 'Sarah's leaving.'

'I know, at the end of the holidays, Christine told me.'

'No, she's going today.'

'Today!'

'Her dad's taking her to stay with her Nan, because of what happened at Raymond's. It's her mum and dad who are going at the end of the holidays... Billy?'

I'm suddenly too weak to stand and sit down on the kerb.

'Oh Billy.' I press my fists into my stomach to stop my hands shaking. Josie sits beside me and starts rubbing my back. 'Let's go and see, at least we can say goodbye or...'

'No, I'm one of the reasons they think London's no good for them.'

Her face is so close, I can see only her blue eyes. 'And I think you're one of the reasons they should *stay*. Come on, come with me.' She takes my hand and we get up.

From down the street, John shouts, 'You playing or not?' I shake my head without looking back.

We stop a few doors along from Sarah's. Josie wants to carry on but I hold back. We grip a railing each and face each other as if we might be talking, but we've nothing to say. Josie has her back to Sarah's house but I'm keeping watch.

Mr Richards comes out carrying a scratched brown suitcase and puts it in the boot of the Humber. On his way back, he sees us. His frown triggers a growl in my chest that becomes a whine in my mouth.

'Billy? What is it?' says Josie.

I have never felt more angry, more powerless, more like a kid. I hate Sarah's dad, I hate being thirteen and I hate living in a world where what adults say goes.

Sarah comes out on to the doorstep. She's wearing her light green frock and a dark green cardigan. She's been crying. Her mum emerges and hands her a small cream bag. Josie squeezes my hand.

Mr Richards crosses to the car again and trails his fingers across Sarah's shoulders as he passes to tell her he's ready. He opens the passenger door and walks around to get in the driver's seat. Her mum straightens Sarah's cardigan and holds on to it as if she doesn't want her to go.

Josie rushes forward, 'Sarah!'

They hug. Josie says something and they hug again. Mrs Richards pulls them both close and strokes their hair. Josie leans forward and whispers in Sarah's ear. They both turn to look at me. Sarah's face crumples. She has given up, accepted that there's nothing we can do. She bites her lip, reaches into her bag and takes out something that she gives to Josie. I want to go over to join them but, even now, I don't because her dad is watching from the car.

The engine rumbles into life and Josie gives her a final hug. Mrs Richards leads Sarah to the car, kisses her forehead and stands back. I take a step forward but Sarah raises a hand to stop me. Josie comes hobbling back. 'Oh Billy.'

Sarah gets in the car. I hurry to the kerbside, where I stand giddy with frustration. The Humber sets off. Sarah shifts in her seat ready to look at me as she passes.

In the slow seconds that follow, I find time to remember what we've done together, what we've talked about, what we planned to do, one day. And time to step in front of the car.

The Humber plunges to a halt an inch from my shins.

The driver's door flies open and Mr Richards jumps out. 'What the hell do you...'

Sarah throws open her door and screams, 'No, dad!' He comes no further and waits with his arm over the door. She climbs out and stands on the pavement with her arms hanging at her sides, as if all her strength is sapped.

'I'm sorry, Billy.'

I cross to the pavement and stand feebly in front of her, unable to say anything, choking with anger that she's being taken from me, and at what adults are doing with our lives.

She looks across to her dad and the thought that she might be about to get back in the car gets me talking. 'Are you OK? The other day, you hardly spoke.'

'I'm fine, I couldn't talk about it ... didn't want to. Is Raymond all right?'

'Don't know, his mum's taken him somewhere. Sarah, why are you going?'

'We're all going. Mum and Dad have arranged

it. They say London's not for us.'

'And what do *you* say?'

'I don't know, Billy.'

Don't know?

'Why don't you know?'

She shakes her head the way adults do when something is too difficult to explain.

'I have to. Maybe they're right. Anyway, maybe we're *not* old enough. We...'

'What?'

'We can't ... we can't do what we talked about, not yet anyway. I'm not even thirteen yet.'

'I know that but we said we could, later. Didn't we?'

'Yes... Oh I don't know, *one day* is too far away.'

'It doesn't feel that far away while you're here, but if you go...'

She looks around at her parents. Their impatience feels like a door waiting to close. 'I have to go now.'

'Sarah, don't let them tell you that we can never...'

She touches my arm, 'Oh Billy, at Hillswood it seemed like everything could come true one day. But now, I'm not so sure.'

Was Rooksy right when he made her admit she couldn't promise to love me always?

'But we promised.' This is a whine. I'm a small boy again.

Mr Richards calls from the car, 'Come along Sarah.' He speaks gently, for her sake, not mine.

'I have to go, Billy.'

I can barely hear her. We're wrapped in the same cotton-wool calm that enveloped us at the

300

bottom of the great slope, and in the chalet. I can't take my eyes from her face. I'm desperate to tell her why we *can*, why we *should* have our 'one day'. But clever Billy Driscoll, who's read all those books, who has all the right words some-where in his head, can only say, 'One day?'

'Hope so. I'll miss you, Billy.'

She squeezes my hand and gets into the car. No embrace, no kiss. She remembers to wave back to her mum and I don't know why this hurts so much. As the car rolls past me, she clutches at her short hair, trying to turn crying into smiling.

I close my eyes. When I look again, the car has gone. Mrs Richards is still there, watching me with her hand clenched in front of her mouth. She's going to come over. I walk away.

Josie comes up behind me, 'Here Billy, this is for you.'

She hands me a piece of exercise book paper. On it is an address: *The Stones, Lower Sinton, Somerset.* Two kisses underneath. I put it in my pocket. With one finger, Josie flicks at the tears on my face and throws her arms around my neck.

'Don't be sad, Billy, you'll see her again.'

'Thanks Josie, you're...'

I can't finish telling her what a good friend she is but I hope she understands. I leave her and start running; I don't care where. Victoria Station, West-minster Abbey, the Tate Gallery, Vauxhall Bridge all appear and disappear in blurred, rainwater grey through my tears. I eventually get home and push open the gate at the top of our steps. Mrs Richards is talking to Mum at the front door. Mum looks up and pushes past her. 'Billy, come here love. Don't be upset.'

I run away.

It's closing time when I reach the library. The remaining kids are queuing in front of Miss Birkett. Few would risk being told a second time that 'the library is closing, please put books on the shelves and bring those you are borrowing to the desk.'

I approach my table but her raised eyebrow warns me not to sit down when she wants everyone on their feet. I patrol the shelves, pretending to look for a book.

After stamping the last book, she gets up and follows its borrower to the door. I sit down at the table and bury my head in my arms. I hear her close the main door and the sound of her rubber-soled shoes crossing the wooden floor. There's a scraping of a chair and, for the first time, Miss Birkett sits down beside me.

I don't lift my head from my arms. She clears her throat. 'A bit late aren't you? And no book, I see.' There's no disapproval in her voice.

I cough to get control of my voice. 'No, Miss Birkett.'

'Do you still want to find one?'

I shake my head.

'Billy? What is it?'

I raise my head. 'I can't wait to grow up, to do what I want, live where I want, be with who I want, when I want. And not have anyone, anyone tell me what I can't bloody-well do!'

Her eyebrows arch. 'Bloody' is a swearword for people like Miss Birkett.

She's nodding slowly, 'I see. But isn't that rather a tall order? It's something that few of us ever manage, you know.'

'Oh?'

'Do you think that kind of freedom comes just from growing up?' I do. 'Billy, what has upset you?'

'Someone I like, a girl, has left, gone to live a long way away because her parents say so.'

I said 'like', not 'love'; this is Miss Birkett and I'm only thirteen.

'How very sad for you.' I'm struggling to hold back tears. She sits back. 'Dear me, how special she must be.'

'She is and there's nothing I can do about it because I'm too young, because she's too young and whatever I … we feel, adults can smash it up.'

Miss Birkett is an adult and I want her to know.

'I see,' she says.

I get up to go. 'No you don't.'

'No, I don't suppose I do. But I do know how painful it is to lose someone you love, for them not to be there when being with them is all you want.'

She said, 'love'. She stares down at her clasped hands and rubs her thumbs together. 'You haven't been here for days, have you been spending time with her?'

I nod.

'Wonderful, isn't it?'

What? How does *she* know?

She looks past me. 'It can be such a special time. Everything seems extra bright and... Oh dear, what *am* I saying.'

She *does* know!

'Yes, it does, doesn't it? And you feel like you weigh almost nothing, and you're full of energy, and clever and observant … and smiley.'

'You do, don't you,' she says, in a tone that tells me she thinks she's already said too much.

But I don't want to stop. 'Do you know, Miss Birkett, there's a part of me that has been sort of waiting, waiting to be given away ... and I didn't even know I had it. It's like finding a present in a cupboard just as the person it's meant for comes along.'

'Yes Billy, very like that.' She sits back. 'But you can write to her, can't you? You, more than anyone, can write.'

'I suppose so.'

She's almost jolly. 'Of course you can.'

'Yes, I can ... I will.'

'She'll be a lucky girl to receive letters from a young man like you. You must keep in touch, write, and wait. But don't give up.'

She says this forcefully as if it's advice that she once followed.

'Miss Birkett, have you ever?'

Her look flashes from soft to sharp and back to soft. 'During the War, there was someone, but then so many young women had their "someone". It's a precious thing, you know ... to have someone.'

'And did *you* give up?'

'I did, at least in this life.'

Her eyes brim with tears. She stands up. 'Closing time. Would you like to pick a book?'

I wouldn't.

'Well then, home you go.'

I'm about to tell her that her library feels like home but she's already crossing to the main door. She opens it for me and waits. 'See you soon, I hope?'

'Yes, thank you Miss Birkett.'

She pushes her glasses up her nose and plants her hands on my shoulders. 'Love is a tricky thing, Billy. There's no right way of being in it, of feeling it, or of showing it. And there is *no* age, young or old, at which love cannot take you to pieces. Your feelings aren't any the less for your being a young boy. Let no one, no one, tell you that you're too young, or too anything, to feel the way you do. How dare they!'

She steps back to let me out and closes the door.

I roam around until I reach the open bombdie and sit down on the low wall behind the soot house. I rock backwards and forwards until the ache in my stomach eases. I take out the scrap of paper with Sarah's new address on it. I touch the two kiss crosses and wonder if it's OK for boys to put them on their letters. Writing might be better because I won't be tongue-tied. And I'll tell her, properly that I love her because I haven't done so yet – although I think she knows.

I close my eyes. I'm thinking of how to start my first letter, when a thump in my back takes my breath away and arms clamp around my chest. Griggsy?

'Get off me!'

'Don't cry, Billy.' The words are muffled, spoken from a mouth pressing against my back. The arms release me and I jump to my feet, wiping my eyes. Behind the low wall, John is on his knees.

'What are you doing?' I scream.

He looks at the ground. 'Don't cry, Billy...' For

once, he sounds like my little brother. 'Mum's really worried ... she asked me to find you.'

He gets up. His guard is down and I wonder if *he's* going to cry. I put out a hand to him but he steps back – already reverting to a toughie. We stand facing each other. After a minute or so, I get his smile. This time it isn't saying that I look scared; it's telling me that I'm his brother, that he knows what I'm like, and that he loves me anyway. I've seen something similar in the smiles of Sarah, Rooksy, Josie, my parents, Miss Birkett and even Madge Smith.

And I realize how much time I've wasted, trying to be someone I'm not for those who don't want me to be anyone else. And that you don't have to be as good, or brave like Audie Murphy to be a hero to those who love you.

'Please, Billy let's go home.'

John almost takes my hand but he recovers in time and spins around to walk home ahead of me.

## LAST REQUEST

I wait for the nurse to disappear into the main ward before pushing open the door to Rooksy's room.

'Back again Billy, no show today, I'm afraid.' He eases himself up to a sitting position. 'How'd you get in?'

'Said I had an important message from your

mum. How are you feeling?'

'I'm OK. So, what's new?'

'I saw Madge in the market.'

'Oh yeah? What'd she say?'

'We were wrong about her, you ... I mean, we shouldn't have.'

'Oh I don't know.' He smiles, and I could punch his face.

'Well I *do*. It was a rotten thing and I feel ashamed, like she said we should.'

He holds up his unplastered arm, 'OK, OK.'

'It's not OK! She was nice to me. After what we did to her, she was nice! Do you know what she said? What she did? She forgave me, Rooksy. It was like I was her Jojo, and she didn't want me to worry about it anymore.'

'She's got nothing to worry about either.'

'Oh no, except that she's shown her breasts to her son's mates.'

'Look, I meant about Siddy. The police were here with Mum. I said it was an accident and even, listen to this, that I might have been a bit lippy and made him mad. It's settled now. The coppers weren't bothered either way.'

'And Yorath's?'

'I'm glad Siddy's sweating about that, the bastard. But if we say nothing, no one will know, OK?'

'OK.'

I sit on the side of the bed. He taps me with his plastered arm. 'What's up?'

'Sarah's gone, to Somerset. Her dad's taken her.' Then I'm gabbling about how her family didn't want to live in London any more, how everything might be different if I hadn't made the big-headed suggestion to go back to Swole's.

I get up and cross to the window. In the square below, an old woman has her hand in the blue gingham wrapping of a Lyons sliced loaf, waiting for circling pigeons to settle. A man wearing a bowler hat sits on a bench, reading a newspaper. Half-a-dozen off-duty nurses in cotton half-capes are laughing as they pass in front of him.

'Billy?'

'When she got out of the car I wanted so much to hold her but I didn't because her mum and dad were there. She was crying and I should have told her that I love her because I've never said so properly – but I didn't.'

'Billy, Billy.' He beckons me back to his bed-side. 'She knows you love her.'

'Hope so. Look, sorry about this Rooksy.'

'I'm sorry too. But it'll be all right. It won't be for long. You two, you're...'

'We're what?'

'Well, you're lucky, really. I mean, it's nice to have someone, someone special to like, love even. I hope I will too, one day, and that they'll be...' He doesn't finish, but he was going to say, *like you*. And this no longer bothers me. I hope he does find someone.

He settles back on the pillow and the sadness in his face reminds me that 'finding' isn't enough, because if you're not loved in return it can break your heart. In films, they lead you to believe that being in love and being happy is the same thing, but it's not. I love Sarah but I've never been so unhappy. Perhaps you can only look forward, or back, to being happy.

I wait for him to make things lighter, for his 'fuck-it-so-what?' look. Instead, he stares past me as if, through the window, he's glimpsed a future where there isn't someone special for him because of who he is. But I know who he is, Sarah knows, Josie knows – and Rooky is special for us *because* we know. And it cheers me up to think that he's bound to find someone special among those who really get to know him.

I stretch out on the bed beside him. He crooks his arm around my neck and the cast lies heavily across my chest. I try to sit up but he resists and says what Sarah said. 'We're still kids, Billy.'

'So what?'

'So, perhaps it's not so bad. I'm not sure growing up is much to look forward to. How many adults look happy to you?'

Until recently, I thought that if they're smiling or laughing together they must be happy, but I know now that it's not so simple. 'Well, what about your mum and dad?'

He laughs. 'They're together about two months a year. Maybe that's enough.'

'Oh.' Perhaps Beryl Street is right after all, that being apart makes for more happiness when you do get together again. I hope this is true.

He joggles my head from side to side. 'Still, if you've got friends…'

I wish Sarah and Josie were here, too, to tell him that that's what we are: his friends.

We lie there, saying nothing. The air is heavy, a sickly mix of surgical spirit and the thick smell from lilies in a vase on the windowsill.

309

My thoughts drift back to Hillswood, to lying on the camp bed with Sarah and holding her, just holding, and inhaling the scent of her hair and the new-chewing-gum smell of her skin. How easy it was to fall asleep, until Rooksy woke us with his broad smile, inches from our faces, and how he sat back with his arm around Josie, while she hugged her knees, and how we talked of how I might go to university, how Sarah might be a nurse, how Rooksy would be a purser on the *Queen Elizabeth*, and how *all* of Josie's face would be beautiful. On that special day, the future we dreamed of slipped back to reveal itself so clearly that it felt like we could get up and walk out into it.

'Wakey, wakey. I was thinking. Fancy going to Somerset? To see Sarah?'

'Oh yes.'

'Can't be too difficult.'

'Yes, let's.'

'We'll make plans when I get out.' He yawns. 'Now *I'm* feeling sleepy.'

I ease off the bed. 'Yeah, I'll get going.'

The door swings open and the nurse bustles in. 'Taking a long time to deliver a message isn't it, young man?' She picks up Rooksy's tumbler of water and hands him two tablets. 'You need to take these for your headache, Peter.' Rooksy knocks the tablets back. 'You're supposed to be resting not talking to friends.' She taps me on the shoulder. 'He's had a very serious injury, you know.' She winks at me. 'When I come back I don't want to see you here, understood?'

She sweeps out.

'I'd better get going, Rooksy. Look ... if there's

anything you want.'

He thinks for a few seconds. 'Well, you could, just this once, give us a kiss.' He offers up his cheek, grinning, expecting me to be embarrassed. I am, but not like I would have been before; now it doesn't seem such a big thing. We're friends, after all.

He opens one eye and we laugh. I'll never be like Rooksy but I do want to be *more* like him. He shuts his eyes again, waiting. I take a deep breath and lean close to kiss his cheek but he grabs my head in his good hand and kisses me on the mouth. It's clumsy, hard and horrible. I recoil, wiping my lips. He watches, expecting me to look away, but I don't because I want him to know that I don't love him in the way he'd like but that I do love *who* he is. He blinks and smiles. There's no need to say anything.

He yawns. 'Just the one, Billy. It's all I wanted.'

'See you, Rooksy.'

He starts singing, '*She loves you, yeah, yeah, yeah.*'

'Hope so. Let's go to Somerset ... and we'll take Josie.'

He yawns again. 'You're on.' He starts rocking his head side-to-side on the pillow. 'Blimey Billy, I think I'm getting what Mum calls one of her "splitters". Time for a kip.'

'I'll come tomorrow, all right?'

He barely raises his hand to give me a sleepy OK sign and closes his eyes.

The nurse comes in again. 'Time you were leaving, young man.'

She bustles past me to Rooksy's bed, 'Just going to do your blood pressure, Peter.'

I've reached the door when she says his name again, I start to tell her about his headache when her voice changes. 'Peter … Peter?' She grabs his wrist to feel his pulse, and puts two fingers to his neck. 'Oh my lord!' She presses a buzzer, shoos me from the room and rushes down the corridor calling for sister.

I dash back through the door. 'Rooksy!'

His head has flopped to one side and his eyes are open. At the corners of his mouth saliva has gathered and there's the beginning of a smile. Is he having us on?

I pinch his cheek. 'Rooksy, stop it! Rooksy!'

I want this to be a cowboy film in which my wounded partner pulls through. But it's real and my legs are giving way. I prop myself on the bed and lift his hand. His fingers still loosely form the OK sign and I hope that it's to let me know that he, too, is going to be OK.

Then, like the moments before I stepped in front of Mr Richards' car, I have all the time I need to take in what has happened and to know what I want to do. The footsteps in the corridor grow louder. I give Rooksy another kiss.

Just the one, Rooksy.

'What *are* you doing?' screams the Sister. She jerks me out of her way and one of the nurses behind her puts an arm around my shoulders to steer me to the door. 'You'll have to wait outside, love.'

'I'm his best friend.'

# EPILOGUE – OCTOBER 1975

Across the years, a girl says to a boy, *Yes, Billy Driscoll, I will marry you*. Even Rooksy and Josie hadn't known of our pledge: that one day I would ask and Sarah would say, *yes*.

In 1970, I was at home from university for Christmas. Mum had had too many Babychams and casually referred to my 'puppy love' for Sarah Richards.

I'd been drinking too. 'Puppy love!'

Alarm flashed in her face and she held my arm, 'You were so young, thirteen for goodness sake, and with all that had happened – Mr Dunn and Peter and everything – things had got too serious. Sarah's mother and I thought it would be best to nip it in the bud ... that you'd get over it in time.'

Get over *it*. As if Sarah and I had had some kind of illness.

'What? Oh god, Mum, no!'

'Sarah wrote a couple of times you know, but I...'

And I had written too, many times. I pulled my arm from her grasp and her 'hope you understand' expression disintegrated. 'Know? Of course I didn't bloody know! But what *you* should know is that you couldn't have been more wrong, and that nothing, *nothing* has ever come close to how wonderful I felt then, before Sarah left.'

Dad crossed the room and put an arm around

Mum's shoulder. 'Easy, your mother, we, thought it was for the best. I'm sorry. You were children.'

Dad, too, with the familiar, cruel excuse. Even the kindness of parents can betray you. We faced each other without speaking and I calmed down. They were sorry and could say no more. When I asked if the letters had been kept, Mum shook her head and started crying. All I could do was hold her close and tell her it didn't matter.

The next day, I returned early to university – and a girl who reminded me a little of Sarah.

I never lived at home again.

I rarely go back to Pimlico.

A couple of years after Sarah left, Michael's family joined their relatives in America. After some brief exchanges – my letters for his postcards (including one with a photo of Paul Newman as Billy the Kid) – we lost touch.

John took up labouring with Dad after he was expelled from school for knocking down a prefect who mocked his Cockney accent. He went on to become a successful amateur boxer. When he was nineteen, he married the daughter of one of Aunt Winnie's friends, a keen Salvationist. He's a reluctant attender of Sunday services and has no intention of wearing the uniform; it would involve having a rank and someone trying to tell him what to do. When Aunt Winnie died of lung cancer, she left him all she had, including twenty years' worth of the *Reader's Digest*. On my rare trips to see Mum and Dad, John and I meet in his local. He comes alone, as his wife won't go into pubs unless it's to sell *The War Cry*. We don't talk much but each time we part, I get the crushing handshake that he's inherited from Dad, and his smile in lieu of the hug he can never quite manage. Whatever brotherly love is, I have all that John can give.

Josie has always kept in touch with me. She also wrote to Griggsy when he went to borstal and, later, visited him in prison. After several trips with her mother to holy shrines, including Lourdes, she failed to find her 'new face' but did find a deeper faith. Today, she wears the uniform of a lay nun and spends much of her time shuttling between the Cathedral and the Children's Hospital. On the wards, after the initial shock at seeing her face, the children ask to see 'Auntie Josie' whenever she visits. And when they're well again and playing in the street, they run to her and compete to hold her hand. I don't think Josie ever got over Rooksy dying and whenever we meet she makes only one or two brief references to him: light touches on a painful wound to confirm it's still there.

I miss him too, the Great Rooksy, and often wonder how it would be to have his friendship today. Over the years, I've tried to be like him: to say what I'm thinking, to be more honest, more carefree. I've fallen a long way short.

Lower Sinton isn't as Sarah described it. The sun isn't shining. There aren't many window boxes, and I can barely make out *The Stones* on the faded sign above the little Post Office. I pull in behind a Ford Corsair that stands where her father's magnificent Humber should be.

Sarah, too, will have changed. I have one black-and-white photo of her, taken by Mr O'Rourke at

315

the street party. She's gazing straight at the camera. There are two pale ribbons in her hair. Her mouth is closed but she's smiling because Josie is linking her arm and whispering something into her ear – a simple way of keeping her birthmark out of the picture. Next to Josie, Little is giving a thumbs-up sign and a wink to avoid revealing his squint. I'm on the other side of Sarah. Our hands are an agonizing inch apart and I'm looking down as if willing them to touch. Soppy stands behind me with his huge arms draped over my shoulders; in one hand he holds a half-eaten sandwich. Beside him, Michael – chin up and eyes narrowed – could be looking for Indian smoke signals. John is missing, even though he's nearby. Rooksy is somewhere else.

I enter the Post Office. The harsh ding of the old dangling bell startles me, and I grow weak at the thought that Sarah might be here.

Behind the counter, a white-haired lady in a floral pinny gets up from a chair. 'Good afternoon, can I help?'

I take a bottle of Coke from a shelf. 'Hello, one of these please.' I hand over the money. 'By the way, do the Richards still own this shop?'

'Until a couple of years ago, but they haven't left the village.'

'And their daughter, Sarah?'

She eyes me closely. 'Yes, she's here too ... with a little one you know.'

Hope, which has kept a boy's dream alive, fades on the lips of an old lady with a Somerset accent. She hands me my change – and confirmation

316

that Sarah's life has gone on without me.

'Are you a friend of hers then?'

'Yes ... at least, I was.'

She studies my face as if she might have met me before. She relents and smiles. 'You might catch her down at the school about now.'

'Thanks.'

I pull open the door, the bell dings and she calls out.

'If you miss her, shall I say who was asking after her?'

'Oh, just tell her Billy called in and wished her well.'

*And said, hello, do you remember him? And that you were his first and best love. And that when you were a girl you said you'd marry him. And that he's never stopped loving you. And that every girl he's cared for since has had to have something of you*

'I will my dear. Bye.'

Outside the primary school, mothers and children are milling around, disentangling for home. And there she is, at the kerbside, the only woman in focus, reaching out to a toddler who is talking to his classmates. I bring the car to a halt.

Sarah. A woman, with long hair again. She notices the car and starts to look away but I catch her attention with a wave. Recognition creeps around her eyes and she shakes her head, disbelieving. I open the car door.

The toddler tugs at her. She leans down to listen to him and releases him to go over to a nearby friend. But when she turns back to me, doubt flickers across her face, as if talking to the little boy is bringing her back from our past to an

317

equally unchangeable present.

Gradually, everything around her – the women and children, the school, the village itself – seems to be rallying behind her, enclosing her with belonging, anchoring her life here.

For a second time, I'm losing her to Lower Sinton.

I ache to talk to her but she will be able to say little more than we already know: that we were children; that life bypasses the once-glimpsed and longed-for futures of childhood; that she is someone else now; and that our memories cannot take us beyond today.

Her shoulders slump and she closes her eyes like she did when Dunn climbed towards her on the woodpile. Once again, I know how to help her. I close the door. Her eyes open and I nod to reassure her, to let her know that I understand. She nods too and through her tears comes the smile that once made me brave and so light that I wanted to run and never stop. The smile she gave me in the chalet at Hillswood when, in front of Rooksy and Josie, she confessed that it was me that she loved, and again, later, when we were alone and we made our promise.

And back from that time comes the man who would know what to do, the kind of man I wanted to be for Sarah. Audie Murphy would flick his hat, turn his horse about, and ride away from the woman he loves because she belongs to another.

I start the engine.

A woman clutches her hair as a one-time cowboy hero prepares to saddle up and ride into the Somerset dusk.

The publishers hope that this book has given you enjoyable reading. Large Print Books are especially designed to be as easy to see and hold as possible. If you wish a complete list of our books please ask at your local library or write directly to:

**Magna Large Print Books**
Magna House, Long Preston,
Skipton, North Yorkshire.
BD23 4ND

This Large Print Book for the partially sighted, who cannot read normal print, is published under the auspices of

## THE ULVERSCROFT FOUNDATION